STONE OF FIRE

Vitarian Chronicles Volume 3

S. L. WATSON

STARGAZER PRESS

S. L. Watson

www.slwatsonauthor.com

ISBN 978-1-954440-08-1 (print) ISBN 978-1-954440-09-8 (hardcover) ISBN 978-1-954440-07-4 (ebook)

Cover Design by Rena Violet

For my Family. You are my rock, my compass, and my inspiration. I love you infinity times infinity infinities forever!

Bree's cheek flared with a crimson handprint. I flexed my fingers, shaking off the numb tingle, and kicked over a box of towels. I Snatched the box cutter from the desk situated in a corner, then swiped the sharp tip across the line of tape securing another box. Resistance bands of different shades, lengths, and widths were rolled and stacked neatly inside. Doing the same to another box, I found rubber massage balls and blankets.

"Hmm." I glanced sideways at Bree. "I suspected your yoga studio was just a ruse to spy on me. But then, why order all this if you weren't planning to actually hold classes?"

I sighed and leaned against the edge of the desk. The gray-washed walls of the room were becoming suffocating. "I'm tired of playing games, Bree. It's time to talk, or else—"

"I told you," Bree whimpered. "I don't know where Orien is, but—"

I held up a hand, cutting her off. "But you want to help me find him," I finished for her. "Yes, so you've said. But why should I believe you? You're the reason Orien has my ancestral ring, and—" I ground my teeth together, and the next words came out in a low rumble. "You're the reason Lucas is dead."

"No, no, no—" Bree shook her head and twisted beneath the rope that secured her to the metal folding chair.

Flames coiled from my fingertips.

"Please, Everly. I'm sorry about your boyfriend. I swear, I didn't have anything to do with what Orien did to him."

"Sorry?" My nostrils flared.

Bree trembled. Her eyes grew wide as hissing flames drifted near her, and the scent of burnt hair filled the room.

"Do you know what it feels like to watch someone you love get murdered? Let me show you."

I gripped both of her arms. The throbbing ache of raw flesh being torn apart rippled through me and passed into Bree. The crushing weight of a broken heart pounded inside my chest. The dark well of self-mutilating thoughts burst to the surface.

Tears flooded down Bree's quivering cheeks. Her head shot back, and an ear-splitting wail sent a shiver of satisfaction through me.

"That's what it feels like to watch someone you love become an empty shell of themselves after the essence of their being has been stripped from them and a knife has been buried in their liver. And knowing, as you watch the life drain from their eyes, that it was all your fault."

Bree's head fell forward and bobbed with her groans. I released her arms and smoothed her platinum hair, then gripped her chin and tilted her head back up. Her green eyes shifted to meet mine, and I recognized all too well the pain she felt. I'd lived it these last few weeks. Unable to stand the stifling feeling for a second more, I backed away from Bree and waved my hand. The coiled flame responded to my command and wrapped itself around Bree, staying far enough away to keep from burning her further, but close enough for her to feel the searing heat of her prison.

"Remember." My hand lingered on the doorknob. "Scream all you want. I've spelled this room, and no one will ever hear you." I twisted the knob and turned my back on Bree's strangled cries.

When the door was securely closed behind me, I slumped against it and slid to the floor with my face buried in my hands. I tried putting the cap back on the storm of emotions running rapidly inside me, but reliving the pain of losing Lucas was too much. My body shook as salty tears streamed past my lips. Who was I becoming? Kidnapping and torture? The person Lucas had loved would never have done such things. But I was not that person any longer. I couldn't be, not if I planned to succeed in finding Orien and doing what had to be done for the safety of my family. I ground my fists into my eyes, quelling the tears. I had to get out of here.

I pulled open the door to Neil's place. The host Neil had recently hired glanced up and nodded. This new guy was quiet and didn't try to rope me into idle chitchat, like some of the others had. I strode past him and slid through the red velvet curtains. The sense of feeling lost immediately wrapped itself around me as I made my way through the sea of bodies.

Female vocals swept across the crowd, carried by heavy guitar licks and drumbeats that rattled the walls. Flashing lights made it impossible to focus on any one thing. I turned my attention toward the bar and pushed my way to the front of the crowd.

The bartender spotted me and poured me a double of evernescence. I drained it in an instant and set it down for a refill.

I ran my finger across the vapor that floated atop the glowing lavender liquid. Images of Bree wrapped in flames filled my mind. My fingers tightened around the glass. Why should I feel guilty? She may not have held the knife that had taken Lucas's life, but she was just as responsible for Lucas's death as Orien was. If she hadn't taken my ancestral ring, Lucas might have made it out of that tunnel alive.

My teeth ground together as I squeezed my eyes shut, trying to block out the memories. The sound of Lucas's body crashing to the ground and the empty stare in his eyes as life left him would haunt me forever. I should never have taken the ring from its hiding place at Felix's cabin. Then Bree wouldn't have followed me and found it. Was I really just blaming her for my own guilt?

No! I tossed the contents of the glass to the back of my throat, barely tasting the floral notes that tingled across my tongue. *Bree made her choice to help Orien, and now she has to pay the price.*

The bartender glanced nervously at me as I slammed the glass down. He carried the bottle of evernescence toward my glass, but I shook my head, already feeling the potent effects of the magic infused in the drink.

The music pulsed through me as I made my way among the dancers. I swayed back and forth, welcoming the crush of bodies against mine as I lost myself to the feeling of weightlessness.

When slender fingers wove through mine and warm breath brushed my cheek, I smiled to myself.

"I've missed you, love."

I bent my head back in reply, and soft lips trailed over my ear and down my neck.

Memories of another person threatened to flood my mind, but I pushed them away and spun. My fingers wove through her dark waves before I pulled her face toward mine, ready to forget everything outside this moment.

"Kamara." Our mouths collided, and the intoxicating scent of her enveloped me. The sweet taste of her tongue filled my mouth as she met my reckless desire with her own.

She pulled back, and her dark skin shimmered with a golden dust. "There's a full-moon party in the woods. You game?" She gripped my waist, her nails digging through my clothing.

I drew her mouth back to mine, then breathed, "Let's go."

We finished our dance before making our way out of the building. I followed behind Kamara's car. Her glowing red taillights blurred as she sped around the dark, twisting road. I let my foot off the gas when her blinker flashed ahead, and she slowed, turning onto an unmarked dirt road that led into the forest.

Night swallowed us as we parked among the towering trees that cast shadows everywhere. Cool air rippled across my skin, and I lifted my hair into the breeze, letting it fan the back of my neck.

"We can walk the rest of the way," Kamara said, and she wrapped her fingers around mine.

A dusting of pine needles covered the forest floor and filled the air with a fresh scent. Their bright green color glowed under the luminous full moon that lit our way as we trekked deeper into the forest. Mud squished under my black boots, and fallen twigs snapped as we climbed through damp, dense foliage.

We had hiked for about a mile when music and laughter echoed in the distance. Then red and orange sparks flickered between the trees ahead.

Kamara sped up. "Come on." She pulled me alongside.

We broke through a line of trees and emerged into a circular clearing. The sparks we'd seen from a distance belonged to a raging bonfire. About thirty people surrounded the fire. Some were dancing in pairs or small groups. Others sat on logs, making out.

Eyes glanced sideways at me, some curious, others indifferent. My shoulders went rigid as I trailed a hostile vibration to the one it belonged to.

I spotted a small group pricking their fingertips and feeding drops of blood to each other. A pair of dark brown eyes glowered at me. Their owner's tongue darted out and licked the remainder of blood off the finger she was fondling. The guy it was attached to winked over the girl's flaxen head when he saw me watching them. The girl lifted her face and drew her brows down into a furrow. "What's she doing here?" Her question sounded more like an accusation.

Kamara grasped my hand. "I invited her. If you have a problem, you and your blood fiends can leave."

I kept a steady gaze on the girl while taming the heat burning at my fingertips.

She lifted her chin, ignoring Kamara and speaking to me. "Don't think you're better than us. The council may have declared you queen, but Siobhan was our real queen. You're just some girl who was born on Earth. You might have the blood of the royal Ever line, but you'll never be a true Vitarian."

Her words dug deep. The Vitarians would never accept me as their queen, and this girl was proof.

Kamara marched forward, but I kept a tight hold on her hand and held her back.

"Let me handle this." I took my steps slowly as I neared the girl and her group.

She tried to mask her apprehension by sneering as I

approached, but the black mist of her fear seeped into her aura as I released a tiny flame from my fingertip.

"There's something familiar about you." My gaze narrowed as I examined her pale hair and dark eyes.

She scooted back as I inched closer.

"Her name is Greer. She's kin to Siobhan," Kamara said from behind.

"Ahh." I smiled at the girl. "That's it! I see the resemblance." I bent down so I was at eye level with her, and a flash of the same fear I'd seen in Siobhan that night on the beach shadowed Greer's expression. The fire festering inside me eased, but I still had to teach this girl a lesson.

"The same envy festers inside you. You better be careful, Greer"—the fire swirled higher from my fingertip—"or you might end up following in Siobhan's footsteps, and we both know how things ended for her."

Her eyes pinched into slits as mine raked over her, but she said nothing as she stared at the fire that responded to my silent command. "You know what it means to be the heir of Oria, Greer?"

The music died down as others drew near.

Her friends inched away, showing their lack of loyalty, while Greer sat frozen, still trying to hide her fear.

"I can take power without belittling myself in"—I flicked my eyes at her bleeding finger—"your pathetic bloodletting ceremony."

When her eyes grew wide at my insinuation, I blew out the flame coiling from my fingertip and laughed as I stood. "Don't worry, Greer. I'm not interested in you and your friends."

"Blood junkies," Kamara hissed. "They're addicted to getting high off the exchange." Kamara's lips lifted into a devious smile. "It is forbidden. And ... you are queen." A sparkle glinted in her sharp ebony eyes.

I shrugged, trailing my finger along the soft caramel skin of her arm. "I don't think I'd be welcome at many more gatherings if I started enforcing ancient laws."

"True." Kamara giggled, tossing her long, dark curls over her shoulder. "But it was awesome watching you put Greer in her place. Her entire clan thinks themselves superior to the rest of us."

Someone turned the music back up, and a dark, haunting violin note swept over us, followed by a dramatic series of guitar chords laced with feminine vocals. The crowd erupted with shouts to turn it up louder as they dispersed back to their groups. Even as the party regained some of its earlier enthusiasm, an anxious energy lingered that was hard to ignore.

"Maybe I should go. I seem to be making everyone nervous."

Kamara shook her head. "Nonsense! They just don't know you. You're a mystery to them. The queen who was born on Earth. Oria's chosen heir. Our people are learning of you, and they don't know if they should fear you or love you or both."

"Neither! I just want to be like everyone else." I swung my hand out in an arch.

A patient smile tugged at the corners of Kamara's lips, revealing her dimpled chin. "You'll never be *just* like everyone else, but that doesn't mean you can't have fun." Kamara grabbed my arm, and flashes of burnt orange and shadowed trees twisted across my vision as she twirled me into the group that was dancing around the fire. She laughed and howled up at the moon. Her skin glistened with a sheen of sweat, and she lifted the sides of her long skirt up past her knees and shook her wild curls in the wind.

The tension melted from my shoulders, and I slipped loose the elastic band that I'd used to twist my hair back on our hike up here. Brisk air fluttered through my long raven waves. I threw my head back and let the sound tear from my lungs as I joined Kamara.

Others began howling at the moon, until the entire crowd had joined in, and the forest filled with wild energy. Bodies swarmed around us as we merged with the other dancers. And in that moment, I felt like I belonged.

A leather pouch was passed to Kamara, and she dipped her hand inside. Her fingers came out covered in a shimmering gold dust. Her eyes questioned me as she reached a tentative hand toward me. I nodded, and she ran her dust-covered fingers down my arms, covering them in long streaks. My skin glittered gold under the moonlight, and my head swam as the ever resin was absorbed into my bloodstream. Kamara handed me the pouch, and I performed the same procedure on her.

Cheerful shouts erupted as someone threw a handful of the gold dust into the fire. Flames shot high into the sky, streaking across my vision. I glanced around the full clearing, and everyone was covered in the glowing gold resin made from ever trees on Aenoas-Vita. Its psychedelic effects kicked in, and everything seemed to move in slow motion. Halos of color bloomed before my eyes. I stumbled as my mental shield slipped and auras burst into existence all around me.

My stomach tightened with a queasy feeling. A bottle was pressed into my hands, and I squeezed my eyes shut as I chugged the herbal liquid.

Vibrations drew near me, but I pushed them away as I forced my shield back into place, and the cloud of colors faded.

"You okay, love?" Kamara's voice echoed in my ears.

"Yeah." A flash of silver caught my eye, and my gaze flicked to the side. A blade was being passed around, and each person who handled it cut themselves and offered drops of their blood to the flames.

When the blade made it to Kamara, she sliced her hand. "It's a releasing ceremony," she explained, and she flung her blood into the writhing fire. The flames accepted her offering with a hiss. She held the handle out to me.

My fingertips brushed the smooth silver handle. "How does it work?"

She stroked my arm and spoke softly. "I forget that you know so little of our traditions." Kamara tilted her head back and glanced up at the sky. "It's the last full-moon cycle before the winter solstice. When the moon reaches its peak, we start the spell, and the power of the moon may draw from you that which haunts you emotionally."

I met her dark stare. "For good?" My fingers trembled.

"It doesn't have to be." She glanced over her shoulder. "Zacharia! The stones." She reached out her arm and motioned with her hand.

I'd met Zacharia several times at the club. He was a part of Kamara's crew and her cousin. He had the same deep brown skin and almond-shaped eyes as Kamara.

"Hey, Everly." His perfectly full lips lifted into a smile, revealing bright white teeth. He held out a leather pouch to Kamara that looked weightier than the one that carried the gold ever dust.

Kamara's hand came out of the pouch holding a familiar milky-white stone that was filled with specks of color. Air caught in my lungs, and I took a step back. My heart rate quickened as memories flooded my mind: images of me cutting the ever stone from the dead Shimera, of watching the light dim in the stone as Lucas's life faded away, of using my magic to siphon Darion's life force into the stone to save him from Orien.

My eyes tightened, and my jaw twitched. "What are you doing with those?"

Kamara's brow furrowed as she studied my reaction. I hadn't shared with her much about my past, so she didn't know what had happened to Lucas or the role the ever stone had played.

I latched onto her aura, observing her vibrations carefully as she spoke. I no longer restricted the use of my magic or naively trusted others, like I had in the past.

"You know what this stone is?" Kamara asked.

I nodded. "And why do you have them?" My left hand instinctively tightened its grasp on the blade handle while my right thumb twisted the onyx ring on my right forefinger.

The light blue, brown, vibrant yellow, and rich magenta of her aura made no major shifts, and her vibrations remained fluid as she answered my question truthfully. "My clan has used these stones for generations for different spells and rituals. We collect them from a cave on our land. They are used to safeguard the emotions attached to the energy you choose to release during the ceremony, in case you change your mind. Or if you choose to destroy the stone, your emotions are lost forever."

My shoulders relaxed. "These stones can be dangerous and used for harmful magic."

Kamara's expression softened as she stepped closer to me. "I'll heed your warning." Her breath tickled my ear as she whispered. "You never speak of your feelings, but I know they torture you. You can distance yourself from them and keep them safe in here." She ran her fingers over the stone she held, then brushed her soft lips against mine as she tucked the stone into my hand. "It's your choice. Participation in the ceremony is completely optional." She handed the pouch back to Zacharia, who circled the party with it, handing out stones to those who wanted them.

I gripped the stone and stared into the roaring fire, but all I saw was the blue-green eyes that stalked my heart and haunted my dreams. Each night, I dreamed of our last moment together, when I had left him staring after me with a broken heart. A battle still raged inside me to set things right and tell Arden my true feelings for him. But I had done what was necessary. Death hunted my loved ones. My father ... Lucas ... I glanced at Kamara as a carefree laugh rippled from her beautiful mouth while she conversed comfortably with other Vitarians. A tightness formed in my temples as worry settled into my bones. I hadn't meant to spend as much time with her as I had. If Orien thought she meant anything to me, her life could be in danger. I twisted the point of the blade into my palm.

What had happened to Lucas was my fault. If it hadn't been for my feelings for Arden, things could have turned out differently. Lucas wouldn't have left my apartment upset that night, and the shifter wouldn't have had the opportunity to take him.

Orien may have taken Lucas's life, but my betrayal had provided him with the weapon. I had vowed to never allow myself to feel love again, but turning off my feelings for Arden had proved impossible. He'd invaded every cell in my body, and my love for him refused to wane, no matter how much time I spent losing myself with Kamara. I had to do something. My feelings were getting in the way of focusing on the only thing that should matter: finding Orien and killing him once and for all, before he was able to hurt anyone else and accomplish the destruction he planned for all of Aenoas-Vita.

I turned the knife and sliced through the existing wounds on both of my palms. When my blood sizzled against the flames, my resolution hardened. Distancing myself from my emotions was for the best.

Kamara's white teeth flashed in the night. "It's time," she called out over the crowd. The others quickly joined her chants until everyone had circled the mounting fire. My own voice vibrated deep inside my chest as I recited the words Kamara chanted.

Sparks of blue and white light shot out of the flames. The moon's light brightened and shifted overhead as if it only shone down on us.

My breath quickened and my heart raced as images flashed before me. The first time I'd met Arden, when he'd come into my mom's café, and I'd instantly been drawn to him. The flutters that had consumed me when our eyes had met moved through me now and drifted away in a glowing wisp of light. My first training session with Arden in the forest, and the way I'd ached to touch him when he'd smiled mischievously after I'd propelled him into a tree. Our first kiss, when every touch had sent waves of desire coursing through me. The way my heart pounded in my chest when all I wanted was him. The touch of his lips on mine, sending shivers racing down my spine. The words *I love you* weighing heavily on my heart as I'd told Arden that there was nothing between us. The crushing ache I'd felt every day of his absence since he'd returned to Aenoas-Vita believing my lie. It was all fading with the bolts of light traveling away from me and entering the ever stone I held.

My chest rattled as someone began beating a drum. They circled the crowd, pounding their fist harder and harder against the instrument while the chanting grew louder. The sound reverberated among us, sending shivers racing down the back of my neck. An explosion burst from the fire, and cheers erupted all around.

I wiped my wet cheeks and glanced at the stone cradled in my palm. It glowed bright and burned hot with my trapped emotions. I drew in a sharp breath and realized I felt ... good.

The heavy weight that had burdened me for weeks was nothing more than a dull ache—not entirely gone, but easily ignored.

My head tilted back, and I closed my eyes under the luminous glow that shone down over us. Energy sizzled in the air and pulsed through me as the crowd exploded into raucous laughter and howls.

Kamara came to me and cupped her soft hands over mine. "If you want to reclaim what you put inside"—she squeezed my hands over the stone—"return the stone to the flames at the new moon before the spring equinox, or the energy inside will be lost for good. If the stone is destroyed before then, you will not be able to retrieve what you released."

I shrugged and pulled my hand away. "I don't want it back." I swung my arm high and was about to pitch the ever stone into the roaring fire, which still sparked with lingering magic.

"No!" Kamara caught my fist. "Give it time until you're sure. If you destroy the stone now, there's no going back." She lowered my arm and extracted the glowing rock from my fist and slid it into my pocket. "What's the harm in holding onto it? If you do nothing before the equinox, then your emotions are gone for good anyway."

Someone turned the music back on.

I caught Kamara's hand as she extracted it from my pocket. "Dance with me," I said, and pulled her slender body against mine. Her laugh was infectious, and within moments, we were both giggling and twirling each other around until the forest spun in circles.

We danced until sweat drenched our hair and trickled across our skin. When our bodies collided in a dizzy tumble, our lips crashed together, and we fell to the ground in a tangled embrace.

The sun cracked through the early-morning sky in a rippling blaze of garnet. I leaned against my car, hesitant to go inside my quiet apartment, as my body still vibrated with the energy of the party. My gaze drifted to the moving shadows cast by the tall arborvitaes bordering the outer fields. The pointed treetops swayed and thrashed in the night breeze as if they suffered from my same restless state.

My fingers dipped into my pocket and brushed the stone that vibrated with a precious piece of life. I trembled as the charged energy inside the stone beckoned me, as though it yearned to return to its source. I tore my hand from my pocket and turned for my apartment.

Tiny pebbles crunched softly under my feet as I slowly neared my deck. I'd sensed the energy of the shadowed figure sitting alone and knew he quietly watched me approach.

"What are you doing here, Darion?"

Silver eyes stalked my movements as I took each step with apprehension. He spoke softly, but his words held a harsh undertone. "What have you done, sister?"

I stood against the railing and shrugged. "I don't know what you're talking about."

Darion jumped up. "Don't give me that crap. The curse woke me in the middle of the night." He grabbed both of my arms and studied me. "This is more than just turning your emotions off." He snatched his hands away and wiped them down his black jeans, smearing gold handprints on the front of his legs. His face turned up to the sky. "You were at a releasing ceremony?"

"So what? I had to do something about my feelings for Arden. I can't love him! It's a betrayal of Lucas's memory. And you know what, *brother*? It feels damn good to be rid of those imprisoning feelings. All they did was hold me back, and now I'm free to focus all my energy on finding Orien." I paced away from Darion and slumped down into the chair he'd vacated.

Darion ran his hands through his black hair. "What happened to Lucas was a tragedy, but you have to stop blaming yourself, Ev. You didn't kill him; Orien did. And Lucas wouldn't want you destroying a vital part of yourself because you think you owe it to him. You knew him. He would want you to have love in your life."

"It's too late for that." I pressed back against the chair, wishing Darion would just leave me alone. "All that matters now is that I find Orien."

Darion shook his head. "You're going down a dark path, Ev. You know as well as I that playing God with others' emotions or your own can do no good. Please tell me you kept them safe."

I cast my gaze down, ashamed to admit that I hadn't dared to destroy my feelings for good after Kamara's warning.

Darion sighed heavily. "Well, at least we can restore them. Give me the stone."

I stared at his outstretched hand incredulously. "No! I don't want them back, Darion. I like the way I feel without the burden of loving and missing someone I can't be with every second of my day. You don't know what that's like. You have Molly, and there's nothing keeping you apart."

"Give me the damn stone, Everly." Darion arched over me.

I shot up out of the chair and forced Darion back. "This has nothing to do with you. What I do with my own emotions is none of your business." My skin burned hot, and I tightened my abdominal muscles to try to keep the fire at bay.

Darion's eyes glowed as he struggled with his own rising temper. "It has everything to do with me. Orien wants my power as much as he wants yours. And you've been making reckless decisions for weeks. You're not in this alone, Ev, and I have more than myself to think about now."

Darion turned. A splinter of wood cracked as he gripped the railing, and for a moment, I thought he might tear the top board off.

I took a cautious step toward him. "What are you talking about? What aren't you telling me?"

The ribbiting of frogs harboring in the plants beneath the balcony filled the silence as I waited for Darion's answer. The earlier streak of garnet stretched across the sky and was now splashed with billowing wisps of orange and yellow.

Darion turned to look at me. His expression softened with his words. "Molly's pregnant."

"What?" It was my turn to crack splinters in the railing.

Darion placed his hand on top of mine. "With twins."

I stared up at my brother. A mix of emotions circulated through me. I ignored the pinch of jealousy that needled its way into my thoughts. "I'm going to be an aunt. How could you let this happen?"

Creases rippled across Darion's forehead. "Thanks for the support. It wasn't planned, and the timing couldn't be worse, but I'm happy. I love Molly. We're getting married."

A lump surged up the back of my throat. I had to turn away from Darion before he saw the anguish I guarded. "Wow," I croaked. "I'm happy for you both. I really am." A deep ache settled within me. "Does Mom know?" I glanced over at the main house.

"She does, and she's over the moon, but we're all terrified of what this means. Orien needs the blood of Ever twins, and we're not the only ones anymore." His hands rubbed the back of my shoulders. "I need you to come back to us before you do something you can't take back."

I stiffened and shrugged Darion's hands away as I turned to face him. "You think I'm a danger to your babies?"

Darion's eyes widened. "That's not—"

"Really? You know what? I'm tired, and it's time for you to leave."

He took a step toward me. "I'm sorry. That's not what I meant. Please. Just think about what I said, and don't make any hasty decisions."

"Go, Darion."

I walked into my apartment and closed the door. When Darion's footsteps faded into the distance, I slid to the floor. How could he think I'd ever do anything to put his and Molly's babies at risk? I reached into my pocket and clasped the pulsing stone, and the air left me. Maybe Darion was right, and he had every reason to worry. We both knew what Orien was capable of, but was it reckless to want to unburden myself from being tethered to feelings that I couldn't and wouldn't allow myself to express?

I sighed and pulled the ever stone from my pocket and watched the tiny bolts of electricity ripple across its surface with the energy I'd put inside it.

What does it matter if I don't have these feelings anymore? Arden's gone, and he believes I don't love him.

A light shone within the stone as I thought of Arden. The surface warmed and vibrated against my palm when his image filled my mind.

The way his eyes gleamed with the blue of the deepest ocean waters when he was happy and content brought a smile to my lips. But they hadn't been that color when I'd left him staring after me that night in the woods.

My chest ached as I remembered the pain that had filled

the fiery pools of emerald when I'd ripped out his heart with my words.

"Ouch!" Heat seared my palm, and I turned my hand over, letting the ever stone fall to the floor. As the stone dimmed, so did the ache in my chest, and I realized that contact with the stone kept me connected to my emotions.

I pushed myself to standing and pulled my sleeve over my hand before retrieving the stone. The barrier helped some, but as long as the stone remained near me, I felt the connection to the emotions I yearned to escape.

Indecision tore at me as I cradled the stone in my sleeve and glanced around the dark room. A lonely silence pervaded the apartment, and I felt detached as I moved through the rooms that had once felt like home. Now they were just spaces formed by walls, decorated with items that no longer held meaning for me. I went to the kitchen and filled a glass with water and noticed the dishes I'd left piled in the sink yesterday morning were gone and the counters had been wiped down.

Thanks, Mom.

Guilt tugged at my insides. Instead of being the leader I'd been prophesied to be, I'd become a burden of concern to my family. It was time to make a change, starting with this. I snatched the hand towel from the counter and wrapped it over the stone. Without the constant weight of these emotions, I could focus on what I needed to do to protect my family.

My legs ached as I wobbled into the bedroom and sat down on the bed. Luna stirred from her curled-up position on the opposite side of the mattress. She rolled over, her eyes drifting open with curiosity.

"Sorry, girl." I smoothed her long, pointed ears.

Her snout opened with a deep yawn, and she plopped a

heavy paw on my lap. I bent down and kissed her furry fore-head. "Go back to sleep, girl."

I leaned back and sank my head into my pillow, not having the energy to bother changing or even lift the covers and climb under. Rolling over to my side, I yanked open the drawer to the bedside table, tossed the wrapped stone inside, and slammed the drawer shut. I'd figure out what to do with the stone later.

2

The bell chimed as I pushed through the café entrance. All the tables were filled with the usual Saturday morning crowd, but that was okay, because I'd called ahead to pick up my order.

"Everly, honey." My mom waved from a table and called me over.

Damn! I knew I should've just got bagels from down the street.

When I saw Darion scowling up at me from the table he shared with my mom, Molly, and the sheriff, I cringed.

"Join us, sweetie." My mom scooted her chair over to make room for the extra one Sam was sliding over for me.

"Thanks, Sheriff." I plopped down and lifted my sunglasses onto the top of my head.

The sheriff smiled. He'd given up on trying to get me to call him Sam since he and my mom had been dating. Sam was a nice guy, and I adored his sweet little girl, Piper, but as much as I wanted my mom to be happy, I just couldn't bring myself to accept him the way Darion and the others had. He was human and vulnerable, and knowing about us only brought danger to him and his daughter. But my mom had let Sam in, and there was nothing I could do about it.

"I can't stay long, Mom. I have a class this morning."

Molly glanced sideways at me. Since she had taken up teaching yoga at my studio, she knew my schedule, and also knew I had plenty of time before my class started.

"I have some news." My mom glowed as Sam cupped his hand over hers.

I shifted in my seat. "There seems to be a lot of that lately." I snuck a peek at Molly and noticed the blue stripe of dye she had added opposite the pink in her hair, and knots twisted in my stomach. She and Darion were expecting twins, and Darion must have sensed the genders through their Vitarian connection with him.

A crushing weight pressed on top of my foot, and I kicked Darion's boot away.

"Sorry, Mom." The bitter knots turned into pokes of guilt when the smile faded from her face. "What's your news?" I tried to infuse some enthusiasm into my words.

"Well …" She perked up.

Oh God. Please don't tell me you're getting married too. The back of my throat went dry. I took a quick gulp of water from the glass the waitress had brought me.

"Sam surprised me this morning with tickets, and we're taking a trip to Mexico."

I released an anxious breath while my mom reached inside her bag and pulled out a stack of colorful pamphlets.

"He's got it all planned out." She unfolded a glossy layout of pristine photos of sandy beaches, craft markets, museums, and the rainforest.

"Wow." I leaned back in my chair, tilting it onto the two back legs. "That sounds great, but what about the café?"

Darion hunched forward. "Mom doesn't need to worry

about anything but enjoying herself. I'll have everything under control."

My mom reached over and patted Darion's hand. "Thanks, honey. I know I'm leaving the café in good hands, and, Ev—" Her sapphire eyes beamed. "I was hoping you'd manage the greenhouse while I'm away."

"Of course, Mom."

"It's settled, then." The sheriff scooted his chair back. "Cacsha, honey." He bent over and kissed her cheek. "I'll see you tonight for dinner. Duty calls," he said as his radio beeped. "Nice to see you kids." He took one more long sip from his cup of coffee, then hurried outside.

The new waitress delivered my bag of to-go food to our table. "Well, looks like that's my cue." I jumped up.

"That looks like a lot of food for only one." Darion eyed my takeout order.

I shifted the bag down by my legs. "I'm hungry."

Thankfully, my mom distracted Darion from his annoying observation when she asked, "Will you be at the house tonight for dinner? Everyone's coming." She leaned closer. "I'm so glad Darion told you the good news. Isn't it exciting?" My mom glanced toward Molly, and her lips turned up. She was going to be a grandmother, and her aura sparkled. "I'm the luckiest mom, and soon to be grandma on all the planets." She winked at me.

I hadn't planned on attending tonight's dinner, but now there was no way I could miss it and let her down. "I'll be there."

Darion continued to eye me as I shimmied around the table, trying not to bump into any nearby customers when I bent down and gave Molly and then my mom a hug.

A cool blast of air calmed my nerves when I finally got outside the café. The door chimed behind me just as I stepped away.

"Ev!" Molly caught up to me. She fiddled with the hem of her shirt. "I'm sorry about how Darion told you the news. We had planned to tell you together." A frown formed across her brow, and she cast her oak eyes down to her feet.

"It's okay, Molls. I'm really happy for you. You've always been like a sister to me, and now you will be, and I'm going to be an aunt." I glanced around, suddenly worried about anyone hearing us.

Molly's shoulders tensed as well. "I hate this," she whispered. "I hate that we have to be so afraid when this is the happiest time in our lives." Molly's back slumped. She looked down and settled a hand on her belly.

I set my bag of food on one of the vacant patio tables and wrapped my arms around her. "We won't let anything happen to your babies."

She sniffled into my shoulder. "Sorry. I've been emotional lately. My hormones are all over the place."

"Don't be sorry. You're going to be a mother, and you're going to be amazing at it. And someday, I'll get to tell my niece and nephew how badass their mom is and how she took a shifter down with a frying pan."

Molly's head bobbed on my shoulder as we both laughed. "How did you know the genders?"

I touched the blue and pink stripes in Molly's blond hair.

"Oh, yeah." Molly giggled and straightened. Then she wiped her eyes with the back of her hands. "Don't be mad at Darion. He loves you, and neither of us thinks you would purposely put the babies in danger. It's just ..." She chewed her lip.

"Tell me, Molly."

"Well, we're worried about"—she paused while a couple walked past us and into the café—"the type of magic you've been using. It's ..." She looked me straight in the eye. "It's changing you."

The silence that hung between us could have frozen a wildfire.

A car horn honked at a bicyclist dashing in front of its vehicle as it pulled into a parking spot. The distraction gave me a moment to calm my irritation. I glanced past the parked vehicles and gazed out at the Columbia River and took a deep breath.

"Ev—"

"I'll see you at the studio." I grabbed my bag of food and dashed down the block without turning back. I didn't need anyone's approval for how I tracked Orien. Finding him was all that mattered. He was more of a threat now than ever. The twins would never be safe as long as Orien remained alive.

❧⳼❧

"Take a bite." I shoved the breakfast sandwich against Bree's mouth.

She chewed, then croaked, "Water."

I held the bottle to her lips. Drops of water dribbled down her chin as she gulped. "I have to go to the bathroom."

I sighed. "Fine, but you know the drill."

"Yeah, yeah, I get it." She risked an eye roll. "Try anything, and I burn."

After she'd been to the bathroom, Bree settled back into her chair and rubbed at her wrists. She'd wiped the crusted blood from under her nose and redone her platinum braid. It astonished me that even in captivity, she primped herself.

I reached for the rope, and Bree flinched.

"Look, we both know I can't escape, so can you please leave the rope off for a while? I can't feel my wrists."

I dropped the rope and leaned back in the chair opposite

her. "Tell me everything you know about Orien. How did you meet?"

"We've gone over this a million times already. It was at Neil's human club in Eugene, where all the college kids hang out. Orien was meeting with the king. Do we really need to rehash this again?"

Bree stared wide-eyed at the ball of fire that formed in my palm. She released a breath. "Fine. It started as an innocent flirtation. He was watching me dance with friends. He bought me a drink and asked me to dance with him. This continued for a couple of weekends before he asked me out. By the time he told me who he was, I was madly in love with him. I bought every line he fed me about being his queen and ruling at his side. I would have done anything he asked of me. But now, I'm sure Orien scouted me for my power. He needed someone with my gift to help him get close to you. He never really cared about me at all. He was just using me to get what he wanted." Bree's Barbie-like beauty vanished as her cheeks puffed and her face turned bright red.

"You realize how pathetic that makes you?"

Her green eyes flared. "Screw you, Everly. I messed up. I lost myself in him. It was like he had some kind of control over me, but I'm finally thinking clearly, and I hate him for what he made me do. I want him to pay."

"Did you play any part in my father's death?"

Bree's head shook rapidly. "I already told you."

My elbows dug into my knees as I leaned forward. "Tell me again."

"No. I swear. I had nothing to do with what happened between your father and Orien, and I want to hurt Orien as much as you do."

"Oh, I doubt that, but I hear what you're saying."

Standing from my chair, I circled Bree and traced my finger around her slender neck. Her aura hadn't changed from the last time I'd asked her about my father's death. She was telling the truth. She'd played no role in what had happened to him, but she had played a role in what had happened to Lucas. My fingers wrapped around the length of her braid, and I fought the urge to rip her hair out.

Instead, I gently tugged her braid, pulling her head back slightly, and I bent down near her ear. "You want revenge because he played you for a fool." I dropped her braid and went to stand behind the chair I had positioned in front of her and gripped the hard metal back. Then I lifted the chair from the floor and slammed it back down, causing the door behind us to rattle. My voice rose. "But what about what he did to Lucas, or what he plans to do to everyone on Aenoas-Vita if he succeeds in killing me and my brother and taking our magic? None of that mattered to you when you thought you were going to be his bride."

I shook off the red haze that crept across my vision.

Bree stared at the floor. Then her head whipped up. "What do you mean? What's he planning to do?"

I sat and scooted my chair closer, so we were inches apart. "Do you expect me to believe that the entire time you were together, you didn't know his plans to destroy Aenoas-Vita and every living entity on it?"

"My family." Bree's shocked whisper answered my question.

"So you do have people you actually care about. Well, how does it make you feel that you helped Orien get a step closer to killing them? Because that's exactly what he plans to do—if they're not taken as prisoners by the Shimera to be experimented on."

Liquid pooled in Bree's eyes and rolled down her cheeks. "I didn't know." She coughed, and snot dripped from her nose.

I went to the desk and grabbed the box of tissues and handed it to her.

"He told me he needed the ring to claim his rightful place." She blew her nose and wiped her cheeks and mouth, then continued. "He promised that if I got it, we would be married. I believed him. I'm telling you the truth."

Bree sobbed silently as I paced the room.

This merry-go-round had grown tedious. Her answers to my questions were always the same. But she had to be useful in some way. There must be something she was holding back.

"Hellooo!" A voice came from the larger studio space at the front of the building.

Bree didn't hesitate. "Help! I'm back here. Hel—"

Fire shot through my hand and imprisoned Bree, cutting off her plea for help.

Footsteps creaked on the other side of the door.

Shit!

I recognized the energy. It was Molly. What was she doing here?

Darion was coming in behind her.

The doorknob twisted. I gripped it and yanked it open just enough to slide out.

"Hey, Molls." I pulled the door closed behind me and guarded it.

Her heart-shaped face scrunched up into a cascade of wrinkles as she asked, "What are you doing here?"

Darion's expression hardened as he placed his hands on Molly's shoulders and waited for my answer.

There was no way out of this. Darion would know if I lied, because of the damn curse that bound us. I twisted the knob and pushed the door open and lowered the fire shield that guarded Bree.

Molly's mouth fell open. Then her cheeks and neck flushed pink as her brows pinched together. A heavy vibration shrouded her, and she pushed past me and whipped her hand across Bree's face. "That's for what you did to Ty." Her other hand shot out and lashed the opposite cheek. "And that's for helping Orien, and nearly getting Darion killed."

Darion leaned inside the doorframe and snickered as he observed Molly with shining eyes.

Molly spun on me. "What in the hell? How long have you had her here?"

I shrugged. "A few weeks."

Bree cupped her welted cheeks. "She's crazy!" She threw a stare my way. "You two have to help me get out of here."

"And why would we do that?" Darion's admiring expression morphed into that of a hunter as his attention shifted from Molly to Bree. "My sister is queen, and you are her prisoner. Why would we interfere? Besides, you've earned your punishment."

"Darion!" Molly's tone was sharp.

Bree flicked the long end of her braid off her shoulder. "Oh, you're one to talk. Tales of the wicked son of Siobhan have spread all across Aenoas-Vita. Your crimes make me look like strawberry freaking shortcake."

A dark scowl marred Darion's handsome face. But then it was gone. "Siobhan is not my mother, and she used dark magic to control me. I've been pardoned."

"Only because your sister is now queen," Bree spat.

Molly huffed. "Stop it! This isn't a game, and we're not comparing who's done what." She turned to me. "Ev. You can't keep her here like this."

"Have you gotten any useful information from her?" Darion eased off the doorframe and moved into the room.

Molly threw up her hands and sat in the chair I had vacated.

I smirked at Bree. "Only that she's as stupid as she looks. She thought she would be Orien's queen."

Darion's laugh bounced off the walls. "Oh, that's a good one. Orien knows how to pick 'em."

Bree rolled her eyes at Darion's jab.

His humor settled, and Bree squirmed under Darion's silver gaze. "Does Orien have any weaknesses?"

"I don't know." Bree wrung her hands. "He has to drink blood to sustain his youth and magic after what Oria did to him."

Darion walked behind Molly and massaged her shoulders. "We know that much. What else?"

"He never shared anything else with me. Except—" Bree stopped talking and pinched her lips together.

"Talk," I demanded.

Bree shook her head. "Not unless you promise to let me go."

A flame shot from my fingertip. "Or I could just burn you, since you've proved yourself useless."

"Okay, wait. I'll tell you. But if you let me go, I'll help you like I said I would. What if I could get a message to Orien that I can't live without him, and that I forgive him for betraying me? I could convince him I still want to help him, when I'd really be helping you."

"We could use her as bait?" Darion said, an eyebrow raised.

I studied Bree. She had a gift for making people believe what she wanted, but could she fool Orien? "I don't know. Orien planned to kill her when he was done with her. He admitted as much. He's not an idiot."

"No, he's not. But he's egotistical, and maybe desperate enough to need Bree's help again. And if he kills her"—Darion glanced at Bree and shrugged—"no loss to us."

"Jerk! Ouch!" Bree cradled the foot Molly had stomped on.

Molly twirled the heart-shaped pink diamond decorating her left ring finger. "Don't insult my fiancé."

Bree's eyes fell enviously on the ring. The legs of her chair scraped against the floor as she scooted backward out of Molly's reach.

"Hmm." I swirled the flame hovering above my finger. "I don't trust her. She's weak. She fell for Orien's tricks once."

"You have my word." Bree jumped up from her chair.

My hand shot out, sending a blast of energy that forced her back down. She gripped the sides of the chair. Her energy vibrated as she struggled to contain her anger.

Darion whipped a pocketknife out and flipped it open. "If we can trust you, then swear on a blood oath."

Bree's eyes went wide. "A blood oath? But—"

"It's the only way we can be sure you won't betray us."

Red fear hazed Bree's aura.

"What are you talking about, Darion?" He had piqued my curiosity.

"It's a dark spell." Bree answered my question. "If I swear a blood oath and break it, I'll die."

"But she has to agree willingly for the spell to work," Darion added.

I considered Darion's suggestion. "And you know how to perform this spell?"

Darion's eyes slid to Molly, filled with apology for who he used to be. "I do."

Molly gripped his hand, her aura warm with love.

"Okay." I took the knife from him.

His forehead creased.

"No more dark magic for you, brother. You'll guide me through the spell if she agrees." I settled my gaze on Bree. "If you agree willingly to the blood oath, and tell me what you're holding back, I'll release you."

This arrangement would solve the problem of what I was

going to do with Bree, since I'd gotten nowhere with my interrogations.

Bree's shoulders rolled back with renewed confidence. "I'll agree, but first I need something from you."

I quirked a brow.

She smoothed the singed fibers of her teal sweater and crossed her arms over her chest. "If I make this oath, I forfeit my life if I betray you, but Orien will surely kill me if he finds out I'm helping you. I want your protection if Orien turns against me. You have to promise that you'll keep me safe."

A bitter taste filled my mouth as I remembered that night in the cave, when Bree had extracted Oria's ring from her pocket and handed it over to a gloating Orien, while Lucas had dangled, lifeless, in Orien's grasp.

Protecting Bree was the last thing I wanted to do, but finding Orien was more important than my resentment toward Bree for being an ignorant pawn in Orien's game.

I nodded. "You have my word. I'll do everything I can to keep you safe if you help us track Orien."

Arden's image filled my head as I made a plan to send for guards. I expected the aching emotions that usually came with thoughts of him, but his image came and left with nothing.

"Ev!"

I hadn't realized Darion was talking to me. I shook myself from my thoughts.

"Are you ready?" He unfolded one of the extra chairs and set it in front of Bree.

I swallowed past the dry lump at the back of my throat and sat facing her.

Bree's knees trembled, and she fidgeted in her chair, as though trying to calm herself.

Darion stood over us. "You'll repeat after me. Then you'll cut your hand and hers and press them together. When the binding begins, do not move until it finishes. You know your part?" Darion looked down at Bree.

"Y-yes." Her jaw jittered.

I gripped the knife as the words rolled off Darion's tongue in Vitarian.

"Blood of my blood," I repeated as I ran the sharp blade down my palm, and then Bree's as she spoke her part.

We smashed our palms together and interlaced our fingers.

Tendrils of blood emerged from between our palms and glowed bright red as they twisted together and formed an intricate binding around our clasped hands.

As the spell continued, I felt the weight of the darkness in the words I spoke, just as I had the night I'd saved Darion on the bloodied beach, when I'd taken the curse from Siobhan and absorbed it into myself, linking my life force with Darion's. The constant hum of the curse was always present, reminding me that my life was not my own.

For an instant, I pitied Bree as I watched the binding turn from red to black and seep into the skin of our bound hands. There had been a time when I would have refused to place a dark spell on anyone, even someone like Bree. But that had been before I'd lost so much. Now I understood that sacrifices had to be made for the greater good.

"You are sworn by blood and oath." The words took on a life of their own as they came from me.

"I swear by the blood of death," Bree finished with a gasp as the binding vanished and the spell was done.

"You're not finished," I told Bree as she stood from her chair.

She nodded toward the stack of boxes and the spilled towels on the floor. "I'm just getting a towel to wrap my hand."

Molly jumped up. "I'll get them." She scooped up the

mess of towels and shoved them back inside the box, then handed one to me. She paused, still holding the second towel, and scowled down at Bree. "Whatever you did to Ty really messed with his head. When Everly lets you out of here, don't go anywhere near him, or you'll have me to deal with," she warned Bree, handing her the towel.

Darion shadowed Molly, sending Bree his own silent warning.

Bree's shoulders hung limp as she wrapped her hand. Exhaustion weighed heavily in her words. "His sister. She's his weakness."

My foot stomped hard on the floor as I propelled myself out of the chair. "How do you expect that to help us? Oria is of the spirit realm now, and without the ring *you* stole from me, I can't communicate with her."

Bree flinched. "I don't know. But when Orien speaks of her, it's with a mix of love and fear and something else. Once, he spoke of a time when he'd first learned of Oria's death. He told me he longed to join her in the afterlife, but he feared that his spirit would go someplace else for all the evil he'd done." Bree paused, then added, "There are other ways to reach the dead."

"What is she talking about?" I turned from Bree and stared at Darion.

He shook his head and ran his fingers through his hair. "It's not an option. It's too dangerous."

Molly sidled up to Darion and protectively wrapped her arm around his waist.

"That's for me to decide, Darion," I said. "You've known of a way to contact Oria, and you've kept it from me?"

Creases formed around his silver eyes. "You don't understand, Ev. Without Oria's ring, the only way to contact the dead is to cross over, and it's too risky."

"How?"

Darion stood in silent defiance.

"You need a powerful witch," Bree answered from behind me. "A witch connected to all forms of magic, and one who's not afraid to touch death."

The look Darion gave Bree could have frozen a lava pit.

Bree shimmied past me. The acrid smell of burnt hair and coppery blood clung to her. "Now, if you don't mind, I need a shower and a bed, assuming I'm free to go."

"Stay close." I nodded at the door, and Bree didn't hesitate before bolting through it.

Molly wrinkled her nose. "That girl is trouble waiting to happen."

I silently agreed with Molly. Bree was trouble, but she'd provided me with useful information, and now that she was sworn to me, I could use her.

"Let's go, babe. I need to get ready for my class." Molly nudged Darion. "I'll see you at the studio, Ev." She disappeared through the door, clasping Darion's hand.

"Darion."

He paused. Dread shadowed his expression.

"Track the Spider Witch."

Freya Moon's crystal shop was filled with human energy. I'd forgotten how busy it got on the weekend. Patrons perused the shelves, mesmerized by the glittering stones and hopeful of the mystical possibilities.

I inhaled the subtle citrus scent of orange that mingled with the air, uplifting the mood all around.

Anya stood behind the counter, giving a palm reading. She traced the lines of the hand she held, giving a detailed description of the meaning of the lines.

The woman listened intently to Anya's words. She grinned

broadly at some piece of information Anya whispered to her at the end of her reading, and the pale, muddy green hue that clouded the woman's aura brightened to a rich, clear color. Whatever she had learned had just made her day.

"Everly." Anya's full lips turned up in a warm smile. "It's good to see you out."

"Is Freya here?"

"Mother's in a reading, but she should be done soon."

I checked my phone. I had an hour before I had to be at the studio to teach my class on breath work. "I can come back."

Anya walked out from behind the counter. The chain clasping her ankle jingled with her movement, and a bright blue glittered in her aura. Anya was half-human, but the magic of her mother's Vitarian blood flowed strongly within her.

The familiar, rich aroma of her jasmine shampoo filled my senses as she reached for my hand. "She won't be long. I'll read your palm while you wait." Her smooth skin brushed down the top of my arm as she turned my hand over.

"I'm not sure." I glanced up at Anya. At five foot four, I wasn't short, but Anya stood several inches taller than me.

"It'll be fun." Her long nails traced the lines of my left hand.

"Okay, sure." I gave in to my curiosity. Maybe I'd learn something that would make me smile the way the other woman had.

The smile creases smoothed from Anya's creamy, bronzed skin as her work turned serious. A sparkle of yellow shimmered across her aura, and I shifted nervously as Anya studied my lines much more quietly than she had those of the woman before me.

"Your heart line ..." Her finger slowly trailed across the

line just beneath the base of my fingers. "There's a significant break. It's like a part of it has been erased."

An uncomfortable knot formed in my chest at the memory of the releasing ceremony and the ever stone tucked away in my bedside table. A thought kneaded my conscious-ness, that I'd made a terrible mistake, but I pushed it to the deepest reaches of my mind. There was no other choice. I'd done what I'd had to.

Anya's forehead creased as her brows knitted together. "And your lifeline ..." She drew her fingertip down the pad of my thumb. "It's forked." She sucked in a breath and gripped my hand tighter. Her breath quickened, causing my own heart to race.

"This extra line," her voice lowered to a whisper, "it's the line of death." Her topaz eyes locked onto mine. She scooped up my right hand, examining it. "This can't be right."

Her vibrations seeped into me, and I snatched my hands away, not wanting to feel her mounting concern.

The beads parted behind the counter, and Freya's energy was immediately recognizable.

"Thanks for the reading, Anya." I rushed away from her, feeling the burn of her eyes as they silently followed me. I walked through the parted beads and down the hall into Freya's home, trying not to think about the panic Anya had felt.

Freya tucked her long, flowing skirt between her dark legs as she bent over the familiar rug on the floor and scooped up her tarot cards. She blew on them while reciting a blessing, cleansing the cards of old energy. Then she went to work on picking up the stones and teacups.

I knew better than to offer her help. Her last reading was still fresh in the space, and shadows of the energies of those who had been here remained. I walked around the space as

Freya burned her incense and sprayed the room with a cleansing elixir.

The large windows that faced the mountains and river below were pristine, and the blinds were rolled up so that natural light spilled into the room. I stood in front of the French doors, which led to a wide balcony, and gazed out at the view.

I turned my hands over and glanced at my palms. Goose bumps spread across my arms as a shiver raced through me. I traced the lines of my right hand with my left, wondering what the line of death meant for me. My fingertips curled in, and I shoved my hands into my pockets, trying to forget the worried frown that had marred Anya's lovely features. Instead, I let my attention get lost in the whitecaps that rippled atop the river below the hilltop of historic Victorian homes.

There was a ferocity in the wind today as it shifted madly. I was surprised to see one lonely sailboat on the water. With winds gusting over twenty miles per hour, only the brave and reckless, or inexperienced, took their chances. The waves thrashed the boat, rocking it side to side, and the front sail flapped uncontrollably as the two people, who were just visible from my viewpoint, struggled to reel it in. The boat heeled heavily, knocking the couple to the side, causing the pair to lose their grip on the rope tied to the sail. They scrambled back up and grappled for the rope as it flailed in the wind. At this rate, they'd be lucky to make it into their slip by nightfall—if they didn't suffer a catastrophe first.

Calm. The energy around me grew thick. I held my control on the elements as the couple scrambled to take their sails down as quickly as possible while they had the chance. Once they'd reeled in their front sail and tied down the main, they were back in control of their boat. I released my hold on nature and watched as the couple pointed toward the marina and slowly motored in. They were definitely newbies to sailing, or they would have known to point their bow into the wind while taking down their sails.

"Have you had any luck tracking your uncle?" The violet in Freya's aura lingered, a sign of her connection with the spiritual realm.

"No." My fists balled inside my pockets. "He's eluded me every time, but I'll find him, and when I do, he'll pay for what he's done."

"Here, my dear. This will help settle your nerves."

I accepted the cup of tea Freya offered and followed her to the sofa that faced the windows. The tension in my temples relaxed with each sip of the tea. The combination of nettle with the subtle hint of mint and soft rose petal soothed my tight throat.

"How can I help?" Freya crossed her long legs and leaned back into the cushions.

"As you know, my uncle has my ancestral ring, and without it, I'm unable to contact Oria's spirit."

She nodded, waiting for me to continue.

"Is there another way to reach the other side?"

Freya sipped her tea. Then she leaned forward, placing the delicate cup on her coffee table, and turned to face me. "Oria's spirit remains in a realm beyond my reach."

I carefully set my own cup down. "But is it possible?"

"Possible, yes." Freya narrowed her dark eyes. "But it's extremely dangerous. It's old, dark magic that would take you across the lines, and you would need a witch who is not afraid to walk the path of death to guide you in and out of the realm."

I leaned forward. "What does that mean, walk the path of death?"

Freya scooted closer and gripped my hands in hers. "The spirits I work with for my clients are still of *this* realm." She glanced around. "They haven't moved on and are eager to be contacted. You see, spirits of the Vitarian people move to a plane of existence much deeper than the spirits of Earth do. For you to connect to the deeper realms, your spirit"—Freya gave me a pointed look—"will need to cross over. You will need to be very near the cusp of death to do this."

My body went rigid. *I'd have to die.*

"And without the proper guide," Freya continued, "you might not make it back. I understand you want to find your uncle, but this is not the way. Nothing beyond absolute desperation should take you down this path." She squeezed my hands. "Trust me, Everly. There was a time in my past that I'm not proud of when I used this magic, and the results were devastating, and they continue to haunt me to this day. This is not something I can help you with."

A tremble crept down my spine, and the hope that I'd finally found a way to catch Orien faded. It wasn't just my own life I had to think about. If I died, the curse that bound my life to Darion's would take him with me. That was why he'd kept his knowledge of this a secret. My anger toward him faded and was replaced by a sharp tightening in my chest as I realized the only reason Darion wouldn't have shared this with me. *He no longer trusts me with his life.*

"Do you know of a witch capable and willing to use this magic?"

Freya sighed, and her eyes met mine.

"It's okay, Freya." She didn't need to speak the name; I knew who I needed to find.

The Spider Witch had used her magic to channel through me and warn me of Orien that night when Lucas had shown up with new photos of the man my father had met with before his death. I'd felt her strength then. Finding her wouldn't be easy. She roamed the world, practicing her magic, and kept her location secret. The only way to meet with her was to be invited. Calista had tracked her for months before receiving an invitation. I'd asked Darion to find the Spider Witch. He was the greatest Tracker on Aenoas-Vita. If anyone could find her, he could, but would he? He knew the risk of this spell, and he had Molly and the babies to think about now.

Freya reached for my hands, bringing me back from my thoughts. Her expression gave away her silent worries as her finger pressed the gap in my broken heart line, then trailed over the forked life line. There was no judgment. She tenderly clasped my hands together. "Only you can mend what's broken. Don't let Orien take more from you." She smoothed my cheek, then stood and walked to her altar, where she picked up a crystal held in the stone palms of her life-size Quan Yin statue. She returned and held it out to me.

I ran my finger over the sharp edges of the large rose quartz. The warm pink tone matched the soft vibration it emitted. A low hum of energy moved through me, and nameless emotions tugged deep within. I questioned Freya with a glance.

"A gift, blessed by the goddess to help you hold onto what's forgotten." Freya sat facing me. A deep understanding shone in her midnight eyes. "Pain is not always easy to face, but our experiences shape who we are and how we grow." She slid the shoulder of her blouse down, revealing a raised scar that started at her breastbone, next to her heart, and dove, angry and jagged, down toward unexposed parts of her flesh.

I shivered at the hate and pain that resonated in the scar. "My stars, Freya. What happened to you?"

She put her blouse back in place. "It's okay, child. It was a long time ago. But I, too, have lost someone I loved, and I carry that pain always. The scar serves as a reminder to not give in to the darkness that put it there, but instead to treasure what I have." Her hand rested over her heart. "I thought

I would be broken forever, but then Anya came, and when I held my child for the first time and looked into her eyes, I saw the love of her father looking back at me. In that moment, I was reminded that love heals, but without it, our hearts harden." She lifted my free hand, which had been lying at my side, and cupped it over the crystal I held in my other. "Keep this close. Let the healing energy of love back into your heart."

Freya lifted her hands toward her neck and removed a chain she wore with a miniature version of the goddess Quan Yin, holding a tiny rose quartz. "May I?"

I tilted my head forward, and Freya dropped the chain over my head and settled it around my neck.

"The goddess has seen me through many dark times. May she guide you like she has me."

"Thank you, Freya." I tucked the goddess pendant beneath my shirt, feeling its gentle vibration against my skin, and threw my arms around Freya's neck. "Your friendship means so much to me."

A buzz sounded from my bag, and it suddenly dawned on me that I was late for my class. *Crap! Molly's going to kill me.*

"I'm sorry, Freya." I checked my phone and saw the text from Molly. "I didn't realize how much time had passed, and I'm running late." I placed the rose quartz inside my bag.

"Thank you for your advice and the gifts. I really have to get back to the studio."

Freya stood. "Anytime you need to talk, I'm here." She gave my hand a final squeeze.

I left through the side entrance to avoid walking back through the shop. Questions about Freya's past filled my mind. She'd never shared such personal experiences with me before. I wanted to ask her more about how she had gotten the scar and what had happened to Anya's father, but I had sensed her pain at the memories. I thought of Felix's warning about working with Freya and wondered how much he knew about her. She'd admitted to making mistakes. Perhaps Felix knew what Freya had been referring to when she had said she'd used dark magic that had resulted in something terrible happening. I trusted Felix completely, but maybe he was being hasty in his judgment of Freya. We all made choices we regretted. My hand reached up and felt the goddess pendant beneath my shirt.

"Hey, you." Fingers dug into my sides.

I'd been so lost in my thoughts, I hadn't noticed Jasper getting off his parked motorcycle. Luckily for him, I recognized his energy before I retaliated.

"Jasper! I nearly fried you."

His amber eyes glowed with mischief. "Speaking of frying." His lips turned up. "We still on for dinner tonight?"

I couldn't help but laugh at Jasper's constant thoughts of food. "Yes. My mom is planning a feast for everyone, and before you ask, there will be a plethora of *Monarda* tarts."

"Sweet! I'll bring the handsome stud." Jasper wiggled his dark brows.

"Okay." I rolled my eyes and pinched his side. "I'll see the handsome doofus at six thirty."

"Oh, now you're gonna get it." Jasper lifted me off my feet and tossed me over his shoulder.

My legs dangled wildly above the ground. "Put me down, you ogre!"

He tickled my sides until laughter exploded from my lips. Then he continued until my sides ached. When he finally set me upright, I felt lighter and more carefree than I had in a while.

I stood on my tiptoes and pulled Jasper into a hug. "I love you, Jasp. I'm glad you're my best friend."

"And let's not forget," he added, "that I'm also your handsome stud of a Shield." He wrapped his arms tight around me.

"I love you too, Ev. Now, I've got to go see my other love, who's waiting for me to take her to lunch. I'll see you tonight." He kissed my forehead and headed into Freya's shop for Anya, who he spent most of his free time with these days.

My cheeks lifted as I smiled to myself. I was happy for them both. Anya was perfect for Jasper, and they made a great couple, but I sensed a resistance in Jasper to fully build a life with Anya. He still insisted that when the time came for me to leave this planet for Aenoas-Vita and take my place on the throne, he would be at my side as Shield and protector, regardless of the fact that I'd released him from his oath to my father.

Jasper had been looking after me since we had been small children, and he deserved a happy, normal life, and I planned to make sure he got it.

I tilted my head back and looked up at the thick blanket of gray sky. In order for any of us to be safe, I had to find Orien and put an end to his plans.

※

My hand hesitated on the door to the studio as I imagined Molly's scornful expression when I walked in an hour late. But then cheers erupted from the other side of the door. Boisterous energy filled the room as I slid in unnoticed.

"Oh my God!" I heard a female voice exclaim. "I can't believe you're getting married."

And then another piped up. "I know! And don't hate me for saying this, Molly, but Darion is such a catch. You're so lucky!" The tall brunette waved her hand, fanning her crimson cheeks, getting nods of agreement.

Thank God Darion wasn't here. His head would be the size of a hot-air balloon.

Several students that we'd gone to high school with flocked around Molly, examining her heart-shaped pink diamond with oohs and aahs all around. The only part of her I could see was her blond ponytail with the pink and blue stripes. Molly was known for adding quirky colors to her hair, so no one would guess that the current colors held significant meaning, unless they knew she was carrying new life inside her.

"There's Everly." Someone pointed me out, and Katie, a regular student at the studio, came toward me, looping her arm through mine.

"You must be so excited. You and Molly have always been so close, and now you're going to be sisters!" Katie squealed with delight. She had always been the first to shoot her hand into the air when we'd gone to school together. "Will there be an engagement party?" she asked me. Her enthusiasm was through the roof.

Katie had been captain of the cheer team in high school and never missed an opportunity to help plan events, so of course, she wanted to hear the party details.

Oh no! I'm the worst sister-in-law-to-be. I hadn't even thought about offering to plan an engagement party, but I smiled and nodded, hoping no one noticed the anxiety causing my cheeks to flame. "I couldn't be more thrilled, and of course there'll be an engagement party." I infused my words with confidence.

Or at least there will be now if no one else is already planning one.

I had really been dropping the ball with my family lately. I peeked over at Molly. A halo of bright pink filled her aura. A dead giveaway of her pregnancy to anyone capable of seeing auras. Worried thoughts crept into the back of my mind, but before I could give them any consideration, Molly frantically waved me over.

"Hey, Molls. I'm sorry I'm so late." I reached into my pocket for a hair tie and twisted my long raven waves into a bun and secured it in place.

"It's fine." Molly pulled me close.

"You okay?" I asked, noticing the pale flush to her skin.

She dabbed her forehead, cheeks, and neck with her yoga towel. "I'm fine. Just need some downtime and maybe a cool shower."

I sensed the low hum of exhaustion in her energy. *The pregnancy.* Until now, I hadn't thought how a human body would be affected by carrying a Vitarian embryo, and Molly had two. Several questions rippled through my mind all at once, but the most worrisome was whether or not Molly's human body could sustain the pregnancy. Darion would be crushed if anything happened to Molly or their babies. My stomach twisted with guilt. I felt like such a jerk for being so inconsiderate and leaving Molly to teach my last class.

"Leave it to me." I tossed my bag over the front-desk counter. "Okay, everyone. Please take your places for class and settle into Anjali Mudra. Eyes closed and long, deep breaths in and out. I want to feel your om vibrating the walls."

While the room filled with energizing breath, I placed my hands on Molly's shoulders and released my own energy.

"Thank you," she whispered. The flush drained from her cheeks, and her aura vibrated with a renewed vigor.

"It's the least I can do. I'm sorry, and it won't happen again."

Molly grabbed her things and quietly ducked out of the studio while I guided the students into their next pose.

By the end of class, exhaustion had settled into my bones. The weeks of late nights and little sleep were taking their toll. Even my own body weight felt like a burden to carry.

My reflection in the mirrored walls followed me as I

finished stacking the meditation cushions. I almost didn't recognize the dark sapphire eyes staring back at me. Hard edges had replaced soft features. Anger and grief now shadowed the bright kindness that had once shone through me. I pulled my hair loose and shook it out of its bun, running my fingers through the long raven tendrils that tumbled down my shoulders. I turned my hands over and rubbed the puffed scars on each of my palms. Reminders of so many failed attempts at finding Orien.

My eyes drifted to the broken heart line, and memories flitted through my mind. I squeezed my eyes shut as emotions came flooding in. My hand bumped against the goddess pendant as I rubbed the ache in my chest. What was happening? This morning I'd felt disconnected from any feelings that had come with thoughts of Arden, but now they tugged at me, like they were finding their way back home. Was this supposed to happen after the releasing ceremony?

I pushed all thoughts of Arden from my mind and looked past the heart line, and I traced a finger across the split life line. Nothing had changed since Anya's reading; the forked branch broke off from the main line toward the lower part of my palm. Something dark loomed in my future, but how far away? I shook away the fear that needled me, and squeezed my hands closed. I'd face whatever came, head-on.

One task remained before I locked up the studio for the night. I pressed in the code to the safe hidden behind the front-desk counter and took out the bottle of gold ink, along with the spelled quill and paper. I dipped the quill into the glowing ink and scribbled sparkling gold letters across the page. The tips of the paper smoldered as I scrawled, and both words and paper vanished as I completed each line.

Arden,

There's been a new development in my search for Orien. I'm in need of guards. Two will suffice. I can't explain now. There's too much risk of exposure. I would not request your soldiers leave their homes unless the need was great. Send them quickly.

 E

The quill hovered over the bare desk as the last bits of paper disintegrated. The letter should be in Arden's possession. An ache brought my hand to my chest again as I pictured Arden reading my words.

"Argh!" Why wasn't the spell working? Kamara had said the emotions I'd released would be trapped inside the stone until they were either destroyed or reclaimed, so why were they still tormenting me? I capped the jar of gold ink and replaced it and the quill inside the safe.

A buzz vibrated in my purse as I was locking up. I shifted my bag and dove my free hand inside in search of my phone while I extracted my key from the studio lock with the other. A text from Kamara lit up my screen: *Club tonight? Great band!*

My fingers flew across the virtual keyboard: *Can't! Dinner with family tonight.*

On second thought ...

I sent another reply: *Might drop in later!*

Maybe Kamara would know why the releasing spell didn't seem to be working the way it should.

Kamara's reply came through before I clicked off my screen: *I hope so. Miss you already!*

I tossed my phone back into my purse and spotted the large rose quartz Freya had given me. I thought of the long, jagged scar that marked her flesh. A shiver shook me as I imagined what horror she must have suffered and overcome.

Instead of getting straight into my car and going home to change for dinner, I started walking toward the riverfront to clear my head. The air was cool and barely tolerable without a jacket for most people, but my body temperature ran warmer since I'd developed fire magic.

A thick layer of rumbling clouds darkened the sky, making it feel much later than it actually was. The weekend crowd dwindled, but many of the shops were still bustling with shoppers.

"Ev!" Someone shouted my name from behind.

I turned and saw Ty walking toward me. After Bree had disappeared, I'd thought her influence over Ty would wane, but he had chosen to keep the short-cropped hair and Gucci-style attire that Bree had persuaded him to wear. I had to admit, the look did suit him.

"Hi, Ty. What are you up to?"

He lifted the box he carried. "Harlow's Gifts is going to carry my dream catchers."

"That's great, Ty."

"Yeah. I owe it all to your mom. Once people started taking my class on making their own, the requests started flying in, and now I can barely make enough to fill the orders." Pride shone in his milk-chocolate eyes. "Flora Designs ordered two more cases of my miniature catchers yesterday. Apparently, they pair well with bouquet gifts."

"Well, I hope you plan to bring a box to the studio. I'd love to feature your dream catchers. I think they'd be a real hit with my students."

Ty's high cheekbones plumped up as his smile grew wide. "I'll bring some by tomorrow. I'd better go deliver these. Harlow's waiting for me."

"I'll see you tomorrow, then." I started to turn away.

"Um, hey, Ev?"

Oh no! I prepared myself for the lie I had to tell. "Yeah, Ty?"

He shifted the box in his arms. His dark brows drew

down, nearly touching his long, thick lashes. "You haven't heard from Bree, have you?"

I exhaled slowly and cringed inside. My skin heated as the words left my mouth.

"Uh-uh. Not since you brought her to my and Darion's birthday party. Sorry, Ty." My chest tightened. The desire to strangle Bree made my jaw clench. She was lucky I didn't still have her tied up.

"Okay. See you, Ev." Ty's shoulders rolled forward as he turned with the same disappointed expression he wore every time he brought up Bree. She'd really done a number on him.

Ty hadn't mentioned Molly's pregnancy, or her and Darion's engagement, which meant she hadn't told him yet. Molly hated lying to Ty about Bree, and keeping him in the dark had distanced the three of us. But Molly understood that we couldn't tell Ty the truth without telling him the entire truth. Maybe Molly was right, and I should tell Ty everything. If he knew what Bree had done to him, maybe he could finally get over her. I pushed the thought away for now and waved goodbye.

"See you, Ty."

I continued toward the riverfront park, passing my mom's café along the way. A couple stood talking at the side of the building. The man was tall, and the woman had dark hair. The pair brought back the memory of when I'd stood in that very spot with Arden, fighting my desire to throw myself into his arms. My throat burned at another memory as I crossed the parking area leading to the park. The pained expression on Lucas's face when he'd walked toward me that day, and I knew he'd seen me kissing Arden.

Squeals of laughter brought me back to the present. I shook off the haunting memories of the past as I hopped up onto the top of a picnic table that overlooked the river. Children filled the playground below, running and jumping with delight as their parents lounged on the park's built-in stone stadium seating. They appeared carefree as they watched their children race up to the slides and swing across the monkey bars. Someday Molly and Darion would be watching their own children play here. I tried imagining the twins. Would they have raven hair and silver eyes like Darion or inherit the blond hair and oak eyes of their mother? One thing was for sure: the pair would be stubborn and fierce, like both of their parents.

Would they have powers? Only time could tell. Anya was half-human and had magic, but her mother was Vitarian. Darion's twins would grow in a human womb. For all we knew, that could affect their development differently. We knew so little about our two species creating life together.

I couldn't believe I was going to be an aunt. I chided myself over my earlier jealousy. Molly and Darion had overcome so much and deserved every bit of happiness they had. Before Darion had come into my life, it had just been me, Mom, Calista, and Selkie. Now I had a twin brother, a sister-in-law-to-be, and a niece and nephew on the way. My family tree kept expanding.

I thought of Creagan and how he'd died trying to free Darion from Siobhan. He had never gotten the chance to see his family reunited, but I hoped wherever his spirit had gone, he knew we were together.

Energy buzzed at my fingertips as they glided over the glassy surface of the rose quartz's blushing hue. The crystal sat heavily in my hand. My eyes roamed over the softer, translucent pink color that filled the rougher parts of the stone. You didn't need to be an Empath to sense the healing energy of crystals. Even humans without magic had a certain aptitude for sensing their energy, but with my Vitarian Empath abilities, not only could I sense the energy, but I could see the vibrations and connect to them on a deeper level. The stone hummed a peaceful harmony as the energy of the crystal seeped into my skin. I groaned and shoved the quartz back inside my bag and thought of the ever stone I'd left stashed in the drawer of my bedside table.

The weightless feeling I'd felt when I'd released my emotions for Arden seemed like a distant memory as a nest of heartache wove anew within me. My love for Arden was relentless in its resistance to untethering itself from my core. If Kamara couldn't help me, then my only option may be to destroy the ever stone and what it carried for good. But now I questioned whether even that would work.

A sharp ache tightened in my chest. If destroying the stone did work, every feeling I had ever felt for Arden would be gone forever. My breath caught, and my heart beat heavily. Was that what I really wanted? I'd thought so last night, when I'd been disconnected from my feelings, but now that they were back, I felt more confused than ever.

I closed my eyes, hoping the migraine that pulsed at my temples would fade. My lips parted, and I exhaled a long breath while gazing one last time across the river at the snow-covered mountains. They appeared so close and yet so far away at the same time.

The wind stirred, blowing my hair into a wild frenzy. I caught the thick mass and twisted it over my shoulder while I ran across the street. If I didn't hurry, I'd be late for dinner.

3

A row of vehicles filled the front parking area of my mom's home. I passed Calista's red Mustang and Selkie's catering van at the end of the line as I continued down the driveway. It appeared I was the last to arrive.

As I swung around the back of the property to park near my apartment, I spotted Sam's sheriff vehicle next to my mom's 4Runner under the carport, where it sat so frequently these days when Sam was off duty.

Since I was already running late, I skipped the shower I had planned on taking and went straight toward the house.

My hand froze on the knob, and I leaned my forehead against the door. Laughter and excited conversation echoed on the other side. I drew in a deep breath, putting on what I hoped was a good party face, and pushed the door open.

"It's about time," Jasper mumbled over a mouthful of what I suspected was *Monarda* tart. "Five more minutes, and there'd have been no dessert left for anyone else." His hand darted down to his side, where it slipped Luna a slice of meat from a tray.

My mom laughed as she turned from the fridge, holding a chilled bottle of champagne. The navy-blue blouse she wore made her sapphire eyes pop and complemented the soft, creamy texture of her skin. She tucked a loose wisp of hair behind her ear and smiled adoringly at Jasper. "Jasper, dear, I've learned over the years to make an entire batch just for you. There's plenty hidden away for everyone else."

"Thanks, Ms. C." Jasper shoved another bite into his mouth while my mom ruffled his wavy, dark hair, and Luna rubbed her head against Jasper's leg before she came over to me for pets.

"I'm glad you're here, honey." My mom kissed my cheek, and the scent of lavender lingered in the surrounding space. "Would you mind grabbing some sparkling waters?" She winked. I wouldn't be the only one drinking a nonalcoholic beverage tonight.

"Here, Ms. C. Let me take the glasses." Jasper swiftly transferred the tray of flutes my mom had just balanced on one hand to his hand, and Luna trotted behind us as we followed my mom into the spacious dining room. She'd added the additional sections to the dining table, which now stretched long enough to fit everyone here tonight.

The spread on the table was immaculate, and the rich aroma of Selkie's famous buttered chicken was unmistakable. My stomach growled with a hunger I hadn't felt in weeks.

"There's our girl." My two surrogate aunts sandwiched me between them as they wrapped their arms around me and covered me in kisses, like they used to when I was little.

"Why haven't we seen much of you lately?" Calista chided. "We're putting an end to that now." She quirked a brow. Her bracelets jangled as her hand shot out.

"Selk," Calista said, pointing at the bounty of food on the table. "Dish her up a heaping plate. We need to get some meat back on these bones."

Selkie gave me an apologetic smile as she twisted my long hair into a loop. But by the way her hazel eyes saddened when she looked me over, I could tell she agreed with Calista.

"I have an idea!" Calista announced with a satisfied smile. She tossed her arms over my and Selkie's shoulders. "A spa day with just the three of us."

"Cal, you're a genius. What do you say, kiddo? Make two old ladies happy, and spend a day getting pampered with us?" Selkie touched her forehead to mine, and I nodded my assent, not wanting to disappoint them.

"Perfect! I'll schedule the appointments."

Selkie and Calista began talking excitedly about facials and paraffin dips.

I smiled, even though the last thing I wanted was to sit for hours having someone do my nails and wax my feet.

Glass chimed across the room. "I have an announcement." My mom beamed, and I noticed she wore the jeweled hair clip my father had given her before he'd died. The colors twinkled under the chandelier light.

Everyone quieted and turned toward my mom. She handed Sam her champagne flute and held out her arms. "Darion and Molly."

The pair went and stood on either side of her. The pink hue encasing Molly was radiant, and I couldn't resist the smile that tugged at the corners of my mouth.

My mom's eyes sparkled like the gems in her hair clip as they filled with happy tears. "My two lovelies have given me the honor of announcing to you, my dear friends and family, that I'm going to be a grandmother, and they're getting married!"

Cheers erupted all around as glasses clinked. But the thread of fear vibrating from one area of the room caught my attention, and my eyes fell on Freya, who quickly masked her reaction. She set her glass down and turned before anyone caught her worried expression.

I inched toward her, but Anya was at her mother's side before I reached her.

"Are you okay, Mama?" I heard her whisper.

Freya straightened, picked up her glass, and placed a smile on her face. "I'm fine, dear. Just a dizzy spell, but it's gone now."

She wasn't fine. She was afraid. But of what?

"We're going to be great-aunts," Selkie sang, pulling my attention from Freya. "Can you believe it, Cal? Let's go congratulate the lovebirds." She nudged Calista toward Darion, and to my surprise, Calista welcomed Darion into a hug.

I smiled in amazement. Darion had finally won Calista over.

Everyone began taking their seat at the table and filling their plate. I took bites of butter chicken while sneaking glances at Freya, who barely touched her food. She sipped her glass and nodded to something Sam was saying. But I could tell her thoughts were somewhere else.

Selkie leaned toward me; the scent of warm cherries drifted from her strawberry hair. "I made your favorite for dessert, dark chocolate cherry cake, and the frosting's to die for."

A loud clang vibrated against the table. My mom screamed, and Darion shot out of his chair and leaned over Molly. Her silverware stood erect in her tight grasp and banged against the table as her entire body trembled uncontrollably.

"She's having a seizure!" Sam yelled, and he pulled his phone from his pocket, but my mom clamped her hand over his and shook her head. Molly was pregnant with Vitarian babies, and if the doctors started running tests, we didn't know what they'd find.

Sam nodded but kept his phone clutched in his hand while his worried eyes monitored Molly.

I jumped up and ran to Molly's other side.

Her energy was out of control. Vibrations poured off her like hot waves rolling off a wildfire. I reached a tentative hand toward her arm and touched her skin. The tangled vibrations encasing her weren't just her own. The threads were coming from Vitarian life force within her. *Her babies.*

What was happening?

I put my other hand on her and tried to enter her energy field, but an invisible force shoved me out. My body actually jerked backward. *The babies are protecting their mother.*

"Don't move her," Darion said, his voice rattled. "Just keep her from falling."

Jasper stood behind Molly, his shield pulsing around him as though he was ready to burst into full Shield mode at any moment.

It felt like an eternity before the shaking stopped, and the silverware Molly clutched clanged onto the table.

Soft whimpers issued from Luna as she lay under Molly's chair, staring out with her anxious dog eyes.

Darion slid his arms beneath Molly and gently lifted her from her chair and carried her into the living room. He laid her on the couch while everyone circled around him and Molly at a distance.

My mom ran into the kitchen and came back with a bowl of cool water and a dry cloth. She handed both to Darion. He tenderly dabbed Molly's eyes, then the beads of sweat on her forehead and nose. She moaned, and her eyes fluttered open.

"Oh ... thank the stars," my mom breathed, and she relaxed into Sam's embrace.

Darion kissed Molly, then asked, "Have you ever had a seizure before?"

"No," Molly breathed, and she held onto Darion as he helped her sit upright.

She took a moment to orient herself and catch her breath.

Her skin had lost all color, and the mass of Vitarian energy I'd felt in the dining room had dulled to a low vibration, but it was still detectable.

Molly gripped Darion's hand. "It was the twins ..." She locked eyes with my brother, whose expression had turned to stone. "They showed me a vision. I could hear their warning in my head." She pulled Darion closer. "Hunters are coming for our babies."

A glass shattered behind us. We all turned toward the noise. Freya's hand covered her mouth as she stared blankly at the broken picture frame she'd bumped into.

"What are you talking about?" Darion asked Molly.

Molly latched onto both of Darion's hands. "They have magic. They showed me a vision of armed men who called themselves Hunters, and they—" Molly sucked in a sharp breath.

Calista passed Darion a glass of water. He lifted the glass to Molly's lips. "Here, love. Take a drink and just breathe slowly."

I pushed my way to Molly's side and touched her shoulder, letting calming waves of energy flow through me to her, and this time the twins did nothing to resist as I helped their mother, but I sensed their magic. Its Vitarian essence mingled with Molly's human energy.

Questions rattled around my brain about the twins and their magic, and the vision they had shown their mother. My insides twisted with fear I tried not to show, for Molly's sake. Who were these men, and what did they want with Molly and Darion's babies?

Molly's muscles relaxed, and she patted my hand, then continued telling us what the twins had shown her. "I was tied down. They were waiting for my babies to come, and there was a woman with them. I think she was some kind of sorceress, because she wore a necklace with a glowing pendant, and she was using magic on me to keep me from moving. They planned to take them …" Molly gasped and wrapped her arms around her abdomen. "I couldn't keep them safe," she choked out as tears trickled down her cheeks.

"It's okay," Darion said through gritted teeth. Then he drew Molly into his chest. "I won't let anything happen to you or our twins."

Darion's eyes met mine, and a mix of emotions crashed into me: fear, uncertainty, rage at the unknown, and a fierce desire to protect.

My muscles went rigid, and I drew in a deep breath and let the emotions pass with the wave of nausea that came with being overwhelmed with another's feelings. The curse that bound Darion and me magnified the experience tenfold.

Molly sniffled against Darion's ear, and he turned his head and whispered unheard words to only her.

"Who are they?" Jasper asked the question burning at the front of my mind. "Why would they come after Molly?"

The room fell into a somber quiet.

Sam squeezed his arms around my mom before she separated herself from his embrace and went to huddle next to Darion and Molly.

"I've heard myths," Calista said. "But I thought that was all they were."

"The Hunters are very real." Freya's voice shook as all eyes turned to her. "They are an ancient order. Their origin is unknown, but their sole purpose is to hunt down and terminate any Vitarian child not of pure blood." Freya's hands trembled as she revealed the top part of the scar that she'd shown me. "The Hunter that came for me murdered the love of my life before my eyes. Then he came for me and tore through me with his knife." She traced her finger over her dress, down past her abdomen. "He left me and my child for dead."

Anya's shock was audible. "Mama—" Anya embraced her mother.

Freya soothed Anya. "It's okay now, baby. It's time I told my story, and told you the truth about how your father really died."

Jasper went to Anya's side. She gave her mother space and held on tightly to Jasper's hand.

"The Hunter that came for me was called Zan, and he was my betrothed before the order came for him."

"You knew him," Anya exclaimed.

"I did not love Zan, but my father was insistent upon our match. Zan had a cold heart, but he did not become truly evil until after the order had claimed him. It had been months since they'd taken him, and when he returned, something dark ruled his soul. Their leader knew of my work with the ever stones. He sent Zan to retrieve me. But while I was in a cave, collecting the stones I was to bring, Zan tried to force himself on me."

Anya gasped. "No!"

My own fists balled tight, and I knew the heat burning inside me was more than the outrage I felt at Freya's tormenter.

Freya reached out and smoothed her daughter's cheek. "He did not succeed. I managed to escape the cave, and out of fear that Zan would come for me again, I fled Aenoas-Vita. I arrived on Earth alone and scared, but I met the kindest man."

Freya's features transformed, and her eyes shone brightly as she continued. "He was a sea captain of a massive tourist ship. I'd somehow portaled myself onto a Caribbean island. And Silus, your dear father"—Freya smiled warmly at her daughter and brushed her hand across Anya's shoulder—"had just come into port. He came up to me and said in the gentlest manner that I seemed lost, and asked if he could buy me a coffee. Our time together was blissful, and those are the most treasured days of my life."

Selkie handed Freya a tissue to wipe the tears that slid down her cheeks.

There was no anger in Freya's aura, just love and sadness as she recounted her story. I unclenched my hands and tried to calm the heat burning at the back of my throat. I quickly grabbed the damp cloth hanging on the side of the bowl Darion had cast aside and pressed it to the back of my neck. Darion noticed my action but kept his question to himself.

"We married not long after, on an isolated island," Freya continued, "where Silus had a home that he'd built. The island was private and only accessible by boat. It was inhabited by very few, and those that lived on the island were friendly and kept to themselves. We lived there, peacefully together, for over a year, and I was the happiest I'd ever been. Silus was the most loving man, and he couldn't wait to be a father."

Anya watched her mother tell her story as she swiped away her own quiet tears. Jasper wrapped his arms around her and drew her into a protective embrace, and I knew in an instant that no matter how hard he tried to hide it from himself, Jasper loved Anya, and I could never let him leave this planet with me.

As if somehow sensing my thoughts, Jasper glanced my way, and in that look was a hint of unmistakable doubt that he could leave Anya behind. Guilt suddenly shrouded his aura, and I gave him a slight nod and smiled that I understood. And it was okay.

My stomach tightened as I tore my attention from my best friend as Freya went on.

"Silus had just returned from one of his tours. We were having a picnic on the beach. I can still taste the fresh coconut milk and feel the warm, salty breeze on my skin like it was yesterday. I don't know how Zan found me. Silus—" Freya cupped her mouth.

The room fell utterly silent. Freya stood straight and took a deep breath.

"Silus fought bravely, but his human strength was no match for Zan. A rage consumed Zan. I was unprepared, and my magic could not protect us. The things Zan said …"

She reached a hand toward her daughter and touched her arm. "Forgive me for what I'm about to say, my sweet daughter, but they need to hear what we're all up against."

Anya nodded. "It's okay, Mama."

I admired the strength Anya provided for her mother while hearing the horror of what had befallen her father. Anya possessed a quality that not all did. She had the strength of a warrior, and I couldn't help but think of Rheya in this moment, and how much I missed her sarcastic honesty.

Freya's words brought me back to the present. "He called me filth for giving myself to a human and told me it was his duty as a member of the Hunters to rid the world of my half-breed child, who polluted the Vitarian blood. His knife still dripped with my husband's blood when he sank it deep into my chest, barely missing my heart, and he tore me apart." A convulsion rippled through Freya. She clutched the top of her blouse.

The fire inside me raged at the atrocity she had suffered. If I could get my hands on this Zan, I'd burn him to the bone.

"When my eyes closed," she continued, adjusting her top and smoothing the fabric, "I thought it would be for the last time, but I awoke some days later in a hut. I remember it was dark, and a woman was feeding me broth that tasted like death itself. She took care of me for weeks. She'd mended my wounds and nurtured me and my unborn child back to health. After she delivered Anya, she disappeared, and I never saw her again. That is when I came here, to where my husband was raised. He spoke so fondly of this town. I wanted our daughter to grow up in the same place as her loving father had."

Anya wiped her eyes and reached for her mother's hand.

Freya's head bowed slightly. "I'm sorry, Anya, darling. You should never have had to hear this, but I fear, with the twins' warning, none of us are safe."

Anya squeezed her mother's hand in silent understanding.

I understood the pain restrained in Anya's features. I'd lost my own father before I'd had a chance to know him, and I had yet to exact my revenge on the one responsible for taking his life.

My mom stood up and crossed the room. She pulled Freya into her arms and comforted her friend. "Freya, I'm so sorry for what you've gone through. I know how very painful it must be for you to relive those memories. Thank you for telling us."

Calista and Selkie joined my mother and huddled around Freya in a protective circle.

"We are all here for you and Anya," my mom said. "We are a family, and we protect each other."

Energy sizzled in the room, and I drew up my protective shield to block out the emotions radiating so near to me. "We need to find out everything we can about the Hunters," I said. "Who they are and how to stop them. Do you have any idea what their leader wanted with you, Freya?"

She dabbed her eyes with a tissue. "I never found out. I'm sorry."

I hesitated to ask my next question. After my talk with Freya earlier in the day, I knew it was a sensitive subject for her, but the Hunters had wanted her for a reason.

"I'm sorry, Freya, but I need to ask what type of magic you were using with the stones."

Freya cast her gaze down at the shards of glass from the fallen picture frame and was quiet for a moment. When she glanced back up, a world of regret filled her ebony stare. "I'm not proud to admit that I dabbled with dangerous magic, and I used the stones to bring spirits forth from realms never meant to be contacted. When one of my spells caused the death of a client, I never touched the stones again, and I destroyed my spell book so no other could replicate the exact spell I'd created."

"Did Zan know of the magic you used with the stones?"

Freya nodded. "Before the tragedy occurred, many in our village came to me desperate to connect with their deceased loved ones. Each time I connected to the spirit realms, I felt myself travel deeper and deeper, and something dark clung to me the last time. I didn't realize the evil I'd conjured until it was too late." Freya covered her face with her hands. "I trapped the dark energy in the stone and buried it with a cloaking spell so it couldn't hurt anyone else."

"Why didn't you destroy the stone?" Darion asked, his tone taking on an accusatory note. His energy shifted, and I recognized the silver flash of mistrust behind his calculating stare.

Freya shook her head. "I tried a hundred different ways, but nothing worked. The darkness that climbed out of the spirit realm with me was too powerful. I was young and foolish." Freya croaked and bit down on her knuckle.

My mom shot Darion a look that silenced him as he was about to open his mouth with another line of questioning. "Come on, honey. Let's go get you a hot cloth for your eyes."

She led Freya out of the room but turned just before she was out of sight, giving Darion another warning glare.

I understood Darion's perspective. It seemed he and Felix agreed when it came to fully trusting Freya, but we had no reason to think ill of her. We'd all made mistakes, and Darion, of all people, should respect second chances.

"Why don't we all take a breath and settle down?" Selkie squeezed Darion's shoulder. "I'll grab a broom and clean up this mess." She motioned toward the shattered glass on the floor.

"Thanks, Selk," I said as she dashed out of the living room.

Calista stretched her long arms, yawned deeply, then threaded her fingers through her wild curls. "I think we could all use one of your mom's special tea blends, or maybe something stronger. Dinners around here just keep getting more interesting." She strode over and kissed my cheek, then knelt down and put her hands on Darion's and Molly's backs. "We won't let anything happen to your precious babies, okay?" Her lips curved into a reassuring smile before she stood and headed toward the kitchen, with both Sam and Anya offering to help with the drinks.

"Zan must have told the Hunters' leader about Freya's ability," I thought aloud.

"And he sent Zan to collect her, but for what purpose?" Darion finished, as if reading my mind.

I touched Molly's shoulder. "Did the vision show anything about how the Hunters knew about your pregnancy?"

"No." She shook her head and trembled in Darion's embrace. He smoothed the frizzed strands of hair from her face and kissed her forehead.

"Wait!" Molly's head whipped up, and Jasper inched closer to my side. "I remember something," Molly said. "The woman who stood over me gave orders that the babies needed to be born alive for her spell to work."

My nails dug into the palms of my hands, and fiery tendrils raced across my arms.

"Ev—" Molly gasped and nodded at my arms.

Darion's and Jasper's eyes went wide when they saw what was happening.

"It's nothing," I told them, and I quickly turned for the hooks behind the front door and grabbed one of the cardigans I kept hanging in the house.

"That didn't look like nothing," Darion noted. "What are you hiding?"

I shrugged. "I'm not hiding anything. It's just the fire magic. Leave it be."

Darion fumed silently at me and looked to be on the verge of going into one of his tirades about how my magic was out of control, but then Sam came back into the living room with Calista and Anya, carrying mugs of tea and glasses of amber liquid that must have been the "something stronger" Calista had referred to.

Calista handed Freya a glass as she walked back into the room with my mom, who accepted the steaming tea mug that Sam handed her.

Freya sank onto the recliner and gulped the entire contents of the glass she held. She put up a hand when Calista offered to refill her glass. "No, thank you. But I'd love tea."

Calista took Freya's empty glass and traded it for one of the steaming mugs.

Freya blew on the steam and carefully sipped the hot liquid, then relaxed back into the chair with Anya watching over her.

"Could it be Orien?" Jasper asked, getting back on subject and going to stand next to Anya. He slid his arm around her waist, and she melted against him. "Maybe he found out about the pregnancy and has sent these Hunters after Molly. That would explain why this woman Molly remembers ordered them to be born alive."

Jasper's line of thought had crossed my mind. "With Orien, anything is possible."

My mom sat on the sofa next to Molly and took her hand. "You remembered something more?"

Darion gritted his teeth while Molly recounted her memory for those who hadn't been in the room.

"If only we could have killed Orien in the cave. Then this wouldn't be happening." Darion stood. He twisted the ring on his right middle finger. Light bounced off the fiery gem that Calista had brought him from Bali, which he'd had cut and encased into two rings—the one he wore and its twin, which never left Molly's hand.

I glanced down and snugged my arms tighter around my chest. It was my fault Orien had gotten away. *Molly and the babies are in danger because of my failure.*

Fingers clasped mine, and I met Darion's demanding stare. He shook his head as if he sensed the direction of my thoughts. "Don't blame yourself. It's no one's fault he got away, but we need to find him. Orien only cares about one thing: power. The twins are descended of the Ever bloodline. If he knew they had magic, he'd want it for himself. He needs the magic of Ever twins to reverse what Oria did to him. Orien is a threat to the lives of my children. We need to find out if he's connected to the Hunters."

"You're right, brother. If Orien's not working with the Hunters, he must know something about them. They stink of his evil." My fingers twitched with the urge to be alone with my chalk and magic.

Darion studied me for a moment. He guessed my intention. He'd warned me about practicing the magic I'd been using these last several weeks, but now Molly's life and their babies depended on me finding Orien. Darion glanced away without saying a word.

"I'd feel better if you both moved into the house for the time being. Would that be okay with you, Molly, honey?" asked my mom.

"I'll have my officers patrol the area and keep a watch around the café and studio." Sam went into sheriff mode.

"Sam, honey." A warm glow filled my mom's aura. "I'm grateful that you want to help, but we can't risk exposure."

Sam kissed my mom's forehead. "I understand. I'll do my best to monitor the areas myself."

"Okay," my mom agreed. "But please be careful. These are Vitarians, and they have magic. And you have Piper to think of." My mom tucked her head under Sam's chin.

When she'd told Sam the truth about who we really were, she had been terrified and prepared to erase his memory immediately. But Sam had told her he'd never believed that Earth held the only life, and when she'd shown him her magic, he'd responded, unfazed, "Life wouldn't exist without magic, and magic wouldn't exist without life. Some are just closer to the source than others." She'd repeated his words with wonder.

I'd always sensed something unique about Sam, so it had come as no surprise when he'd accepted us without fear or judgment.

"Sam has the right idea, Mom. Will you contact Felix and see what he knows of the Hunters? And we need a Shield."

Jasper stepped forward at my words. I held out my hand. "You'll protect Anya, Jasp. But I want a royal Shield assigned to Molly as well. I've already contacted Arden about guards. I'll explain later," I told my mom when she wrinkled her brow in question. "But we'll need more than the original number. I'm awaiting Arden's reply, and in the meantime, I'll send another request, for additional guards to keep watch around the property while Molly and Darion stay here."

"I'll talk to my father," Jasper said, a conflict brewing in his amber gaze. "The number of Shields is half what it was a century ago, and the gift is presenting weaker and weaker. He'll know who Felix should send."

I groaned silently at Jasper's reminder that magic was fading from Aenoas-Vita. The council didn't know the cause, but they tracked and kept a secret record of the decline of certain abilities. We didn't know how much time we had before those abilities went extinct.

I pushed those worries to the back of my mind for another time.

Darion helped Molly up. "Let's go pack some things to bring back to the house."

"Sam and I will follow behind you." My mom's tone brooked no argument on the subject.

"And we'll be right behind you." Calista grabbed her and Selkie's jackets.

"Power in numbers," Selkie agreed.

"What about you, Ev?" Jasper asked. He would always put my protection above all, but even if he wouldn't admit it to himself, I knew how much Anya meant to him, and his worry for her was evident in the vibrations surrounding his aura.

"You take Anya and Freya home, Jasp. I'll be fine here on my own." I shot a glance at Darion and relaxed. He was so focused on Molly that he hadn't noticed my lie.

I had no intention of staying home, but they didn't need to know that.

An eerie silence filled the yoga studio. I drew in my energy and sent out my internal command.

Light.

A charge sparked through the air, and a soft glow burst from the wicks of every candle in the room.

I smiled to myself, proud of the new trick I'd mastered. I opened the safe and quickly finished sending Arden another message. It surprised me I hadn't received a reply yet. I shook the concern away and reached for the spelled blade.

Shadows cast in the flickering candlelight crept up the walls as I stood in front of the floor-to-ceiling mirrors. The air stirred. I called out the words I'd memorized and smeared my blood over the mirror in an arc, creating a circle as big as my arms could reach. Then I filled in the center with the all-seeing eye and stood back.

Fire.

Red-hot flames burst from the image as the glass shattered into a tracking portal linked to my blood. I stepped inside the black nothingness and searched.

"Orien!"

The crack appeared. A sliver of light in the darkness, taunting me as I ran toward it. If only it would open more, I could see what Orien saw and find him. The familiar laughter rang overhead, penetrating my ears.

"Do you think I don't sense you trying to get into my head, niece? I admire your effort, but these baby spells are no match for my magic."

"Who are the Hunters?"

The laughing ceased, and I was slammed out of the portal and back through the mirror, which was once again solid glass. I stared at my charred blood, wondering at the sudden expulsion. Orien usually liked to taunt me much longer before proving he could evade my attempt to use my ability of Sight to see through his eyes.

Why can't I break through?

I'd practiced on Darion and the others with success, but it never worked on Orien. I smacked the glass and wiped my hands through the symbol, smearing my crusted blood.

I sighed.

The air left me as I pressed my back against the mirror and slid down to the floor, hugging my knees. I needed to siphon more energy. The leftover dark energy I had extracted from my students wasn't enough. It was a weak energy that fed on fear and insecurities. I needed pure energy to fuel my magic. I'd never crossed that line before, but I had to do whatever it took to keep Molly and Darion's babies safe.

A buzz vibrated from the front-desk counter, where my purse sat with my phone inside.

Kamara. The club.

I knew what I had to do. I'd be breaking the first rule of Neil's club, not to use my magic for mischief while on property, and he wouldn't be happy if he found out. The thought of putting my friendship with Neil at risk made me cringe with hesitation, but what other choice was there? I had to do what was necessary at all costs.

Straightening my black tank top, I pushed myself up to standing and pulled my hair loose from its twist. Waves cascaded down past my shoulders. I crinkled my nose at my pale reflection, then went to my purse and dug around for the tube of lip gloss and stick of black eyeliner.

Backing away from the mirror, I examined my handiwork. The thin, sharp black lines added an edge to my sapphire eyes, and my lips sparkled with the crimson gloss. Satisfied, I snapped my fingers, putting out the candles, and locked up the studio.

The field where everyone parked outside the club was packed.

Perfect!

"Neil around?" I asked the host over the ridiculous bass.

He tilted his blond head toward the red velvet curtain that hid the staircase leading to Neil's flat upstairs. "Boss is upstairs." He shifted his glasses down the bridge of his nose, so his blue eyes peered over the rims. "Do you want me to call him?"

I smiled at the host, who had obviously been inspired by Neil's style of attire. "No, thanks."

So far, so good.

If Neil had been monitoring the bar tonight, I wouldn't have had the guts to break his cardinal rule right in front of him.

After a quick stop at the bar and a couple of shots of evernescence, I searched the crowd for Kamara's energy. My senses took over as I followed the familiar thread to the one it belonged to. I lifted my arms into the air and swayed to the music as I weaved around bodies until I spotted Kamara's glittering skin and long hair. Her curved hips shimmied as her body bounced to the music.

Dancers closed in around us. I twisted and turned to match Kamara's pace. Her fingers swept across my shoulders and torso, and I gripped her waist. Her skin smelled of patchouli and sweat, and her hair of sweet orange blossoms. I breathed it in as my nose trailed the back of her neck, my teeth grazing her flesh. She arched back against me, revealing more bare skin where her top cut off at her midriff. She moaned and turned, her lips finding mine. Our tongues teased each other as we continued our sultry dance.

I released my mental shield, and as I lost myself in

Kamara, I latched onto the energy around me. Vibrations swam through the air, entering me one by one. A dizziness separate from the light-headedness caused by the evernescence consumed me, and a feeling of weightlessness lifted me up as I siphoned more, reveling in the pure ecstasy of Vitarian energy. It was more powerful than the dark energy I drew from my students, almost orgasmic. It held an essence of magic that filled me to the core. With so many Vitarians packed into the club, I was able to fill myself without taking too much from any one source, and no one would suspect that their energy had been siphoned. They might feel slightly hungover tomorrow, but that could be attributed to the late night of dancing and consumption of evernescence.

Kamara's arms locked around me, and she gasped. I opened my eyes and glanced down. Our bodies hovered inches above the floor, and pulses of light flashed up my arms.

I snapped my shield back in place, and our feet softly touched down.

"What have you done?" Kamara's sooty lashes drew down as her eyes narrowed.

"Exactly what you've been telling me to do for weeks. I'm taking what I need to help break through Orien's barriers. It's my only choice. But not from you, love." I licked the curve of her neck, and she ran her fingers into my hair.

Time didn't exist inside the club. As long as patrons remained, the club provided drinks and entertainment. Minutes turned into hours on the dance floor.

Music pounded through my rib cage. I didn't know if it was still night or morning when Kamara tilted her head back and said, "You have an admirer."

"Hmm." My mouth found hers again.

She laughed, separating herself enough to force me to pay attention.

"I don't think he likes what he sees." Her muscles tensed.

That got my attention. I glanced around, trying to force my mind to clear enough to pick out any recognizable features, and then I felt it. I locked onto the thread of energy and traced it to a pair of soul-searing eyes.

My heart pounded against my chest, and blood rushed to my ears, sending a wave of heat down the back of my neck. My hand instinctively flew to the goddess pendant tucked under my shirt. A thunderstorm of emotions rolled through me, and I struggled to breathe. *This shouldn't be happening. I locked these feelings away in the stone.* Before I had a chance to pull my thoughts into a cohesive thread, a familiar voice mocked me from behind.

"Isn't this a surprising twist?" Rheya laughed. "If I'd known I stood a chance, I might've given the commander a run for his money." Rheya's laugh quieted while her gaze raked over Kamara.

I wrapped a protective arm around Kamara's waist. "What are you doing here, Rheya?"

Rheya's stance relaxed. She placed one hand lazily over the hilt of her sword while she twisted the length of her long copper braid with her other. "Why don't you ask the commander?" She dropped her heavy braid over her shoulder and held a hand out to Kamara. "May I steal a dance with your *friend?*"

Rheya winked at me, and the heat at the back of my neck spread to my cheeks.

"Don't worry," I reassured Kamara. "Rheya's got a big bark, but she doesn't bite."

"Ha! Shows what you know." Rheya quirked an auburn brow.

"I think I can handle her." Kamara extended her hand and slipped it into Rheya's, and the two twirled away.

I had to admit, Rheya had moves, and Kamara seemed to enjoy responding to them. I'd have been jealous if the two of us had been serious, but what Kamara and I had was casual and filled what would otherwise be lonely nights.

The crux of my heart stood scowling at me with a tense jaw and hard muscles. Arden masked his emotions with an impenetrable wall, but the anger he felt shone in the lines across his forehead and the shadow of crushed feelings staring back at me. Not a hint of blue remained visible under the fiery green moss that stalked my every move in his direction.

I couldn't blame him. After all, I'd broken his heart without so much as a warning. Yet as commander of Aenoas-Vita's army, he remained bound to answer my every call.

"Why are you here, Arden?" My eyes drifted to his tantalizing lips.

"I received your message," he answered coolly.

"My message was for soldiers. But more specifically, what are you doing here, at the club?"

Arden glowered down at me. "The soldiers wait with Rhal and Malakai at your mother's. You weren't home." He glanced in the direction of Kamara and Rheya. "Darion said we'd find you here. If you're in danger, it's my duty to protect you." His stony features softened as his hand lifted toward me.

I held my breath as he swept a lock of my hair back. My eyes trailed his honeyed five-o'clock shadow and landed on his mouth as images of those sexy lips, searing my skin with every touch, filled my mind.

I flinched away from his touch. I needed to talk to Kamara about what had gone wrong with the spell and why my feelings were still torturing me. There had to be something we could do to fix it.

A strained expression crossed Arden's face at my reaction toward him. He stood silently looking me over, and the all-too-familiar stir of energy charged the air between us.

His eyes wandered once more to Kamara, who was

grinding her hips against Rheya. "What are you doing, Everly?"

I groaned. I couldn't allow myself to be so affected by Arden's presence. I wrapped myself in a hard wall and responded, "I'm having fun, Arden. You should try it sometime." I turned away, ready to march off, but he caught my arm. The energy that zapped between us was explosive. Every feeling that I'd tried to erase with the releasing ceremony stared back at me in Arden's expression and rippled through my being, causing my body to shudder.

He felt too much for me. I nearly faltered as the desire to entwine my fingers around his neck overcame me. I steeled myself and yanked my hand away from his as if a viper had bitten me.

His stare became hard. "When you're done having fun, I'll be at the cabin. Guards will be stationed around your property and inside your mother's home with her permission." He flashed a look in Rheya's direction and turned away.

A freeze iced the area where Arden had stood. His long strides carried him away too quickly as he slipped through the crowd and disappeared behind the red velvet curtains.

Kamara's arms wound around me. "That's him," she whispered in my ear while she nibbled at the lobe. "The one you hide your love from."

My hands tightened around hers. I spun, and our mouths collided as I tried to forget Arden and the feelings that should be gone but still tethered my heart to him.

The guards Arden had stationed around our property remained out of sight, but I sensed their energies as I stumbled from my car and into my apartment. I barely made it to my bedroom before I crashed onto my bed.

"Everly."

My eyes snapped open, but I was no longer in my bedroom. I stood in a dark space, twisting from side to side, and that was when I noticed the cracks. Two slivers of light shone ahead.

Where am I?

The cracks grew and spread like a web expanding all around me. The walls shuddered and light exploded ahead, forcing me to squeeze my eyes shut at the brightness. When I opened them, a forest of color surrounded me. I breathed in sweet air that made my skin prickle with life. Flowers that stood as tall as me glittered with radiant hues.

I reached a tentative hand toward the luscious petals.

"Do it, Orien."

My outstretched fingers froze, then curled closed. I held my breath and waited.

"I don't want to hurt it, Oria. Please don't make me."

I crept around the corner, where two children huddled together on the ground.

"Don't you love me, brother?"

The little boy nodded as he swiped away a tear.

"Then prove it, Orien. Prove how much you love me." The little girl, with sparkling raven hair and shining sapphire eyes, hovered over the boy, whose hand shook. The blade he held descended on a glowing creature that squirmed beneath the boy's knee. Light glinted off the sharp tip as it halted several inches above its target.

I gasped. The transparent skin of the creature rippled with flickering currents of energy, similar to the ever stone. Its wings, which were crushed against the ground, shimmered in multiple layers of color. The turquoise tip of one wing protruding from beneath its back was rimmed in glittering silver and dusted with specks of twinkling gold. It twisted its tiny head unnaturally and looked directly at me with glowing purple eyes that pleaded for help.

My hand flew to my mouth. I stumbled back. Did it see me?

"Don't be weak, Orien. We're royalty. This creature belongs to us, like everything else in these lands. Make it bleed for me."

I cringed at the cruelty in the girl's words and the cold darkness within her aura. This couldn't be Oria. She was supposed to be kind, and this girl was anything but.

The little boy cried harder. "Mother says we're to be the protectors, so we shouldn't hurt it."

"If you wish to rule at my side, you'll do as I say." The girl bent down next to her brother and snatched up his hand. She forced his hand downward, and the shining blade sank into the creature's chest.

"No!"

My body jolted as I woke with a start. My hands flew out and felt my mattress beneath me. I knew what I had seen hadn't been a dream. It had been a memory—Orien's memory. He'd dream walked into my mind. But what he had shown me didn't make sense. Oria had been so cruel. That couldn't have been what had really happened. *Orien's just twisting things to mess with my mind.*

I kicked the blankets back and peeled off my sweat-soaked tank top and went to take a shower.

I was on my third cup of coffee, trying to kill the migraine that buzzed at my temples, when a fist pounded on my front door.

"Okay! I'm coming." I set my mug on the counter and went to the door.

Bree's fist was set for another blow on the door just as I yanked it wide open, and she stumbled forward.

"Argh! Thanks a lot!" She righted herself and glanced around my apartment with her nose high in the air.

I sighed and closed the door. "What do you want, Bree?"

She swerved past me in her tight white pants and red stilettos and tossed her bag onto the kitchen island. She rummaged through my cabinets and helped herself to a mug, then poured herself a cup of coffee. She didn't even glance my way when she cracked the fridge open and took out the coconut milk, which she then left sitting on the counter.

"Huh." I twisted the cap back onto the jug of coconut milk and put it back in the fridge. "Please, just make yourself right at home," I said sarcastically.

Bree swung herself up onto a barstool. "Don't mind if I do." She kicked her feet up onto the vacant stool next to her.

I rolled my eyes and walked around to the other side of the counter and refilled my cup, then lifted a brow while I waited for Bree to tell me why she had barged into my apartment at five in the morning.

"Not bad." She took another gulp from her mug. "What's for breakfast?"

"Oh my God! Just tell me what you're doing here." A sledgehammer banged against the inside of my head.

"Okay! Simmer down." Bree grinned, enjoying the fact that she was irritating me. She sipped her coffee, then announced, "We're going on a road trip."

"Are you high? I'm not going anywhere with you." I winced when I set my cup down a little too loudly.

Bree shrugged. "Then I guess you're not interested in the tip I got on Orien." Her fire-engine red pinkie nail shot high into the air as she drained her coffee mug.

Working with Bree definitely went against my intuition, but I may as well take advantage of this blood oath. "Tell me."

I barely remembered the drive up to the cabin when I parked and got out of my car. The scene with Orien and Oria plagued my thoughts. And then there was the tip Bree had received from her friend at the club where she'd first met Orien.

I pushed through the cabin's front door without knocking and stopped in my tracks when I saw a woman I didn't recognize feeding Arden a bite of something from her plate as the two laughed together.

Words caught in my throat. Heat flushed my skin, and I reached for the goddess dangling against my chest. My grip tightened until the miniature stone cradled in the pendant cut into my palm, and I fought the urge to tear across the room and shove the golden-haired beauty and her forkful of food away from Arden. If only that damn releasing spell had worked the way it was supposed to, I wouldn't feel like I was about to combust.

"I ... I'm—" *Oh God! Say something, Everly!* But my tongue was twisted in knots and wouldn't comply.

I'd wanted him to move on, but seeing him with someone

else hurt more than I had expected, and the guilty expression Arden wore made it even worse.

He straightened and stepped away from the woman as he slipped his shirt on over his head. The soft cotton glided past his muscled abdomen, and a lump formed at the back of my throat as the woman standing next to him watched him with a hungry ease.

The iron-gray fabric complemented the blue-green eyes that were currently locked on mine, and for an instant, nothing and no one else existed, until the woman's voice chimed in next to Arden.

"Hello." She smiled. "You must be Queen Everly." She bowed her head. "I'm Dalia."

I tore my gaze from Arden and forced the edges of my lips up.

Why did she have to be so beautiful and womanly, and have curves you couldn't help but envy? I cringed inside while I offered her a smile. "It's a pleasure to meet you, Dalia."

Her smile was absolutely radiant, and her hair, the color of spun gold, was twisted into an intricate braid that ran down her back. "Your Majesty."

"Oh, no. Please, just call me Everly."

"You're even more beautiful than I expected, Everly." Dalia blushed as she glanced at Arden, who'd further separated himself from her.

"That's kind of you." *I could say the same of you.* I groaned internally.

"Everly!" Malakai darted down the staircase leading up to the second floor at my side.

"Malakai! Excuse me." Relieved to escape the awkward conversation, I shot around Dalia and flew into Malakai's arms. "It's so good to see you."

Malakai's wild energy was a breath of fresh air.

"How kind of Her Majesty to grace us with her presence,"

Rheya taunted as she came down the stairs behind Malakai. "How did I do?" she whispered in my ear, and motioned her eyes toward Dalia. She didn't wait for an answer before she shoved past and followed Dalia into the kitchen and filled a plate with the amazing-smelling food that had my stomach growling audibly.

"Would you like to join us for breakfast, Everly?" Dalia asked. She adjusted the knobs on the gas burners so the flames warming the pans clicked off, and then pulled a baking sheet lined with bacon out of the oven, just in time for Malakai to scoop off a few slices.

"Thanks, D."

Malakai's casual familiarity with Dalia was like another punch in the gut.

This scene felt like a regular occurrence to them, and I couldn't help but wonder how often the beautiful Dalia made everyone breakfast back on Aenoas-Vita, and where she did the cooking.

The salty scent of the meat filled the air, eliciting another growl from my traitorous stomach.

"Dalia's an *amazing* cook," Rheya announced, louder than she needed to, and she effortlessly lifted herself up onto the kitchen counter. She reached behind her and cracked one of the windows, letting in a gust of fresh air.

I ignored the satisfied grin Rheya wore while she shoved food into her mouth with her long legs dangling over the side of the counter, and I answered Dalia. "That's nice of you to offer, but if I could just borrow the commander for a moment …"

Arden followed me out onto the porch.

"Everly."

My hands glided over the worn wood of the deck banister. I took a few calming breaths while I stared past the treetops at the snowy mountains beyond. The pointed peaks were a mesmerizing sight, but it was the flat top of Mount St. Helens that always drew my attention. It stood as a reminder that a serene and beautiful exterior could be a facade for a menacing threat harbored deep within hidden layers.

Arden's energy threaded into mine as he silently drew nearer.

I kept my face turned away from him while I reminded myself that Arden had done nothing wrong. *I'm the one who pushed him away and told him I didn't love him.* I forced a steel wall around me to keep Arden's Empath abilities from sensing any uncertainty in my words. "There's no need to explain. Dalia's lovely, and I'm happy for you." My nails dug into a splinter in the wood.

"It's not—" He reached a hand toward me and paused.

I backed away. "Really, Arden, it's fine."

His hand fell back to his side, and lines of frustration rippled across his forehead. "Darion filled me in about Molly and her vision. She'll have guards and a Shield at all times."

I nodded. "Thank you."

Arden followed me as I walked down the porch steps and toward the path that led into the forest.

"I've heard the myth of these Hunters," Arden said at my side as we continued along the trail. "But until now, that's all they've been, whispers among our kind to keep Vitarians fearful of having intimate relations with humans. Freya is the first I've known to have seen one."

Brushing past a huckleberry bush, I ran my finger over one of its shiny green leaves. "Perhaps that's because the victim doesn't usually survive to tell their story," I offered. "Have there been any updates on the Shimera?"

Arden cut through the trees and leaned against an ancient oak tree. "Our borders are secure, and there has been no sign of threat posed by the Shimera."

He studied me as he leaned against the very spot where

we'd shared our first kiss, and where I had broken his heart. "You're different."

"What do you mean?"

He pushed away from the tree and took two long strides toward me.

My breath hitched when he stopped an inch away and stared down at me. I didn't move when he gently laid his hands on my shoulders.

"I don't know ..." He ran his fingers into my hair, causing knots to tangle in my stomach.

I twisted away, angry at the way my heart began to beat wildly. *This shouldn't be happening. I shouldn't feel a thing toward him, and yet I feel everything as I did before.*

My eyes squeezed shut as I inhaled deeply and doubled the invisible barrier I surrounded myself with to rein in my emotions and keep Arden from sensing my reaction toward him. Instead, I focused on the reason that had brought me here.

"There's been a development with Orien." My words came out hoarse, and I took another step away from Arden to distance myself from the pull he had over me, but the farther I went from him, the more my body desired his closeness. Ignoring my inner turmoil, and the way Arden was staring at my mouth, I went on. "I'm going out of town for the night to a club where Orien's been spotted. I need you to keep Molly safe, and there's another reason why I initially asked for guards. Bree has returned."

A scowl furrowed Arden's brow, and I quickly added, "She's sworn a blood oath to me. She's helping me locate Orien, and in return, I've promised her protection."

Arden slid his hands into his pockets. "Blood oath or not, she's proved she can't be trusted. I don't like this plan."

I sighed. I was tiring of everyone in my life questioning my decisions. "I don't trust her one bit, but she knows what will happen if she breaks the blood oath. Will you do as I ask or not?"

Arden's mouth quirked with a grin as a glint of something lit up his eyes. "I'll place a guard with her." He glanced up at the sky as a loud squawk tore through the forest.

An eagle soared above the trees, reminding me of the time Malakai had shared his gift with me. The large bird dove into the branches, and I wondered if Malakai was inhabiting it now.

"That's why I'm here," I said, shifting my attention from the eagle back to Arden. "Bree and I are going on a little road trip to one of Neil's clubs, in Eugene, to investigate a lead on Orien, and I want to take two of your guards with me. If they need time to prepare, they can meet me at my place, but we leave in an hour."

"I'll have them ready to go in ten minutes. Are you sure only two? Shouldn't we surround the building?"

"Not this time. We don't know if Orien will be there, and I don't want to risk blowing Bree's cover yet."

He nodded. "Do you want to come back inside for coffee or—"

"No," I cut Arden off before he could finish. The last thing I wanted to see was Dalia anywhere near Arden again. "I'll just wait at my car."

Arden strode back toward the cabin. When he was out of sight, I wandered to the oak tree he'd leaned on and trailed my hand down the jagged bark, remembering the feeling of it scratching against my skin that night when Arden had me pressed against it. The images flashed in my mind, and my skin prickled as if the moment had just passed. I really needed to talk to Kamara and find out what had gone wrong with the releasing spell. It had seemed to work perfectly, but now it was like it had never happened. It didn't make sense. I turned from the tree and followed the path back to my car.

As I waited for Arden's guards, I stared at the cabin and thought of Arden inside with Dalia, shirtless and eating from her fork. Dalia made him smile. He cared for her. I sensed it, and she had strong feelings for him. She would be good for him, and she'd treat him better than I had. But the thought of Arden being hers ... A searing heat rippled through my arms just as two balls of flame burst from my palms.

Crap!

I shook my hands, forcing the fire back inside me, and glanced at the cabin, hoping no one had been looking out the windows just now.

The cabin door swung open as I was stomping out the patch of grass that smoldered from the bit of fire that had spat free. Thankfully, I put it out before anyone noticed what I was doing.

My eyes widened when Arden, Rheya, and Dalia came hastening down the stairs.

"Shotgun," Rheya called, and she swooped into the passenger seat.

I narrowed my gaze at Arden. "What's this all about?"

"We're your guards," Rheya barked from inside the car. "Let's roll."

Arden shrugged when I glared at him.

"How exciting!" Dalia slid onto the backseat when Arden opened the door for her. "My first trip to Earth and now a road trip."

"Can I talk to you?" I marched away a few feet. When Arden came up behind me, I spun on him. "I asked for two of your guards."

"Well, you're getting three. We are your guards. Your safety is *my* priority."

"Why is Dalia coming?"

Arden's hand shot through his hair. "Rheya invited her."

I gritted my teeth. "Of course she did." The tip of my

boot slammed into the ground. "She could get hurt. Shouldn't she stay here, where it's safe?"

A battle waged in Arden's expression. He stepped toward me. "Dalia is a trained fighter. She's no longer a soldier, but she remains a part of the royal guard as keeper of the Ever Gardens. She's perfectly capable of taking care of herself. But if you're against her coming, I'll ask her to stay behind."

My lips pinched together tightly. Yes, I wanted to demand that she stay, but I couldn't. If I did, Arden would know that I had a problem with the woman in his life accompanying him. "Let's just go."

He sighed as I shoved past him.

Rheya grinned widely when I hopped into the driver's seat. "This should be fun, huh, Your Majesty?" She sniggered to herself and adjusted her seat back. "You have enough room, Dalia?"

I glanced in my rearview mirror and saw Dalia scoot out of the way of Rheya's seat as it continued backward, forcing Dalia closer to Arden. My cheeks burned when Arden's reflection stared back at me. I looked away and started the engine.

"Real fun," I whispered through my clenched jaw.

B ree was standing outside her studio, tapping on her cell phone, when I pulled up. She glanced at the front seat and then the back.

Rheya rolled down her window. "Get in the back, Barbie."

"It's Bree!" Bree snapped, and she huffed as she tossed in her bag. "Do you mind bringing the back of your seat up so I can get in?"

The seat rose, just giving Bree enough leg room. She

squished into the back seat with her knees pressed into the back of Rheya's seat.

"I'd appreciate a little more room, if you don't mind." Bree shifted, causing Dalia to press closer to Arden.

I growled under my breath as I pulled away from the curb.

"A crew will be out tomorrow to repair my sign," Bree said with an air of irritation.

I hadn't apologized for destroying it. It was the least Bree deserved.

"Oh, what happened to it?" Dalia asked.

I felt Bree's eyes burning the back of my head when she replied to Dalia. "It had an accident and came crashing to the ground."

"That's terrible."

My shoulders trembled with laughter. I'd hoped to never have to see that monstrosity Bree called a business sign again.

"Yeah," Bree answered Dalia. "It's lucky no one was injured when it came down."

I glanced over my shoulder, and Bree flicked her hair back and gave me a pointed stare. I shook my head and turned back to face the road. Bree should consider herself very lucky. It had taken all my willpower not to let the sign fall on top of her. After all, she had helped Orien destroy lives.

Rheya fiddled with the radio. And for the first thirty minutes, I thought maybe the drive wouldn't be so bad—that was, until Bree asked Dalia if she and Arden were a couple and how they'd met.

My eyes found Arden in the rearview mirror, and he shifted nervously.

Dalia had a warm and soothing tone when she spoke, another admirable quality. "I'm the groundskeeper of the Ever Gardens. I've known Arden for many years, but it wasn't until recently that we've spent more time together." She smiled when she glanced sideways at Arden. "For the last couple of months, Arden has been visiting the gardens each day." Dalia paused, and I knew she was thinking of things she wouldn't say aloud to strangers, but a sadness passed over her expression before it was replaced with the glow of hope. "Each day, we talked a little more, until finally I worked up the courage to invite the commander over for dinner."

"And now she cooks for him every day," Rheya added quietly with a wink.

My grip tightened on the steering wheel. The tips of my ears burned while Bree and Dalia continued making conversation, and Dalia described the extravagant meal she'd made for Arden on their first date and the picnics they'd shared since. I snuck glances at Dalia in the mirror as she spoke. Her smooth, pale skin had a soft glow. Gray eyes sparkled with a hint of blue, and I knew from her aura that she always saw the bright side of things. Her face was framed by shining gold hair that she'd twisted into a complicated braid. As I watched her mouth move, I couldn't help but wonder if Arden had kissed those perfectly plump lips.

Suddenly a cold hand clamped around my arm. My head whipped sideways, and I was about to tear free from Rheya's grasp when I saw the glowing red veins creeping up the length of my arm. Rheya released her magic, and a blast of ice raced through me, causing a shiver in my bones as the tendrils faded beneath my skin.

Her eyes narrowed as the white glacier clouding her irises dissipated behind a green blaze, and she shook her head, releasing my arm.

My heart thrummed in my ears. I hadn't even realized the fire inside me was surfacing. It was responding to my ... fury. Seeing Arden with someone else, especially someone as perfect as Dalia, was eating me up inside. The releasing spell was definitely no longer working. A deep ache rippled through me. Had I made the biggest mistake of my life in driving Arden into someone else's arms?

I risked another glance in the mirror, and my chest constricted when I saw Dalia's head resting on Arden's shoulder. A perfectly content smile danced across her lips as she dozed. I drew in a deep breath and clasped my hand over the pendant Freya had given me. It was small, but the weight of it suddenly felt heavy as it lay against my bare skin. Heat surged up the back of my throat. I swallowed hard, forcing it back down, and shifted my gaze to another direction. My breath caught. Arden watched me in the mirror. Our eyes locked, and in that instant, I knew he felt everything I felt. I threw my invisible wall up, and he cast his eyes down at the sleeping Dalia and leaned his head back against his headrest.

The remaining miles passed in a quiet blur of tree farms, cattle fields, and forested hilltops. When the synthetic voice of the map guide came over the speakers, indicating the exit ahead, I changed lanes and exited the highway. Memories of previous trips to visit Lucas shook me as I drove into the town of Eugene, where he had lived, worked, and attended college when he'd been alive.

I slowed as we passed Neil's club. Unlike his club in St. Helens, this one wasn't hidden in the woods with magic, and the patrons here weren't only Vitarians. I gripped the steering wheel and held my breath when someone with sandy-blond hair burst through the doors. Of course, it wasn't Lucas, but for an instant, a flutter of hope tricked me into thinking it could be him.

I pressed the gas pedal and sped past.

"Whoa!" Rheya gripped the door rest as her body jolted to the side at my abrupt turn.

Dalia's head shot up off Arden's shoulder.

"Sorry," I mumbled. But I really wasn't. I was glad Dalia wasn't cozied up to Arden any longer now that everyone sat erect and alert. Except Bree, who still nuzzled her jacket, which she'd folded into a makeshift pillow.

"Are we there?" Dalia asked as I slipped into a parking lot and found a spot to park in between two larger vehicles.

I shifted the gear into park. "The club is just a few blocks away. Bree will go ahead of us, and we'll pair up and split off to go in separately. We're here to guard Bree. If Orien shows, only Bree is to approach him. We don't move on him here."

Rheya fidgeted in her seat. "Why don't we just surround the building with guards and take him down?"

"Because we don't even know if Orien will show up," I told her. "And if he senses a trap, we lose the upper hand with Bree, and he'll know she's working with us. The goal here is for Bree to convince Orien she misses him and wants to help him, while she'll really be leading us to him. And besides, Neil owns this club, and unlike the other one, the patrons are not restricted to Vitarian. Attacking Orien here would be too risky for the humans. If I thought we could capture Orien without anyone getting hurt, the plan would be different, but for now, our job is to blend in and keep an eye on Bree, and that's it."

I waited for Rheya to nod her agreement before turning my attention back to Bree. "If he shows, and you think he's onto you, remember the signal we talked about. I'll have my eyes on you the entire time."

Bree rummaged in the oversized bag she'd brought and passed me a short blond wig with cropped bangs.

Rheya smirked while she watched me secure the wig in place. "Not bad."

"Take your hair down," I told her.

"What?"

"We need to blend in, and you look too ... hard around the edges. And leave your weapons in the car. There's a bouncer stationed at the door to check for weapons before letting anyone inside."

Rheya's face turned crimson as she undid her braid while she scowled at me.

"What's a bouncer?" Dalia asked.

I twisted around in my seat and glimpsed muscled abs as Arden shifted out of his jacket and put on the ball cap that Bree handed him. He'd easily blend in as one of the college football jocks.

Dalia cleared her throat, and I realized I hadn't answered her.

"Oh, a bouncer is basically a guard," I explained.

"Ah … And what about my clothing and hair?"

I looked Dalia over. She wore a casual dress that wouldn't stand out. She had all the soft features of a lady and none of a warrior. "You're fine the way you are." I tried to offer Dalia a smile, until her hand glided atop Arden's thigh as though it was the most natural movement, and I tore my eyes away and spun back around.

Bree left the car. I waited until her energy was out of range. "Okay. Dalia and Arden, it's your turn. Once you're inside, keep Bree in sight but maintain distance."

After Arden and Dalia left the car, Rheya let her tongue loose on me. "Your fire magic is out of control. You didn't even know you were using it."

I sighed. "We don't have time for this, Rheya."

She gripped the door handle. "I felt the fire when I touched you. It rages with your fury. Fire magic is deeply tied to emotion. Until you deal with what you refuse to, it won't be tamed, not even by a queen." Rheya pushed the door open and slammed it shut behind her.

The low light of the club took a minute to adjust to after being outside in the daylight. Neil's Eugene club was a downsized version of his St. Helens club. Since humans were welcome in this establishment, all decor was limited to what was acceptable to the human mind. There would be no shots of evernescence, no floating sconces, and the only swirls of light were created by electronics controlled by humans. But Neil had still done a superior job with the ambience.

Knots pinched my insides when I glanced over at the bartender standing behind the long fish tank, which was a smaller replica of the tank at Neil's other club.

"Here." Rheya handed me a tall glass filled with clear liquid and garnished with a lime.

"No alcohol." I pushed the glass away.

"It's club soda. We're blending in, remember?" Rheya drank from her glass while she looked around the club.

"Good thinking." I squeezed the lime into the bubbling soda water and sipped while I scanned the room for Bree. I spotted her on the dance floor with a group of human girls. They laughed as they swung their hips together, and for the first time since I'd known Bree, she actually looked carefree. I didn't detect a hint of her usual snotty demeanor.

I sought Arden's energy and found him dancing with Dalia. She interlaced her fingers around Arden's neck, and he smiled down at her.

"Careful," Rheya warned, and nodded at my hand.

Crap!

I took a deep breath and commanded the magic back. The red tendril that had crept to the surface of my skin faded.

Rheya flung her long copper hair back with irritation. Apparently, wearing her hair down was not something she enjoyed.

"Isn't this what you wanted?" Rheya nodded toward Dalia, then continued without waiting for my reply. "Someone to make him smile. Dalia's kind and smart and without baggage. She's perfect for the commander, and the stars know I'd love to see him move on from you, but ..." Rheya stretched a hand toward me and clasped the top of my arm. "He loves you, Everly. That hasn't changed, but given enough time, I think he could be happy with Dalia ... if that's still what you want."

What *did* I want? The releasing spell obviously wasn't working. I still loved Arden as much as I ever had, but the reason I had left him hadn't changed. Lucas was gone because of me, and I only caused Arden pain.

Just then Arden spun Dalia and caught her around the waist. Dalia trailed her hand up his arm and pressed her body close to his.

I slammed my glass down on a nearby table and yanked my arm free from Rheya's grasp. "I have to go to the bathroom. Keep an eye on Bree."

I pushed through the bodies that filled the club. I didn't really need to use the restroom, I just needed to catch my breath. If that damn spell had worked the way it should have, I wouldn't have cared that Arden smiled with Dalia, touched her, and enjoyed her company. I'd told him to move on, and that was what he was doing, so why couldn't I just let him go, with or without the help of magic?

"Everly."

I felt his energy behind me as he captured my hand. When I turned, I threw my arms around his neck, and his lips were on mine in an instant. A different kind of fire seared my insides. We backed up behind the wall that separated the restrooms from the dance floor. Arden twisted open the door to the janitorial closet and lifted my legs around his body as he moved us inside and kicked the door closed.

He pulled back, and his eyes blazed with an emerald fire

as he drank me in before his lips returned to mine. His hands pressed firmly against my back so that no space remained between us. I tilted my head back when his mouth trailed down my neck, his tongue caressing the plump curve of my breast. A soft moan escaped me when his teeth grazed my skin.

When his mouth found mine again, he whispered against my skin. "What do you want, Everly?"

"I want you." I locked my legs tighter around his waist, and Arden suddenly froze.

He caught my hands as I lifted his shirt. "That's not what you said before. You said you didn't love me and told me to find another. What's changed?"

Oh God. What am I doing?

"Nothing's changed," I lied as I created a thick barrier around me. "I don't know what this is." I loosened my legs from his waist, and my feet slid to the floor.

Arden shook his head. "You're lying to yourself as much as you are to me. Do you think I don't sense the barrier you surround yourself with every time you tell me you don't love me? But I can't be with you like this. You know how I feel about you. I want more."

"And that's what Dalia is? More?" I shoved away from him.

Arden reached for my shoulder. "So that's what this is all about? You're jealous of Dalia?"

I shrugged Arden's hand off my shoulder, but he latched onto my arm and spun me around. "Look at me," he demanded. "Damn it, Everly. You know how much I love you. You know what I'd give up for you, and yet you still pushed me away." He stared down at me with hard eyes. There was nothing left of the earlier passion he had felt. "Dalia and I aren't a couple," he said through gritted teeth.

"Well, someone might want to tell her that. She touches

you like she has some kind of claim on you. Have you been with her?"

Arden's jaw clenched. His silence told me all I needed to know. I wanted to lash out at him, to shove him against the wall and pound on his chest and demand that he tell me how he could do that to me. But what right did I have? He'd only done exactly what I had made him do. I turned for the door as Arden whispered my name into the dark.

When I rounded the corner, I bumped into Dalia.

She straightened her dress. "Oh, I'm sorry, Your Maj—I mean, Everly. Have you seen Arden?"

Dalia stared at me with her innocent gray-blue eyes as she waited for my answer.

The darkness in me wanted to sting her like a scorpion would its victim, but instead, I bit back the anger raging through me and nodded toward the bathrooms. Then I pushed past Dalia without saying a word, not caring if I was being rude. She'd slept with the man I loved, albeit unknowingly, but it still took all my effort not to give in to the part of me that ached to punish her for taking for herself what I couldn't.

੒

"You were gone awhile," Rheya noted.

I snatched my glass of soda water and gulped it down. "Long line."

"Uh-huh ... Something's put the commander in a foul mood." Rheya motioned toward a solemn Arden as he walked across the club with Dalia. And then she eyed me suspiciously.

"Huh." I shrugged and checked the crowd for Bree. The club had gotten busier since we'd first arrived.

Rheya nodded. "She's over there with her cackling hens. This mission is a bust. You-know-who isn't coming."

"He might. It's still early."

Rheya set her glass down. "We're talking about a man who has survived centuries under the radar. Do you really think Barbie over there is going to outsmart him?"

I propped my elbow up on the table and sighed. "You're right. This was a fool's errand."

"Or not ..." Rheya's eyes narrowed as she gazed past me and then slid off her stool.

She slinked onto the dance floor and started a conversation with a woman who'd been dancing with friends. The slender woman, whose bronze skin was covered in tribal tattoos, reached for Rheya's hand, and the two began swaying their hips as they laughed and inched closer to one another. To my surprise, Rheya seemed to enjoy it when the woman ran her fingers through her flowing copper hair. She slid her own hand down the woman's back as they continued grinding to the music.

I couldn't help but roll my eyes. Leave it to Rheya to find a hot date while on a reconnaissance mission. I huffed out a frustrated breath and slumped back against my chair, my attention gravitating toward Dalia and Arden.

Arden's entire demeanor had changed from when he'd first joined Dalia on the dance floor. The carefree smile he'd had earlier had been replaced by a hard expression, and he no longer seemed to be enjoying Dalia's company. I'd done that. I brought death and pain to everyone I touched.

"Hello, niece."

I gripped the sides of my chair and sat erect as spiders raced down my spine.

"Turn or call out, and I'll leave this place a bloodbath. Shimera surround your friends on the dance floor."

I scanned the dancers. Of course, the Shimera wouldn't be

in their true form. They could be any one of the people inside the club, just waiting to strike.

"Calm your magic," he ordered.

Sparks shot up the sides of my arms.

"That's better," Orien said as I gained control of my magic, and the flickers of electricity vanished beneath my skin.

"I'm going to kill you," I growled.

He chuckled. "Oh, I do love your tenacity, niece. And yes, the time may come when you do end me, but that time is not now. You need my help."

"Ha! I don't need anything from you except your death."

"The Hunters."

My skin prickled. "What do you know of them?"

"I've crossed paths with their order over the centuries. Their leader is the Ghost of Time. Something precious was taken from him, and he exacts his revenge on the innocent while he searches between dimensions. So tell me, niece. Which of my descendants is expecting?" His hot breath touched my ear as he bent over me. "No need," he continued when I remained silent. "I'll take a stab at it. If I had to guess, I'd say my doppelgänger nephew and the feisty little blond have a bun baking in the oven." He laughed when I flinched.

"What do you mean, their leader is the Ghost of Time? And what dimensions? You're even madder than I thought you were."

Orien gripped my shoulder. "Maybe I am a madman, but I speak the truth. Their leader searches between worlds. You should have learned by now that life is more complicated than the eye can see. Now, I'd love to tell you everything I know, niece, but I need something from you."

I scanned the crowd, hoping to catch Rheya's or Arden's attention, but a group of college students flooded in and blocked my view.

I shrugged, trying to shake Orien's hand off my shoulder. "What?"

"I need your blood."

"You're growing weak."

"It's true. My life force is getting harder to maintain on the weak blood source I've used these many centuries. I need the blood of one from my own bloodline to regenerate."

I inched closer to the edge of my seat, preparing myself to lunge and make my move.

"But"—his nails dug deep into the skin of my shoulder—"don't think I'm too weak to follow through on my threat. Everyone in this club will perish if you move against me. Your sparky red-haired friend will be first. The Shimera she dances with waits only for my signal."

Rheya!

His threat halted my movement as bitter hatred surged through me. Attacking him would be too much of a risk.

Boisterous conversation took place all around us as everyone was oblivious to the danger that surrounded them.

"You're crazy if you think I'll let you drink from me. I'll kill you before I give you my blood."

"Don't be foolish," Orien hissed from behind. "Your brother's child will never be safe as long as the Hunters exist. Once they know of the child, and I presume they either do or will soon, or you wouldn't have come to me about them, they will never stop hunting it. I can help you find them and put an end to them. But you must help me first."

Orien had said "child." He didn't know that Molly carried twins. Orien was finally within my grasp, but at what cost? If I attacked him here, innocent people could be hurt or worse, and he had information that could help me find out who the Hunters were. If I could find them before they learned of Molly's pregnancy, I could stop them from ever coming after her. Molly's safety took priority over my thirst for revenge.

Darion would want me to do whatever I had to do to save his babies and Molly, even if that meant working with our enemy.

I sighed as I accepted the only option I had and scooted back in my seat. "How do I know you're not the one who sends them?"

"That's a valid question, and one I think you already know the answer to. I may need the blood of that child someday, and no one goes after my own but me."

Blood rushed to my ears with the pounding of the bass as the music seemed to get louder. My chest grew tight, and I fought the fire that burned to be released. I sucked in a breath of the humid air that clung to my skin. Sweat beaded at the nape of my neck as I gripped the sides of my chair to force myself to remain in place. "You have a sick sense of family loyalty."

Orien laughed. "I suppose I do. What's your decision, niece?"

I gritted my teeth as I agreed to the unthinkable. "There's a janitorial closet behind the wall near the restrooms. I'll meet you in there."

"Sorry, niece, but I don't trust you. It has to be here and now."

I started to turn, but his nails cut deeper into my shoulder. "Ouch! Get your hands off me. There are too many people here. Someone will see."

And then the lights went out, and teeth sank into my neck. I didn't resist as Orien drained my blood. A scream pierced my ears as my body slid to the sticky floor. I tried pushing myself up, but my hand landed in the wet puddle of someone's spilled drink, and then I stood back inside the tunnel from my dream.

"You have to see first to understand," Orien's voice whispered inside my head.

The walls crumbled, and an exotic garden appeared. The

whimper of a child drew me around the corner to where the two children sat next to the dead creature. Its tiny body lay limp while the young girl ran her finger across the blade. She popped her finger into her mouth and sucked the blood off. Her eyes glowed with magic, and her skin sparkled as the creature had when it had still lived.

Footsteps neared, and the girl shoved the knife into the boy's hand. "Children," a woman's melodic voice called from behind.

I stood mesmerized as she came into view. Everything about her was regal and elegant. Her long raven hair shone bright and cascaded past her sparkling skin. Sapphire eyes stared over the children. She gasped when she saw the lifeless creature. "What have you done?"

"It was Orien, Mother." The girl accused her brother with a shaking hand. A false tear slid down her cheek as she lied. "I tried to stop him, but he wouldn't listen to me."

Orien dropped the knife to the ground. He sat trembling, staring at the lifeless creature, but said nothing in his defense.

"I'm very disappointed, Orien. You are an Ever, and these are our people and our lands." The woman's arms spread wide. "Why would you harm this beautiful creature?"

Oria narrowed her gaze at Orien as he glanced up at his mother.

"I—" Orien croaked. Then he pinched his lips together tightly as tears flowed from his cheeks onto the creature's dimming skin.

Their mother bent down. Her words were gentle and kind. "Magic imbues the forest fairies as it does us. They are under the protection of the realm. As an Ever, it's your duty to keep them safe. Do you understand, Orien?" She scooped up the tiny winged body and whispered over it until it disintegrated into dust. "Hold out your hands."

Orien's hands shot out, and his mother filled them with the fairy dust.

"You must give back to the soil the life you took." She nodded at a garden of ever flowers, and I noticed drips of water trickling down the length of the petals, as though the flowers mourned the loss of the forest fairy.

A halo of brilliant colors bloomed to life at Orien's approach.

Orien whimpered as he spread the ashes over the soil underneath the giant flowers. Light reflected off a drip of clear liquid that fell from the tip of a flower's leaf onto Orien. He smeared the drop across his skin and whispered, "Sorry."

"Now, come with me, children." Their mother extended her hands. Orien grasped his mother's hand, but Oria did not.

"I'll be right there, Mother. I forgot something near the trees."

"Don't be long, Oria. It's time for your lessons."

Once her mother and Orien were out of view, Oria ran to the bed of flowers and scooped up a handful of the fairy ashes and shoved them into a pouch she had tied at her waist.

The scene faded, and then I stood within an immense room. The sun shone through high windows and cast rays of light on walls made of what appeared to be a shimmering quartz.

I walked to the massive bed situated in the center of the room. My fingers glided atop silk fabric that decorated a plump mattress. Symbols carved into the headboard caught my eye, and then I noticed that each bedpost of the intricately cut white wood displayed a different set of symbols. Some seemed vaguely familiar, and then I remembered the symbols cut into the stone bordering the fireplace in Felix's cabin.

The scratch of pen scribbling roughly against paper drew my attention toward a girl who sat at a desk made of the same quartz stone as the walls. Her hand moved quickly as she dipped her pen in ink and wrote furiously. She had the same features as the young Oria, only now she was much older, maybe sixteen. Her bedroom door burst open.

"Orien! What took you so long, brother? Do you have what I need?"

"You doubt me, sister." He produced a sack made of fabric and cinched tightly to secure whatever was struggling within.

Oria took the bundle from Orien. "I saw you with *her* again. She takes too much of your time. She plans to steal you from me."

Orien stood tall. He was a striking young man. His sapphire eyes shone with kindness and vulnerability. Both traits he no longer possessed.

"Zelda is kind. She has no plans of any sort. We enjoy each other's company is all. Have you been spying on me again? You promised you would stop using the Sight on me."

Oria's haughty stare narrowed. "You care for her, brother." Her words were gentle as she caressed Orien's cheek, and an unmistakable hint of fear shadowed his features. "Do you care for her more than you do me?" She squeezed a chunk of his skin aggressively.

Orien backed away, rubbing his sore cheek. "Of course not, sister. You know how much I love you. I'll do anything you ask of me. But Zelda makes me feel like I'm ... good," he whispered.

Oria flicked her hand. "Then go. Be with Zelda, Orien, and leave me alone."

Pain splashed across Orien's features before he turned and left.

Oria went to her bed and dumped the contents of the sack atop her mattress. Three small fairies struggled against the thin rope that bound them together. An energy shrouded them as they wiggled their little hands and bare feet, which were shaped no differently from my own. An inner light brightened within their transparent skin, and they twinkled with a mirage of vibrant colors as sounds squeaked from their tiny mouths. They tried flapping their delicate-looking wings, but they were bound too tightly.

They stared past Oria, and each looked directly at me as their melodic voices pleaded in a language I didn't understand.

Oria's hand hesitated as she reached toward them. She turned in my direction and scanned the area with a narrow gaze. She huffed, then turned back and snatched up the bundle of fairies, a dark expression twisting her beautiful features. "It's time to send Zelda a message."

"Stop!" I yelled. I tried to reach for the fairies, but I slammed into an invisible wall and woke with a start.

My head throbbed. I tried fluffing my pillow, but my hand found hard muscle instead. My eyes snapped open. An arm was tucked around me, and my body lay across Arden's lap.

Dalia glanced over from across the back seat. "You're awake. Are you okay? You were calling out in your sleep."

A haze clouded my vision. Dalia's voice seemed distant, though she was only a few feet from me. I squeezed my eyes shut as my mind reoriented itself back to my present surroundings.

Arden's chest lifted as he breathed, and I fought the urge to nuzzle against him and doze off. His scent enveloped me as I shifted, and without thinking, my hand wrapped around his neck, and I breathed him in and nearly kissed him as his hands guided my torso up.

The car swerved, jerking my body to the side. Arden's arms tensed around me, pulling me against him, but not before my head bounced off the window.

"Rheya!" Arden scowled past the driver's seat.

"Sorry, Commander. I thought I saw something in the road."

More like she saw me in the rearview mirror, about to do something that Dalia wouldn't like too much.

My entire body shivered as Arden held me.

A blaze of emerald looked me over. "Are you hurt?"

"I'm fine." I rubbed the back of my head where it had hit the window, and felt a tender spot, but nothing that wouldn't heal in a day or two. "What happened?"

"I was hoping you could tell us that. The lights went out at the club, and when they came back on, we found you passed out on the floor."

It all came rushing back. Orien at the club. I'd let him drink my blood in exchange for knowledge about the Hunters. And then the dream again ... Orien was in my head, whispering about me needing to see. See what? That he was twisting history to turn me against Oria? Or was he showing me the truth? No! Oria couldn't have done those things. *I won't believe it.* And what did any of what he had shown me have to do with the Hunters?

My hand flew to my neck. I felt no wounds and vaguely remembered Orien whispering as he smeared something on my neck. Whatever he'd done had healed the bite marks.

What game was Orien playing? I scratched at the scars on my palms. I needed to be alone with my magic.

"Are you sure you're okay?" Arden examined the area of my neck that I'd been inspecting, then glanced at my hands.

"Yes." I gripped his shoulder as I adjusted myself. His expression grew strained, and his muscles went rigid when I pressed against him and then scooted off his lap.

Dalia watched us closely. Her gaze fell on Arden's hands as they slid from my body. She scooted closer to the door to make room for me in between them.

"I don't know what happened." I wrapped myself in a

thick shield as the lie passed my lips. Arden was an Empath, like me. Though it wasn't his dominant gift, he had honed it well. "Everything went dark, and that's the last thing I remember."

How could I tell them I'd let Orien drink my blood? Rheya would think me a fool, and Arden would be furious. No. I wasn't ready to reveal my deal with Orien. Not until he gave me something worth sharing. *There must be a reason he's shown me these memories of the past.*

Arden didn't say anything as he studied me. The hurt from earlier still lingered in his eyes.

He watched my movements as I reached up and felt for the goddess pendant dangling beneath my shirt and ran my thumb over the soft cotton fabric. I should never have let anything happen between us at the club, but even now, an electric pull sizzled in the air between us. If magic couldn't keep me from loving him, how could I continue to deny him? The way his eyes drifted to my mouth sent a flame burning through me. I jerked sideways and bumped into Dalia who I'd forgotten sat on the other side of me.

"Oh, sorry, Dalia."

An odd look flashed across her features before she smiled and waved off my apology, and I wondered if Arden had ever told her about our relationship. I considered dabbling in her aura, but instead, I repositioned myself awkwardly in the center of the backseat and leaned my head back. My eyes drifted closed as Rheya and Bree bickered over what music to listen to.

$$\text{\textbf{\ss{}}} \quad 5 \quad \text{\textbf{\ss{}}}$$

A roaring wind jolted me from an agitated sleep. I rolled over, expecting to sprawl out, but remembered I wasn't in my own bed when my leg hit a wall. I tossed the blanket back and sat up and glanced toward the dark window.

Dalia had insisted I stay overnight at the cabin. She had worried that driving down the mountain alone in the dark could be dangerous, and Arden and Rheya had both agreed. So I'd caved and taken the spare room, which had once served as a healing room for Selkie, my mother, and Jasper.

The door creaked when I opened it. The scent of freshly brewed coffee drifted through the cabin, a sign that I wasn't the only early riser. I crept into the kitchen and poured a mug of the steaming brew and then went outside onto the front porch.

"Couldn't sleep either?" I sat down on the step next to Arden.

"I don't sleep well on Earth." Fog billowed from his mouth.

A pang pinched my insides when he continued looking toward the forest without a glance in my direction.

"I suppose I'd feel the same way if I was on another planet." Which was exactly what my future had in store for me.

Arden didn't respond. A quietness lingered between us as we drank from our mugs and stared into the shadows cast by the swaying tree branches.

A melodic hoot came from an unseen location and echoed all around us.

When he finally spoke, his voice held a haunting sadness. "Why did you push me away after what happened to Lucas? Why didn't you let me be there for you? If you needed time, I would have given it to you, and you know that."

We turned to face each other, and Arden caressed my face. The wind stirred and ruffled his golden hair.

I allowed myself a moment to enjoy his touch before I tilted my head away, and his hand fell back to his thigh.

"It wasn't time I needed, Arden. After what happened to Lucas, I couldn't allow myself to be loved by you. The way he died ..." A stabbing pain tore through me, and I couldn't fight back the tears that burned free. "It was so wrong, and I can never forgive myself. I can never let myself enjoy the pleasures of loving someone, not when Lucas died because of his love for me."

Arden's thumb caught my tears, and he drew me to him as he wrapped his strong arms around me. I buried my face in his chest, exhaling the tension caged in my lungs while breathing in the comforting scent of him. I'd forgotten how easy it was to talk to him.

"I'm sorry for what happened to Lucas. And I'm sorry you punish yourself for it. But I need the truth, Everly, because what you say doesn't match the energy that surrounds you. I can feel the barrier you wrap around yourself when you're near me. Why? If you can honestly say you don't love me, tell me now, but no more lies." His heart quickened under my touch as he waited for my answer.

I couldn't bring myself to hide the truth any longer. I sat up and took his hands in mine. "The truth is, being without you and not knowing if you believed I didn't love you has been torture. I've been so desperate to release myself from these feelings that I did just that, only it didn't work. I still love you, Arden. I never stopped."

He released a deep breath and lifted me onto his lap. His fingers kneaded my back, neck, and shoulders until they entwined in my hair, and he guided my head down toward his. Our mouths collided, and energy exploded between us.

Arden pulled back slightly and stared up at me, brushing strands of raven hair from my face. His brow furrowed. "What do you mean you released your feelings?"

My mouth quirked. "It doesn't matter now, because it didn't work, but I participated in a releasing ceremony."

"And you were willing to erase your love for me? Just like that?" The blue disintegrated from his eyes, and pools of fiery emerald stared back at me as the air cooled between us, and he set me off his lap.

My own temper flared. "It's not like you're completely innocent. You slept with another woman." My voice rose, and with it, the unreasonable sense of betrayal I felt.

"And whose fault is that?" Arden asked accusingly. "You insisted I was nothing to you but the commander of your army, to do your bidding. You swore you had no love for me, and you enlisted Rheya to find me someone else to spend my time with."

His fist slammed down onto the wooden step, causing our coffee mugs to rattle.

A silence grew between us as Arden looked up at the star-filled sky. The hurt he felt radiated in his vibrations.

I wanted to reach out and touch him and tell him how

sorry I was, but instead, I picked up my mug and cradled it in my hands and let the guilt gnaw at my insides. "Did Rheya tell you?"

"You think I don't know when my closest friend and the person I trust most is acting on someone else's behalf? Rheya wanted me to move on from you, but the lengths she went to were too much even for her." Arden grinned. "I have to hand it to her, though. She played her part well. The only reason I accepted Dalia's invitation to dinner was to get Rheya off my case about it."

The wind stirred around me. "And yet you slept with her, and you brought her here with you. Here! To our place. To where we fell in love."

Branches thrashed behind me. I knew my magic was spinning out of control, but I didn't care. "How could you bring her?" Leaves and debris swirled in the air.

Arden tried to reach for me, but I shoved him back. "No!" I set my mug down and leaped up from the step.

"And what about you?" he demanded, jumping to his feet and scowling down at me. "I saw you with that woman at the club. You're just as guilty as I am," he raged.

"It's not the same. Kamara and I haven't been together in that way. We dance, we kiss, and we caress, but I have not betrayed you in that way. I never would."

The sticks and leaves crashed to the ground as Arden yanked me against his chest and crushed his lips to mine.

For a blissful moment, we lost ourselves in each other, and then reality hit. My promise to Lucas. Dalia sleeping obliviously inside. Too much stood between us.

Our lips parted, and Arden whispered against my ear. "I love you, Everly."

I stiffened and pushed him back. "Nothing's changed. We can't be together."

His expression froze. Then a furrow wrinkled his brow as

he stared at me in confusion. "So we're back to that game? You love me. You don't love me. You kiss me, and then we can't be together."

Arden stepped away from me. "You're making a mistake, Everly, and by the time you realize it, it's going to be too late. I'll never stop loving you, but I won't play this game anymore."

He turned for the cabin and left me standing alone in the night.

I knew what he had said was true. But if I made things right with Arden, I'd be betraying Lucas … again.

I pressed my head into my hands and walked numbly back to my room. The floor above me creaked, and I wondered if Arden was sharing a room with Dalia. The thought made me queasy, and I buried my face in the pillow and squeezed my eyes shut.

Once again I stood imprisoned within tunneled walls that crumbled as voices echoed in my head.

"What have you done to Zelda, Oria?"

Oria casually placed her book at her side and stood from the stone bench she sat upon at the far end of the garden. "I don't know what you mean, brother. Has something happened to Zelda?" She drifted near the ever flowers. The tips of the flower petals curled inward at her touch, as if they, too, sensed her darkness.

Orien marched toward Oria and scowled down at his sister. "She's sick! And I know it was you!"

Oria's features softened when she reached out a hand to touch Orien. "You think so little of me, brother. Why would I harm someone you care about?" She smiled at him as though he were a toddler she was schooling, even though the pair were twins.

Orien shrugged Oria's hand away. "Why do you force me to do things I hate? We're supposed to be the protectors of this land and all its creatures, yet you make me go to the forest and capture that which I'm supposed to protect. You use me to do your bidding, and you're jealous of Zelda because she makes me happy, and you're afraid she'll come between us."

Oria's sapphire eyes glaciered over with a look that sent a chill through my bones. "Zelda will be fine, brother. And if you hate doing what I ask of you so much, then why don't you refuse?"

When Orien offered no reply, Oria smiled and kissed him on the lips. "I suggest you worry less about Zelda and more about preparing for the choosing."

Orien stepped back and wiped his mouth with his sleeve. "That's all you care about. Who will be chosen to rule. The ancestors will see your cruelty, Oria. You can't hide it from them." Orien spun on his heel and strode away from his sister.

Oria picked up her book and threw it across the garden.

"He's right. But I can help you."

Prickles raced across my spine. Something about the voice was familiar, but as I turned to see who approached Oria, a bright ray of sunlight flooded my vision, and my eyes fluttered open.

Sunlight poured through the floor-to-ceiling windows that made up an entire wall in the cabin's living room and looked out onto a blanket of green forest and blue skies. I glimpsed silver fur blurring through the trees. The wolf stopped. Its head shifted toward the window, and sharp eyes stared back at me as I reached into its energy field, sensing Malakai's wild vibrations inhabiting the animal. I wondered where his body rested while his consciousness shared the body of the wolf. He lifted his snout to the sky and howled before turning and disappearing into the forest.

I went to stand in front of the crackling flames that filled the fireplace, and studied the symbols carved into the stone that bordered the hearth and mantel. I reached out and traced the deep grooves with my finger, remembering similar ones burned into the bedposts in Oria's bedroom. The memory of the magical fairies bound on her bed haunted me. What had she planned to use them for?

The fire hissed as a log collapsed from the center and turned to cinders and ash. I bent down and plucked a fresh log off a stack and tossed it into the flames. Scents of cinnamon and sugar drifted into the living room, and riotous laughter vibrated from the kitchen. I adjusted the log with the fire poker, then went to see what all the commotion was about.

"Hey, Sleeping Beauty," Rheya teased. "You're just in time for Dalia's delicious cinnamon rolls."

A groan rattled inside me. I wasn't in the mood for Dalia and her amazing food. And I definitely didn't appreciate Dalia and her voluptuous curves, which she was currently brushing up against Arden as she carried a full platter of cinnamon rolls, shining with fresh glaze, to the table. Her golden hair cascaded past her shoulders in waves, and a smile lit her face. "Help yourself. There's fresh coffee too, or tea if you prefer."

I mumbled a thanks and made my way into the kitchen.

Arden glowered from the counter he leaned against and hastened to the table when I nudged past him to get a mug for coffee.

"I hope you slept well." Dalia handed me a plate.

My cheeks burned as I nodded and glanced at Arden, who refused to look at me.

I tore my eyes away from him and plopped down into a

chair and devoured a cinnamon roll. "These are delicious, Dalia. Do I taste orange?" I washed the gooey bite down with a hefty gulp of earthy brew. The nights spent experiencing Orien's memories had left their mark on my energy level.

Dalia beamed. "It's my secret ingredient. A hint of orange zest." She handed Arden a full plate, her hand lingering on his shoulder.

I set my cup down a little too forcefully, earning a mocking grin from Rheya, who tossed me a towel for the spilled coffee. Dalia scooted her seat over to Arden while I soaked up the drops of coffee on the table. I tried hard not to pay attention to the fact that Dalia rested her arm against Arden's. When she leaned into him with a relaxed familiarity, I had to cross my legs to keep them from kicking her chair back. She turned and said something only he could hear, and his frown transformed into a smile that made me ache to be in her place. When a lock of her hair caught on his shirt and remained there as the two continued in a private conversation, it was all I could do not to reach across the table and tear it off him.

Rheya kicked my leg and nodded toward my hand when I grimaced at her.

"Oh," Dalia breathed. "Are you okay, Everly?"

Smoke drifted from the wooden table beneath my fingertips, and when I snatched my hand away, charred fingerprints remained.

My chair scraped against the floor as I abruptly stood. "I'm sorry. I ..."

I stared across the table at Arden, who watched me through hooded eyes and guarded emotions. Dalia's hand rested atop his, and red tendrils snaked up my arms as my fire magic burned beneath the surface of my skin. "I have to go." I ran back to the room I'd slept in and grabbed my bag and rushed outside, colliding with Malakai as I catapulted down the porch steps.

He caught my shoulders and steadied me.

The cabin door banged open, and Arden's energy enveloped me.

Malakai glanced past me, then squeezed my arms as understanding emanated from him.

"Sorry, Malakai." I darted past him and ran to my car.

"Everly!" Arden called after me.

My hand froze on the door handle.

"What was that back there? Your powers are out of control?"

I spun. "I don't need you to tell me that, Arden. I'm dealing with it." I opened the car door and tossed my bag inside. "Go back to Dalia."

He flinched. Then his features hardened under a glow of sunlight. Pain shadowed his aura before he blocked me out.

The voice inside my head urged me to go to him and run my fingers through his golden hair, which sparkled in the light of the sun, and claim what was mine. But I ignored her silent pleas.

"You can't have it both ways, Everly. You push me away and tell me you don't want to be with me, yet your actions speak otherwise. I think you need to question if punishing yourself for what happened to Lucas is worth everything it will cost you."

When I didn't respond, he encased himself in a wall of ice. "I'll be at your mother's today." His tone took on the sternness of a commander. "Rhal set wards around your property last night. Tonight, Malakai will survey the area from the sky. It's unknown how these Hunters find their victims, but we'll be guarding from all angles. Felix is researching their order, and he'll send word when he's found something."

I nodded with a tightness in my chest. Everything I wanted to say stayed locked inside.

Disappointment shrouded Arden's features when he turned away and walked back to the cabin. Dalia waited for him at the front door. A golden-haired goddess, free to love who she chose. Her aura bloomed in a familiar hue when Arden approached her.

I slammed my car door and sped down the mountain, taking the corners at reckless speeds.

⚜

I drove straight to Neil's, eager to burn off some agitated energy. I felt at home in the sea of bodies under the dim lighting and floating sconces. When I released my mental shield and fed on the powerful Vitarian energy surrounding me, a laugh echoed in my mind. "You are my blood after all." I pushed away the memory of Orien's words and reveled in the power that coursed through my veins and made me forget about Arden.

"Hey, love." Kamara's slender arms snaked around my waist. When her mouth moved toward mine, I backed away.

She smiled with a hint of sadness. "It's okay. I knew the one that stole your heart would return to you. Friends?" She twisted me around.

"Of course." I pulled her into an embrace. "Always."

We danced together as we always had.

Patchouli and orange blossom scented the air as Kamara's hair lifted, and the image of Dalia brushing up against Arden tortured my mind once more.

"Your skin is burning up." Kamara drew her fingers down my arm. She clasped my hands. "Are you okay, love?"

"I don't think so," I admitted. "Is there a reason the releasing spell would stop working?"

Kamara's brow drew down. "What do you mean, stop working?"

"Well, after the ceremony, I felt great. For the first time in a long time, I didn't feel shackled to my feelings for Arden, but ever since he showed up the other night, everything I felt for him came crashing back. It's like the spell never happened, and I can't let him go."

Kamara was silent while our hips continued to move to the music. Concern rippled across her forehead as she shook her head. "I've never heard of this occurring before. Do you carry the stone with you?"

"No." I shook my head. "I've left it in the same place since that night."

"Hmm ... If the stone isn't in close proximity, the emotions you released into it shouldn't affect you at all. I'll need to speak with my uncle when I return to Aenoas-Vita. He has more experience with the stones than I do, but this is strange."

"Thank you, Kamara."

She grabbed my hand and tugged me toward the bar, but I halted our movement when a flash of platinum and familiar features caught the corner of my vision.

"I'll be right back." I kept my eyes on the blond head as I followed it through the crowd.

Someone snagged my hand and ground against me, blocking my vision. When I finally escaped the dancer and glanced around, she was gone. I pushed through the gyrating bodies and scanned every corner of the club, but the person I thought might be Bree was nowhere to be seen.

I sensed Kamara coming up to my side. "What is it?" She followed my line of sight and surveyed our surroundings.

I blinked and rubbed my tired eyes. "I thought I saw someone, but I guess not. Come back to my place with me. I'll make breakfast."

Kamara locked her fingers with mine as we made our way out of the club.

"My queen." Neil's words echoed in my mind just as we pushed through the red velvet curtain to the foyer on our way to the exit.

I sensed by Neil's demeanor and the formal way he addressed me that he wasn't happy about something, and I suspected I knew what.

"I'll meet you in the car." I separated from Kamara and handed her my car keys.

"Neil." I glanced up the staircase to where he stood at the top.

He nodded for me to follow him into his apartment above the club. He wore his usual black shirt decorated with a red tie, black skinny jeans with red Converses, and the black square-framed glasses he didn't need but wore anyway.

The disappointment that shrouded his expression as he turned sent my stomach plummeting to the floor. Neil was my friend, and I'd betrayed his trust by breaking his club rules.

I followed him into his apartment. It'd been some time since we'd visited, and this particular visit would be very different from the ones of our past.

Neil's posture was tense as his dark brown eyes roamed over my face. "I understand how much you've gone through." He took my hands. "You're my dear friend, and you know how much I care about you, and I respect how much you've done for me. As queen, you can do as you choose, but I ask you, as my friend, not to use your magic the way you have been inside the club. I keep these rules to protect my clientele. If they knew what you had done, I could lose everything."

"How did you know?"

Neil quirked a brow. Of course Neil would have someone

monitoring magic in his clubs. His reputation was everything to him, and that was why Vitarians felt safe inside his businesses. If I had been anyone else, I'd have been banished with magic from ever entering the premises again.

"I'm sorry, Neil. It won't happen again. You have my word."

"It's okay, darling. You know I'm here for you whenever you need me. Come here." He squeezed his arms around me.

I'd missed Neil. I hadn't realized how much until this moment. "I'd better go. Kamara's waiting."

Neil nodded and walked me out. "Anytime you need to talk, Everly, I'm here."

"Thanks, Neil." I gave him a quick hug and then ran down the stairs and out to my car.

⸙

Tension knotted my shoulders as I pulled into the driveway of my house and scanned for Arden's energy. He'd said he would be here today, and I both dreaded and desired the sight of him.

"You've never invited me to your place before. It's lovely." Kamara stared out at the field of wildflowers while I parked.

Guilt seared the tips of my ears. I'd invited Kamara for selfish reasons.

An excited bark echoed from the field. Luna bounded to my side and bounced around for pets, then circled Kamara with enthusiasm.

Kamara laughed and rubbed Luna all over and tickled her ears. The two became fast friends while I surveyed the property.

Vitarian energy permeated the air, and an eagle soared unnaturally low to the house, but there was no sign of Arden's guards anywhere around the property or among the trees bordering the field. I wondered how effective Arden's soldiers would be if the Hunters had an Empath among them—though not all Empaths could sense Vitarian energy the same way I could. The magic of the Ever bloodline flowed stronger than any other.

"My apartment is this way."

Kamara followed at my side as we crossed the gravel path. "You have an expansive garden. I'd love to see inside the greenhouse."

I took her hand and veered off into the greenhouse. The door was open, and Luna raced inside.

"Oh, hello." Dalia stood with my mother and Arden. She glanced to my side at Kamara, but my eyes were locked on Arden and how close he stood to Dalia, smelling an herb she held up to his nose.

How could he have brought her here after everything we had talked about last night? I'd told him how upset I was that he'd brought her to the cabin, and now he'd brought her here, to my home. Who was playing games now?

My nostrils flared as I reeled in my rising temper and met his challenging stare.

"Hey, sweetie. Are you going to introduce your friend?"

A light pressure squeezed my hand, and Kamara shot forward. "I'm Kamara. You must be Everly's mother. She's the spitting image of you."

My mom beamed. "It's lovely to meet you, Kamara. This is a day filled with making new friends. Are you a lover of herbs too?"

"I am." Kamara glanced around the greenhouse in wonder as she took in the abundance of herbs and edible flowers growing all around, and this offered me a moment without my mom's and Dalia's attention focused on me. But Arden's gaze remained fixed on mine.

"Dalia," said my mom, "help yourself to whatever you like

while I give this lovely young lady a tour." She turned her attention back to me, and I tore my eyes from Arden and cleared my throat. "Dalia's kindly offered to make us all dinner tonight." My mom smiled at Dalia before she drew Kamara to a selection of *Monarda* flowers and laughed as she told her of Jasper's obsession.

Dalia's hand dangled at her side, and she brushed Arden's fingers with her own as she signaled him to follow her.

I dashed out of the greenhouse, unable to take a second more of seeing the tenderness Dalia showed Arden that I couldn't, and I lashed out at a nearby lavender bush, tearing stalks from the ground.

The floral scent of the purple buds filled the air, mixed with earthy patchouli as Kamara bent over me.

"Are you okay?" she asked.

"Not really. But I will be. Come on."

We dashed into my apartment with Luna at our heels.

I opened the fridge and took out two soda waters, handing one to Kamara. Then I unwrapped some cooked bacon and fed it to Luna, who took her treat over to her dog bed beneath the living-room windows.

"I can't go to dinner with them alone. Will you stay and come with me?"

Kamara scooped up my long hair and twisted it over my shoulder. She smiled. "Of course."

"I'm grateful for you." I took her hands and led her to the living-room sofa and pulled her down next to me, breathing in her perfumed hair as we snuggled.

"Why do you deny him?" Kamara asked. "Only a fool wouldn't be able to see how madly in love he is with you. The woman he's with sees it too. She willfully denies it, hopeful to gain his affection."

I rubbed Kamara's back, not wanting to explain about Lucas and what had happened to him, and how it was all my fault. So instead, I tried changing the subject. "Are you sure you're not an Empath?"

She laughed. "I'm serious, Everly. Why are you hurting yourself like this?"

I sighed. "There's a lot I just can't talk about right now. But all that matters is Dalia can make Arden happy. His feelings for me will fade over time."

Kamara spun to face me and flung a leg over mine. Her dark curls cascaded into my own raven waves as we lay with our bodies mashed together.

"You underestimate the power you hold over others." Her mouth turned down, but then she quickly recovered herself. "You were honest from the beginning with me about where our relationship stood, but even knowing you loved another, I couldn't help but fall for you."

A weight settled on my chest. "Kamara, I'm—"

"No, no. That's not where I'm going with this. We're not having *the* talk. My point is I don't think he'll get over you that easy. You're not an easy one to get over, and the way he looks at you ..." She closed her eyes and breathed in. "If someone looked at me that way, I don't know how I'd resist."

I was about to argue, but Kamara placed a finger over my lips. "He doesn't look at her the same way. I just hope you're not sacrificing your happiness for the wrong reasons, and that's all I'll say." She smiled and rubbed her nose against mine.

"It is the way it has to be," I said to Kamara as much as to myself.

Lines appeared at the corners of Kamara's bright ebony eyes, but she said nothing more on the subject as she tucked her head into my shoulder, and it wasn't long before we both dozed off.

The walls crumbled, and the familiar luscious garden appeared.

Flowers on Earth held no comparison to these majestic blooms, and their intoxicating aroma was like nothing I'd ever experienced before. The rich scent lifted me up and made me wish for a floating cloud to sink into. I reached toward one of the massive ever flowers, and its brilliant hues burst to life as it bent toward me. Did it sense my presence, like the fairy had?

"How can you help me?" Oria's voice sounded from around the corner of the garden, drawing me away from the ever flower.

I drew in a sharp breath as I peeked around the edge of a flower bed, eager to see who she spoke with.

A masculine figure towered over her. Something about his physique seemed so familiar, but his face was turned away.

"I can provide you with a transference spell. With this spell, you can displace your brother's aura during the choosing."

"An aura swap." Oria's sapphire eyes gleamed as she considered the man's proposal. "Yes, that could work. When the ancestors test me, they will sense Orien's aura, and him mine." A wicked smile played on her lips. "Genius! But that kind of spell has been outlawed for centuries. How do you know this magic?"

"Never mind the how. There will be consequences to the spell," he explained. "Parts of you may not return as they once were."

Oria placed a finger on her lip. "You mean I may be stuck with my brother's annoying weakness for love."

The man nodded.

I inched closer.

"And what do you want in exchange, Hunter?"

Hunter! Was he one of the order?

"You know what I am?"

"Of course. I dreamed of you before this moment. I knew the Ghost of Time would come to me."

The Ghost of Time? That was how Orien had referred to the leader of the order of Hunters.

Orien was living up to his side of our bargain. A part of me had doubted he would.

I crept closer but froze when Oria stared in my direction.

Her gaze returned to the man, and she brushed her fingertip across his cheek. From where I now stood, I could see the side of his cheek had a scar that ran a finger's length.

Oria leaned into him as she placed a kiss at the base of the scar.

He snatched her hand and stepped back. "Not that!"

"You deny your future queen?"

His jaw clenched. "I'm searching for someone, and you're going to help me find her." His tone was cool, with a harsh edge.

Something in the back of my mind told me I knew that voice. But whose was it?

"Tell me your name, Hunter, and I'll consider your offer." Oria circled him and ran her hand across the back of his maroon cape, then twirled her finger over the wolf head carved into the hilt of his sword as she eyed his assets hungrily.

"Cade Wolf."

I shot up from the couch cushion. Kamara still lay asleep and undisturbed at my side.

Sweat trickled down my brow. I wiped at it with the back of my hand and stretched my damp tank top, which clung to my skin. *Who is Cade Wolf?*

Orien's mind games were getting old. *Tonight, he gives me answers.*

I made a mental game plan to get through this ridiculous dinner that Dalia had planned. Then I'd meet with the devil.

6

"**Y**ou look absolutely scrumptious," Kamara purred from behind as she stood in my bedroom doorway.

I twisted in the full-length mirror, examining my outfit. The black leather pants hugged me perfectly in all the right places, and the white silk blouse I wore dipped daringly at the chest, showing just enough to make the eye linger.

Kamara came into my room. Her caramel skin and dark, wavy curls reflected in the mirror as she lifted the back of my hair and placed a soft kiss at the nape of my neck. "If I had to guess, I'd say you plan to keep a certain pair of eyes on you all night. I know mine will be." Nostalgia laced her tone, but she laughed and nibbled my ear. "Let me do your hair, love."

The gentle breeze tickled the skin on my back as we walked from my apartment to the main house. Kamara had styled my hair in a beautiful braid and tucked the end up into my hair to reveal the open back of my shirt.

"I still think you should have gone with the heels." Kamara glanced at my black combat boots. "But I suppose those do add an edge to your look." She entwined a finger around mine.

I took a deep breath as we entered the kitchen through the back door. I didn't know why I felt so nervous.

My mom turned from the fridge. Her brows shot up when she saw my outfit. "You two are just in time."

"It smells wonderful," Kamara said to Dalia, who was extracting baked dishes from the double oven. "Can I help?"

Dalia peeked sideways at me. Her cheeks brightened as her eye followed the dive of my top. "You look stunning, Everly."

"Thank you." I returned her smile while noticing how flatteringly her dress snugged around her curves.

"Kamara, dear. If you wouldn't mind helping us carry in the platters, that would be lovely. Ev, sweetie, could you run down to the cellar and grab some chilled bubbly?"

"Sure, Mom." My hand slipped from Kamara's as she jumped in to help with the food, and I turned for the door leading down to the cellar.

Darion's voice drifted up the stairs as I made my way down. I paused on the bottom step. My brother stood with Arden, Malakai, and Rhal. Their attention shifted from the paper they were examining toward me. Darion's silver eyes popped when he glanced at my top, and a knowing smirk splashed across his face.

"Sister ... aren't you ravishing tonight?" He grinned. "This letter just arrived from Felix. It's a detailed list of sightings of those suspected of belonging to the order of Hunters that the council has kept a record of."

"Is there any information we can use to track them?" I chanced a glance at Arden and smiled inwardly as I joined their group. Not a fleck of blue shone in Arden's narrowed emerald gaze as he watched me cross the room. He tore his attention from the dip in my shirt, and a vein bulged at his temple as his jaw clenched.

Malakai drew my hand to his lips and winked as he stood. "'Ravishing' is an understatement, my queen."

Multiple shadows darkened the floor as Rhal's massive form dipped in front of me. I'd been amazed when I'd first seen the shadows separate from Rhal in battle and fight side by side with him, each as its own entity.

Rhal's lips peeled back to reveal a bright white smile. Sparks of purple danced in his ebony eyes, and the overhead light shone on his midnight skin. "Your beauty is unmatched." He kissed my hand.

"It's so good to see you, Rhal." I squeezed his massive hand. "I've missed you all."

He clasped his hands over mine. "And I you, my queen. We all look forward to the day you arrive at the palace."

"Ahem." Arden cleared his throat. Agitated energy vibrated all around him. "You two have ogled the queen long enough."

Malakai and Rhal shared an amused glance while Darion passed me the letter with Felix's familiar scrawl.

"The sightings date back centuries."

I scanned the list of names.

"Where are these people now? Can any of them be found?" I asked.

"That's the odd thing," Darion answered with a frown. "No one on this list has been located, not dead or alive. It's like they've all just vanished. No evidence exists of their deaths, or current locations for those that could still be living."

I thought of the nickname Orien had given Cade, the Ghost of Time. Oria referred to him by that title as well, in Orien's memory. What did that mean, and did it have something to do with the disappearances of all these Vitarians? I read the list again. The number of names was great. Dozens of Vitarians had vanished over the years and later been sighted as a part of the order. But where did they all go if they weren't on Earth or Aenoas-Vita?

My deal with Orien was turning out to be my only lead on who Cade Wolf was. His name wasn't among those listed. I nearly brought it up but then changed my mind. I needed to know more first, or at least talk to Darion about it alone before telling anyone else. Darion would be angry, but he'd understand. I'd learned much about my twin since he'd been reunited with our family, and we'd been tethered by the curse that linked our lives. His loyalty to his family and his love for Molly knew no bounds, even if that meant crossing lines and breaking rules. Darion would do whatever it took to keep Molly safe, even working with Orien. Arden, on the other hand, would disagree with my plan, and I didn't feel like having another argument with him. And telling my mother I'd brokered a deal with the man who had murdered the love of her life, and I'd let him drink my blood, was not at the top of my to-do list.

"We need more to go on than this," Arden said. "I've dispatched a team to interview any living family members of anyone listed." He nodded at the parchment. "In the meantime, guards will be stationed around the premises and with Molly indefinitely. I've assigned guards to watch over Freya and Anya as well."

Darion nodded. For once, he and Arden saw eye to eye on a common goal.

"Gentlemen." Darion gave Malakai and Rhal a meaningful glance as he nudged my shoulder and brushed past me with a wink.

"Darion, wait." I gave him a pleading look. "I need to talk to you."

He glanced over me at Arden and smirked. "Later, sister."

Malakai and Rhal followed Darion up the stairs, leaving Arden and me alone.

"I should be going." Arden stepped forward, avoiding further eye contact with me.

"Wait." I blocked his path and placed my hand flat against his chest. His heart thumped a steady rhythm beneath hard muscle.

The air stirred, charged with electric energy.

Arden reached up. The tips of his fingers briefly caressed the Quan Yin pendant hanging between my breasts before his arm fell back to his side. "Has anything changed with where we stand?"

We stared at each other for a long moment. Arden took my hand from his chest and released it. "Dalia's waiting for me." He dashed past me without another word, leaving an icy breeze in his wake.

I leaned against the laundry machines and gripped my chest. How long could I keep this up? At least when Arden was on another planet, I could ignore my feelings, but now, seeing him every day and with Dalia ... I choked on the earthy air that saturated the basement, and forced myself to walk to the cooler where my mom kept the champagne.

Everyone was gathered in the dining room when I carried the bottles in. Molly and Kamara chatted gaily with Dalia, who seemed to win over everyone she came into contact with.

I scanned the elaborate feast spread across the table and caught Darion watching me with a mischievous grin.

"You really should try these tarts, sister. Dalia is quite talented. Wouldn't you agree, Arden?" Darion leaned across the table and popped a stuffed olive into his mouth.

Molly nudged Darion in the shoulder.

Arden's hooded gaze shifted my way and then back to

Dalia, who smiled coyly at him. "Dalia has many talents," Arden agreed.

I chewed the inside of my cheek when Dalia ran her hand down Arden's arm and entwined her fingers with his. My skin burned hot when he didn't pull away from her.

The memory of the previous night filled my mind with images of Arden holding me on the porch steps and touching me with those hands, and other stolen moments from our past came rushing to the surface. The two of us in the woods, pressed against the oak tree. Arden lifting me onto my kitchen counter before we were interrupted. Had he touched Dalia in the same way he had touched me?

The chandelier flickered above the table. Plates, glasses, and silverware rattled in place. My body temperature had risen to a boil when suddenly a chill so cold hit me that I froze to a shiver.

Rheya came from behind and clasped a hand over my shoulder. The clattering on the table settled, and my jaw jittered from both the cold shell that cocooned me and the shock at what I could have done had Rheya not come in. I shrugged her hand away, and my body instantly warmed.

She gave me a warning glare as she took a seat next to Kamara.

Darion distracted everyone's attention with more of his meddling. "Dalia, are you still teaching young Vitarians plant magic at the gardens?"

Dalia lit up as she spoke of the children she tutored and how their skills grew.

"I'm sure you're missed at the palace." Darion flashed me a ridiculous grin and added, "But you served the royal army well, and I can't think of a better place for your retirement, and now you'll have time to start a family."

"Darion," said our mother from the head of the table. "Let the poor woman enjoy the meal she's prepared."

Darion's expression was apologetic when he nodded at our mother, but I knew what he was doing. He wanted me to feel jealous of Dalia. *He thinks that if he can force me to see what I'm losing to her, I'll change my mind about pushing Arden away and destroying my emotions.* I hadn't told him yet that the releasing spell no longer worked, but that didn't matter. Nothing could change my mind about Arden and make me break my promise to Lucas, not even Darion's pestering.

Molly's eyes went wide when I snatched a bottle of champagne and filled a glass. The chilled liquid burned my throat as I gulped it down.

My mom's brow wrinkled, but she kept her comments to herself. Her mouth smiled at our guests as she tucked a wisp of raven hair behind her ear, but her eyes shone with an entirely different emotion as she looked from me to Arden sitting next to Dalia.

The muddy violet hue blotching her aura gave away the distress she kept hidden from anyone without my ability. My muscles tensed, and I stared numbly at my hands. She had enough to worry about with the threat to Molly and the twins. She didn't need to worry about my emotional well-being.

Tendrils of energy crept my way as my guard slipped with the effects of the alcohol.

Kamara slid my glass of champagne in front of her. "You don't want this." She squeezed my hand.

"You're right. I don't." What I wanted was sitting across the table, giving his full attention to Dalia. I pushed my chair back, suddenly feeling dizzy. "I need some air."

Kamara started to get up.

"You stay and enjoy your meal while it's warm. I just need a minute."

Rheya scooted her chair closer to Kamara. "I'll keep her company."

Candles flickered as I cut through the living room and rushed outside to the front porch. I gripped the porch railing, lifting my face into the cool breeze. A cold prickle swept across my sweat-dampened skin. The icy blast of wintery air helped clear my hazy thoughts but did little to calm the frustration that gnawed at me.

A splash of light spilled onto the front porch as the front door opened and closed. I didn't need to turn to know who had followed me outside. Arden's unmistakable energy sent sparks jolting down my spine, like it always did, and a fresh wave of heat flushed my skin.

Screw it! I turned and threw my arms around Arden's neck and kissed him. He responded briefly before pulling me away.

"I can't do this anymore, Everly."

My heart tightened like someone was squeezing it in their fist. "Are you still sleeping with her? The way she touches you. It's—" I sucked in a sharp breath.

Arden glanced down before meeting my eyes. "It happened just the once. Before we came to Earth. It was a mistake and hasn't happened again. I barely remember it. We were having dinner, and then I woke up—"

"That's enough! I don't need specifics." I latched onto my anger, since it seemed to be the only thing that worked to harden my heart against the man scowling down at me.

The wind stirred, and the bare wisteria branches slapped against the side of the house.

"You told me you weren't a couple, and yet she fondles you like you are. So much for your love and loyalty."

A howl accompanied a gust of air as its ferocity responded to my fury.

He grabbed my arm. "How can you say that to me? You told me you didn't love me, that we'd never be together, and now you're angry that I've found someone who wants to be with me?"

Arden sighed and rested his forehead against mine. "I'm not with Dalia. I just wanted you to see that you're making a mistake, and I'm not sleeping with her. But I'm starting to think that she wants you to think that there's more going on between us."

"And you're happy to play along with her theatrics?" I gritted my teeth.

Arden shook his head. "What do you want, Everly? Because I have no idea anymore."

I sighed, suddenly feeling sick to my stomach. Arden was right. I was being completely unfair. I had no right to be upset about Dalia. I'd broken his heart. What had I expected? I'd asked Rheya to push him toward another, and she'd followed through on her promise. I only had myself to blame for all of this.

"Do you have feelings for her?"

Arden snatched my other arm and crushed me against him. "I love *you*! I've loved you since the first day you came to my table at the café, tongue-tied and fumbling with the menu. When you blasted me against the tree during our training, all I could think about was pulling you against me and kissing your beautiful mouth. I loved you when you wanted to remain on Earth. And when you had feelings for another, and you broke my heart. Even after you walked away from me." His voice dropped to a whisper. "I've loved you through it all." His mouth crushed mine, and his kiss was hard and deep and passionate.

The ground slipped away, and I lost myself in our kiss. When Arden pulled back, the world spun, and my heart raced uncontrollably.

His breath warmed my cheeks as the weight of his words sank deep into my core. "But my heart can only take so much." Arden released my arms and went back inside the house.

I had to lean over the railing to catch my breath.

"You've really made a mess of things." Rheya came outside.

I sat down on the top porch step and buried my face in my hands.

"The man finally starts to move on, and you reel him back in for another beating." Rheya scowled at me.

I couldn't argue with her. She was absolutely right.

Rheya stretched her long, toned legs over the steps as she sat down next to me. "He doesn't love Dalia, but you're going to lose him for good if you keep this up." She glanced toward the sky, and her copper braid fell from her shoulder and dangled behind her back. "You can barely see the stars on this planet," she mused as she stared at the distant twinkles in the sky.

"Huh." She leaned against the pillar on her left. "I've known Dalia for many years. We're not exactly close, but she's a good person, and I don't want to see her get hurt, so figure it out, Everly, and stop acting like a little girl. Be the queen you're supposed to be." She glanced sideways at me. "I've given the commander a piece of my mind as well."

I brought my knees up and tucked them under my chin. "You're right. I've really screwed things up. Dalia is a kind woman, and I don't want to see her get hurt either—although she definitely wants me to see that she's staked her claim on Arden. The thought of him with her ..." Fiery tendrils snaked to the surface of my skin.

Rheya reached out with a cooling touch. "Dalia is a woman who knows what she wants, and she's not afraid to fight for it. You have to decide what you're willing to lose and what you're willing to fight for. Now, tell me how you could do something so foolish as releasing your emotions into an ever stone."

I groaned and dropped my head onto my folded arms, then peeked sideways. "He told you?"

"The commander is quite furious with you." She smirked and drew her legs up, turning her body to face me. "Something is bothering me, though."

I laughed. "I know you won't hold back, so let's hear it."

"Hmm." Rheya smirked. "I'm glad you accept me for who I am. Here's the thing: I'm familiar with the releasing spell, and it doesn't just stop working until you've destroyed the stone properly at the designated time after the spell was performed." Her green eyes roamed over my face and settled on the goddess pendant dangling at my neck. "Something is amiss. I don't know what it is, but we need to find out. This is not a spell to be toyed with. Your emotions could be lost for good if not properly restored. Is the stone safe?"

I nodded. My throat clenched with the weight of Rheya's warning. I'd thought taking away my feelings for Arden was what I wanted, but now, with the threat of losing them for good, I wasn't so sure I did want that anymore.

"Good," Rheya breathed. "Keep it that way. I've sent a message to someone who may know more. You know how dangerous the magic of the stones can be." Rheya grabbed my knee. "Well, enough with the pep talk. I hope you don't mind, but I'll be stealing your date for the rest of the night." She jumped up just as Kamara came outside.

"I'm sorry I spoiled dinner." I hopped up and hugged Kamara, breathing in her earthy citrus scent.

"You did no such thing, love." Her soft hands cupped my face. "I've had a great night. We're headed to the club. You feel like joining?"

Rheya shook her head from behind. She wanted Kamara all to herself, which worked fine with my own plans.

"You two go on. I think I'll call it a night." I had no intention of telling anyone where I was going or who I planned to contact.

My blood glistened across the mirror in an arch. I stood back and examined the large eye that was encased in the Sight rune. I placed my hands on the outer edges of the blood circle and chanted the spell that now came from memory. The glass exploded inward, and I stepped into the portal, searching for cracks in the darkness.

"I'm here, Orien. Show yourself."

"Your bravery knows no bounds." Orien's words echoed in the dark.

"You won't hurt me."

"For now." His breath warmed my ear.

I twisted and stood face-to-face with the man who had taken everything from me. Flames shot through my fingertips, and a mirage of light encased us.

"I could end you now," I hissed.

Orien smirked. His features were so like Darion's it was nearly impossible to tell the two apart, but for their eye color and Orien's signs of aging, and the anger and resentment that had burrowed into the contours of Orien's face and leached into his aura.

"You could end me, niece, but then how will you ever save your brother's child and its mother from the Hunters? And they *will* come for her."

The sapphire eyes that questioned my next move mirrored the color of my own. I couldn't help but wonder if mine now held the same hardness that Orien's did.

"Why are you showing me these twisted visions of Oria? I don't believe that she did those things."

"Hmm ... If only that were true, niece. I would not be the

man I am today. Oria turned me into this monster. And it's time for you to see what you've sworn your fealty to."

"Enough with these games! Who are the Hunters, and how do I defeat them?" Flames coiled near Orien, but he paid them no attention as he considered me. "Patience. You need to see to understand. But you know the price."

Fury coursed through me as I stared at the mocking glare Orien wore. He knew it killed me to need his help, and he enjoyed it. I struggled to draw the fire back as I lifted my arm and turned my wrist up. "Show me."

I barely felt the tear of Orien's teeth piercing my skin when Oria flickered into existence. A dark forest surrounded us, and Oria stood chanting over an explosive fire. Shrieks tore from the flames, and I saw the last sparks of life fade from the fairy she had tied to a stake.

"Drink," a voice ordered.

I searched but saw no one in the darkness and turned my attention back toward Oria.

She brought a crystal goblet to her lips and drank. Crimson liquid dripped past the corner of her mouth as she tilted the goblet upward.

"Finish the spell and bring me the stone," he growled.

Oria rose, her arms overhead, and chanted. An aura of color burst from the lifeless fairy, and a bolt of electricity shot through the sky, piercing Oria's chest. Pure, raw power rippled across the forest, sending up the hairs on my arms.

The roaring flames dimmed to cinders as Oria brought her arms down, and I sucked in a breath as she stepped barefoot into the glowing embers of ash and retrieved a stone. When she held it up, it drew in the hovering energy expelled by the fairy, and a bright, fiery hue burst from within the stone.

Heat seared my insides. I bent over and dug my nails into a tree trunk to keep from crying out. Panic took hold of me as my skin flickered with the same glow that came from the stone. My magic was reacting to the stone. But why?

"Orien! What's happening to me?"

His image flitted into existence beside me. "Just watch and listen." He nodded toward Oria.

"Bring the stone of fire to me." A man's voice ordered from the darkness.

The stone of fire?

I wrapped my arms around my chest and tried to focus my attention on Oria instead of the searing ache spreading through my body.

Oria did as he commanded. "Why is this so important to you?"

A tall figure emerged from the forest, but he stayed within the night shadows, just out of view, keeping his features a mystery. Even though I couldn't see his face, something nagged at the back of my mind that I knew him. But how?

When he remained silent, Oria asked, "How do you know of this magic, Hunter?"

His answer came as barely a whisper. "My wife."

"Where is she now?" Oria inched closer to him.

He glanced up, his eyes awash with the bright blood-orange glow of the stone. "Lost in time, but I'll find her, and with this"—he held the stone up—"I'll have the power I need to bring her back to me, and you now hold the power you need to take your brother's place."

"And in exchange," Oria whispered as she reached up to the silver clasps at her shoulders, "I will protect your secrets." She unclasped her white gown and let it fall to the ground.

Her pale skin glowed in the night as she stood, offering herself to the man who called himself Cade Wolf.

His eyes roamed over her young body.

My breath caught when he gripped her waist and pulled

her to him. He licked the blood that stained her lips. "Your beauty is painful to resist, but what you offer, I cannot accept."

Oria stood on her tiptoes and bit his lip, then sucked at the blood that surfaced. A light tremble shook her limbs, and she stumbled away. "I see now." She bent down and lifted her gown up, securing the clasps. "Many lonely years will darken your future before she returns to you."

Cade stared down at the stone of fire clasped tightly in his hand. "I'd suffer an eternity to have her back."

"And suffer you will. When you find her, she will love another." Oria turned and left Cade staring after her while she slinked alone into the shadowy forest.

"I'll make her remember our love," Cade whispered to himself.

Something about him drew me to him. Without thinking, I moved in his direction, but just as I got closer, and his face began to lift from staring down at the stone, the scene faded, and another appeared.

Oria stood in her bedroom, admiring herself in a tall mirror. The gown she wore sparkled with hundreds of tiny crystals that cast off prisms of light with her movements. She smiled at herself, lifting her raven hair and twisting it up, then released the dark bundle and twirled her body as waves cascaded past her glitter-dusted shoulders. The streak of sunlight that bathed her in a warm glow seemed unfitting for the darkness that she embodied.

An eerie laugh that sent knots to my stomach burst from Oria's glossed lips, and she picked up an ever stone from the dressing table, cut from a quartz-like crystal.

"Only one ingredient left to retrieve, and I'll have everything I need to be chosen," she whispered to herself.

My nails dug deep into my palms as I realized that the energy flickering within the opalesque stone was the very same I had sensed within the fairies. She'd stolen the lives of innocent creatures to perform her wicked spells. Oria was not the queen we'd all thought she was.

The knots in my stomach pinched tighter as I thought of how I'd taken energy from other Vitarians at the club for my own selfish need. Was I not just as guilty as Oria?

I jumped at a loud thud, and Oria spun in surprise when her bedroom door burst open. "Orien!"

Orien glowered at his sister as he took patient steps toward her.

Oria's posture stiffened, and she tucked her hand that held the ever stone behind her back.

"Sister." Orien's lips turned down as he studied her. "I saw you. I know your plan."

"Humph." Oria stared her brother down. "So I'm not the only spy in the family. You surprise me, Orien. I didn't think you capable of such an act."

Dark circles shadowed Orien's eyes, and lines rippled across his forehead as his brow furrowed. "I did it for Zelda. I knew you were up to something." His arm shot out. "Take it! Take my blood and take my place on the throne. I don't care about ruling. I just want Zelda back. You must promise to heal her. Promise me now, and you'll have everything you've ever wanted, and I will say nothing of your treachery. I never have."

Oria's lips peeled back. "And what about your treachery, brother?"

Orien stepped back. His hand flew through his hair. Then he gripped the sides of his head. "What do you mean? I've always been at your side. That hasn't changed."

I tried to swallow, but my throat felt like sandpaper, and I cringed as Oria's cheeks lifted high with a demented smile. It made me nauseous how she enjoyed toying with her twin brother and tormenting him.

Her tone was laced with great pleasure when she spoke. "You must swear your loyalty to me, and promise to never see Zelda again if I heal her."

Orien sucked in a breath, and his arm fell back to his side. He grabbed his sister's shoulders. "Haven't I proved myself to you, Oria, time and time again? I've done unspeakable things for you. I've taken the blame all these years for your cruel acts. Mother expects you to be chosen. It will come as no surprise when the ancestors sense your aura within me and choose you to rule. This has been your plan all along. Why won't you allow me the tiniest bit of happiness? Have you ever loved me, sister?"

Oria didn't bat an eye when she answered coolly. "Swear to me, or Zelda will pay the price."

Orien released her shoulders. He stared at his sister as if she were a stranger he'd only just met, and then he lifted his arm and turned it over. The same as I had done with my own in the portal. "I swear."

Orien hardened himself in a protective shield as Oria drew a blade across his wrist and drank his blood. Then she cut her own wrist and held it out to him. Orien did as his sister beckoned him to do, and when he lifted his head from her wrist, she licked her bloodstained lips and nodded toward her bedroom door.

"I'll see you at the choosing, brother." She turned, dismissing Orien with a flick of her hand.

My stomach flipped as I was yanked from the past and placed once again inside the portal with Orien.

I shook my head. "I don't understand. How could Oria have been so cruel? I sensed her aura in the afterlife. She's good."

Orien shrugged. "Oria had always had wickedness inside her, but she changed after the choosing. Part of what once belonged to me became a part of her. When her daughter was born, and she finally understood real love, she came to me. She begged my forgiveness and professed her regret. But it was too late."

"Why? Why was it too late?" I demanded. "If she healed Zelda and changed, then why did you kill your family and come after mine? Did you take my father's life and Lucas's because your sister stole your chance to be king?" My voice rose and filled the tunnel. "Why are you showing me all of this? So I'll feel sorry for you? Your sister was cruel and conniving, but you are worse. You're a murderer!"

Orien turned away into the shadows. "There's more." A sadness laced his words, and something shifted in his aura. A lingering hint of a long-forgotten emotion broke through the black ice of Orien's shell. "I've not shown you everything Oria did to me."

"Damn it! No more!" I stormed toward him. "I don't have time to psychoanalyze your past, and I don't care why you turned into a demented killer. We made a deal. I gave you my blood. Now tell me who Cade Wolf is. What was he searching for? And why did I react so strongly to the stone Oria spelled for him?"

Orien laughed the same sardonic laugh as his sister had when she'd forced her ultimatum on him, until his eyes fell on the fiery tendrils snaking up my arms.

"You are by far my favorite descendant, niece. If only we didn't have to be enemies."

I shoved him hard, and he stumbled back. "You chose to be my enemy when you came after my family."

"True." Orien regained his footing and caught my fist before it landed square in his eye. "But perhaps I've made an error in judgment." He forced my arm down.

I roared. "An error in judgment is taking a left turn when you should have taken a right, not killing someone for power or some centuries-old vendetta. You're a monster! Every second I let you live is a betrayal to my family."

Fire blazed from my palms, and my vision hazed in a red cloud like it had the night I had chased Orien before he'd vanished through a portal.

"Oria linked the stone to her bloodline," Orien rattled off.

The flames rescinded to a low flicker. "Why would she do that?"

An orange hue lit Orien's pensive features while he twisted the onyx ring he wore that we both knew protected him from my Empath abilities. "I think a better question is why would a time traveler want a stone that could control a member of the royal family, someone he knew would have fire magic?"

"What are you saying? And what do you mean by 'time traveler'?"

Orien faded into the darkness. "No more for today. You know my price." The portal closed around him and blasted me backward, and I stood, staring at my crusted blood on the mirror. *No!*

"Orien!" I pounded the mirror with my fist, causing a crack to splinter down the glass.

"Argh!" I picked up my spelled blade and was about to make a fresh cut to my palm to create another Sight rune and recast the spell, but an insistent buzz vibrated from my purse.

I tossed the knife aside and crouched over my bag and dug my phone out. A notification with several missed calls from my mom and Darion lit up my screen. *What's going on?*

A text from Darion came through: *Molly's gone. Where are you?*

I sat on the floor and responded. My pulse beat madly, and a high-pitched ringing filled my ears while my shaky fingers fumbled the letters as I typed.

What do you mean Molly's gone? It's the middle of the night. Where is she? Did you try calling her?

Darion's reply came instantly: *Of course I did! Just come home. I need you!*

I tore through the studio, using my magic to put out the candles, and barely remembered to lock the studio door as I flew out of the building and ran to my car. There wasn't much traffic out at this time of night, so I didn't hesitate to run any red lights I came to that were clear, while glancing in my rearview mirror to make sure no sirens flashed behind me.

Damn! I'd forgotten to clean the blood off the mirror, and my part-time instructor opened in the morning. I'd have to think of something to tell her.

I pressed the gas pedal, not caring about speed restrictions. *Molly, where the hell are you?*

The house was ablaze with lights when I pulled into the drive. I parked in the front instead of my usual spot back by my apartment.

"Everly!" Darion's voice came from around the house, and then he and my mom came into view, carrying a limp body by the legs and arms.

Dirt and rocks kicked up as I tore through the gravel and ran to help them.

"Oh my God! Is that Malakai? Why's he unconscious?" I scanned Malakai's energy. My hand flew to his neck to check his pulse. *He's so weak.* "What happened?"

"Where were you?"

"I—"

Darion scowled. "Forget it! Just get the door!"

I leaped up the steps and threw the door open.

Darion and my mom shuffled in with Malakai and heaved him up onto the sofa.

"I'm glad you're safe, honey." My mom hugged me and rushed off into the kitchen.

I reached for Malakai's dangling arm and squeezed his hand, searching his face for any response.

"Malakai!" I tapped his cheeks, hoping for an eye flutter, but he remained motionless. Beads of sweat covered his bronzed skin, which was turning paler by the second. I leaned over him and placed my hands on either side of his head. His energy was nearly undetectable, and his breathing shallow.

"What happened to him? He's so cold and weak."

"We found him like that outside," Darion said as he rummaged through a basket on a bookshelf. "And the guards are all dead. It's the Hunters. It has to be." He slammed the basket back onto the shelf, causing the entire bookcase to rattle against the wall. "Damn it! Where are all the phone chargers?"

"Here, son." My mom handed Darion a long white cord and then dashed back out of the living room.

"What? How could they all be dead?" I glanced at Malakai, willing him to hold on.

"We don't know," Darion said, shoving the end of the charger into the phone he held. "There were no signs of injuries. They were just all dead. All except Malakai. We found a dead owl on the ground beside Malakai's body, so my guess is he was inhabiting the bird when they were attacked. Maybe that's why he's still alive." He stared at the phone screen. "I've never seen anything like it."

"Is that Molly's phone?" I recognized her glittery pink phone case with I LOVE AN ALIEN printed on the back. Darion had gotten her the phone case as a joke, but Molly had loved it and snapped her phone into it immediately.

Darion nodded while clicking the power button. "I found

it outside." He turned it over for me to see. "The screen is smashed, but if I can get it to turn on, maybe I can find out why my fiancée left our bed in the middle of the night and went outside into the freezing cold alone."

A turbulent wave of Darion's emotions gripped me, and I found myself wanting to pound a hole in the wall or shred the skin off someone's body. I forced back the nausea that came with being overpowered by someone else's emotions, and I managed to bring up a minimal barrier to shield myself. The curse that linked my and Darion's lives made it impossible for me to completely guard myself against his vibrations.

My head swam, and even though my temperature ran hot from the fire magic inside me, a chill iced my bones. *I've failed.* I'd betrayed my family and made a deal with our enemy, and it had all been for nothing, but maybe I could help Malakai.

I climbed over and straddled his torso.

"What are you doing?" Darion paced. His agitation had the hairs standing up on my arms.

"His energy is weak, like he's been drained." I cupped my hands over Malakai's temples and moved through the outer layers of his aura, searching for the thread of energy I could connect to. "I'm going to transfer some of mine into him. I did this to Molly after we performed the blood spell on her. It worked, and she woke up. Maybe it'll work again with Malakai."

"Yeah," Darion said without looking up from Molly's phone. "And maybe he can tell us what the hell happened out there."

I took a deep breath when I found the thread and latched onto it. An invisible force tugged at me, and lightning bolts of electricity charged down my arms as my energy transferred into Malakai. He was so depleted I wasn't sure how much I could give him without causing myself harm, but I held on and kept going, pushing harder as more and more pulses of my life force channeled away from me.

Something banged against the wall, and I glanced over to see Darion stumble backward. "Ev! You need to stop." His voice cracked.

My arms shook as my energy flowed through me. "Just a little more. I can feel him coming back." A tremble jarred me forward, and I collapsed on top of Malakai's chest just as a crash sounded across the room. I could barely move my head when I saw Darion slumped on the floor.

No! The damn curse!

"Darion! Everly!" My mom rushed in and set down the bowl and cloth she carried.

"I'm okay," I assured her when she came toward me. "Check on Darion."

Darion moaned as my mom helped him up. "Damn it, Ev. I told you to stop. You could have killed us both."

Malakai shifted beneath me. It took all my effort to lift myself off him.

"I'm sorry, but I had to keep going. I couldn't just let him die. What kind of magic could suck the life out of the guards and Malakai all at once? Even I don't have that kind of power."

"Uhh." Malakai's arm flew up and across his forehead. His thick black lashes fluttered as his eyes moved rapidly behind his closed eyelids. I touched his skin, which had gone from cool and clammy to burning hot.

Darion shook his head against the bookcase he leaned back on. "I don't know. It could be dark magic, but if it is, it's new to me."

My mom gave a slight nod.

None of us had seen this magic before.

Darion's grim expression mirrored my own fear as a dead silence lingered between the three of us.

I knew we were each thinking of Molly and the babies.

I glanced back at Malakai, whose eyelids still twitched, but his skin was no longer as pale as it had been.

My mom brought the bowl and cloth over, and the air was filled with the scent of herbs and black licorice. She dipped the cloth into the infused water, then wrung it out over the bowl. She dabbed Malakai's face and then carefully moved his arm and laid the cloth across his forehead.

I scooted to the edge of the sofa and slid down to the floor, pulling my knees into my chest, then let my dizzy head crash into my folded arms. The scent of the herbs helped calm the nausea a bit, but I wasn't sure I could safely get up yet.

"Have you contacted Arden?" I mumbled into my arms.

"He's on his way now." My mom dipped her fingers into the bowl and dribbled the water down Malakai's arms.

My stomach flipped as a new mix of emotions stirred within me at the thought of Arden. What if he'd been here tonight, guarding the property? He could have ended up like the rest of the guards. If anything happened to him, I ... My hands pressed against the hardwood floor as I pushed the thoughts away. I couldn't let myself think like that.

"Could it have been Orien?" my mom asked while resoaking the cloth and wringing it out once more.

"It wasn't him," I answered. *He was with me.*

"But how can you be sure?"

I turned my head and met deep pools of worried sapphire. I had to tell them about my deal with Orien.

"It's on!" Darion yelled before I could answer my mom's question and reveal my secret. His fingers tapped in Molly's passcode, and a deep scowl darkened his features. "What the hell?"

"What is it, son?"

Darion's eyes narrowed, and without looking at us, he

said, "It's a bunch of texts from Ty asking Molly to come outside and talk." He swiped his finger up. "He said he can't go on without knowing what happened to Bree and that his life feels empty."

"Let me see." I crawled over and leaned against the bookcase next to Darion and took the phone. I knew Ty had been sad, but he'd never talked this way before. A hot wave of anger coursed through me. I'd been a terrible friend to Ty. He'd been suffering, and I'd been too caught up in my own problems to notice.

I scrolled to the end of the messages to Molly's reply. She'd texted back that she was coming right out. My eyes closed. Molly had always been a good friend. Her ability to put others first was both her strength and her weakness.

"But if Ty was here"—I glanced up as different scenarios raced through my mind—"then he could have been taken too, or worse." I turned toward Malakai, who still lay unconscious, but his energy was much stronger.

"Oh dear." My mom rubbed Darion's back. "We'll find Molly, honey. She and the babies will be okay." Her voice shook as she tried to reassure Darion.

Darion snatched the phone back from me. A storm of fury brewed in his silver gaze. "I'm going to Ty's. Maybe they're there."

The desperation in his tone rattled me. I clenched my fist, and my teeth jittered as I tried shielding myself from the violent vibrations rolling off Darion.

My fingers clasped his arm. "I'm coming with you." I wobbled to my feet and grabbed my purse and keys. I suspected we wouldn't find Molly and Ty at Ty's place, and I sensed that Darion did too, but at least going there gave us somewhere to start, and maybe we'd find something.

"We can't leave Malakai alone," my mom said. "I'll stay with him and wait for the others."

I paused. "What if whoever did this comes back? You're not safe alone."

"The others will be here any minute, honey. I'll be fine."

I nodded, still feeling unsure, but followed Darion outside.

"Still no answer," I said after trying Ty's cell for the fifth time. A terrible feeling gnawed at my insides as Darion accelerated, and the jerk of the car pressed my head back against the headrest.

My fingers gripped the door handle as Darion yanked the steering wheel and whipped into the marina parking lot. We bolted from my car and ran toward the marina gate, which was kept locked at night. The gate clicked open as soon as I punched in the final number of the passcode, and we hurried down the ramp.

A restless wind blew hard, and choppy water caused the boats to rock back and forth in their slips. Every sound had us on edge as we made our way to Ty's boathouse while staying watchful. Goose bumps swept across my skin when we passed a massive barge that had always given me the creeps. Shadows crawled across its blackened windows, and its rusted sides creaked while the barge sloshed side to side with the current, tugging against its ropes and causing the dock to rock under our feet.

When we turned down the dock leading to Ty's place, we both paused. Ty's door was wide open. His dad worked grave-yard and was never home this time of night, and it wasn't like Ty to leave his front door open in the middle of the night.

"Molly!" Darion burst into the boathouse and tore through the living room.

There was no answer. Besides a couple of lamps turned on

and the main menu of a video game glowing from the TV screen, the house was pretty much dark and completely silent. We searched the bedrooms and bathrooms, but all were empty. A large pizza box sat open on the coffee table, with several pieces eaten. Two cans of open soda and two video game controllers were on the table next to the pizza box.

Darion kicked Ty's trash can, and it crashed against the wall, spilling everything out onto the floor.

"Something's not right about this." I motioned toward the items on the coffee table. "Does this look like Ty was sitting here sad and lonely and feeling like the world was ending? He was eating pizza and playing video games with someone. There are two sodas and two controllers. Someone was here with him."

I slid my phone out of my pocket and dialed Jasper.

His voice was groggy when he answered. "Ev ... What time is it?"

"Were you with Ty tonight at his place?"

"Huh?"

Muffled movements came over the phone speaker.

I heard Anya's voice in the background, asking Jasper for the phone.

"Hold on, babe," Jasper whispered to Anya. Then he said into the phone, "What's going on, Ev? It's the middle of the night."

I sighed, trying not to get frustrated. "Were you with Ty tonight? I just need to know."

"No," Jasper said, more alert this time. "I've been with Anya all night. I haven't seen Ty since this morning. Why?"

"Did Ty seem off to you?"

"Okay, now you're freaking me out. Tell me what's going on."

I heard Jasper start moving around. It sounded like drawers were opening and closing.

"Molly's missing, and now we can't find Ty, and we think they may have both been taken together."

The phone went silent, and for a minute I thought I'd lost the connection. Then Jasper's voice came through the speaker. "Back up. How is Molly missing? What about the guards?"

"They were attacked. They're all dead but Malakai."

Another dead silence. And then a loud noise like a drawer slamming shut echoed over the phone.

"How is Ty involved?"

"Darion found Molly's phone," I explained. "It was smashed outside our house, but he got it working. We found messages from Ty. He told her he felt sad and hopeless, and he asked her to meet him outside my mom's to talk, so we came to Ty's place, hoping there was a chance they were here. When we got here, we found his front door wide open and an empty house. But something's not adding up. There's a pizza box and sodas, and two game controllers out. It looks like he was hanging out with someone. Why would he go from hanging out and playing games to needing to talk to Molly in the middle of the night? What was he like this morning?"

"Perfectly normal," Jasper said. "Hold on. Anya wants to talk to you."

"Everly," Anya said on the other end.

"I'm here," I answered.

"They've taken them both. I've just seen it in my dream. They're alive."

The phone slipped from my ear, and I locked eyes with my brother. The air caught in my lungs, and I had to remind myself to exhale.

"Tell me!" Darion demanded, looking on the verge of tearing the walls of the boathouse down.

"Anya had a vision." My words came out in a whisper. "The Hunters have them."

Darion roared and slammed his fist into the wall, punching a hole straight through the drywall. "How could she have gone outside alone, knowing the risk? She should have woken me up and shown this to me." He shook Molly's phone in the air.

I pulled Darion into my arms. "She had no way of knowing the guards had been attacked. And you know Molly. She's fearless and loves hard. She'd do anything to protect the people she cares about. And that's one of the reasons you love her. Now, listen to me, brother. You are the best Tracker on our planet. If anyone can find her, it's you."

Darion's metallic silver eyes glowed with magic, and our hearts beat as one as the curse that linked our life forces coursed through us.

"You're right, sister. It's time I started acting like a Vitarian again." He sped away at inhuman speed.

I lifted the phone to my ear. "Anya, are you still there?"

"Yes."

"Tell Jasper to meet me at my yoga studio, and can you call your mother and ask her to come as well? We'll need all the power we can bring together for what I'm about to do."

"Your uncle?"

"It's time I followed through with my promise to my family."

I scanned the marina parking lot for any energy signatures while I ran up the ramp. Shadows flashed across the dark windows of tenant vehicles that filled the lot, but I sensed no one else as I hurried into the driver's seat and slammed my car door shut. I had no idea where Darion had rushed off to, but I hoped he could find something that would lead to where Molly and Ty could have been taken.

My head sank back into the headrest. The scene we had found at Ty's played over and over in my mind. The drinks had still been cold, and the pizza hadn't appeared to have been sitting out longer than a few hours. And the game controllers had been sitting on opposite sides of the pizza box, each next to a soda can, a sure sign that there had been two players. Nothing about that scene struck me as depressed behavior. Sure, Ty had been bummed when I'd told him I hadn't seen or heard from Bree, but I hadn't noticed anything alarming in his vibrations. He'd been excited about his dream catchers getting picked up by local shops.

"Huh." If only my own gift of premonition were more useful. It was the one piece of my magic I hadn't been able to summon control over. I'd only had the one vision when I'd touched the ever stone I'd cut out of the Shimera's chest. I still wasn't sure if everything we'd done would be enough to prevent that event from taking place.

A vicious wind howled, and the tall masts of the sailboats visible from the lot rocked back and forth, causing a flurry of creaks and whining sounds as ropes and hooks clinked against the metal parts of the boats. I didn't know how anyone living in the marina homes got any sleep. The sound had always kept me and Molly up at night when we'd had sleepovers with Ty, while he slept undisturbed through all the noise.

My phone buzzed in my lap, and my head jolted off the headrest.

"Mom," I answered.

"Did you find Molly or Ty?"

I inhaled a deep breath, wishing my answer could have been good news. "No." I filled her in on everything we had found at Ty's and told her about my conversation with Anya.

"This can't be happening." Her voice croaked. "Our sweet

little Molly, and the babies." She sucked in a harsh breath. "After what Orien did to her, and now this. And poor Ty. What if we're already too late?"

"We're going to find them, Mom. I have a plan, but there's something I need to tell you first. It's about Orien."

The silence stretched for what felt like an eternity while I waited for her to react to everything I'd told her.

"He can help us, Mom. He's seen their leader."

She still said nothing. I checked my phone screen to make sure I hadn't lost the call, but we were still connected. My legs jittered as I imagined the depth of her disappointment.

When she finally spoke, her words were tense and sharp. "He can't be trusted."

"I know, Mom. But he has information about the Hunters, and if what he showed me about Oria is true, then—"

"Stop. That's enough! Oria ruled our people with compassion. Everything Orien says is a lie. I'll call Calista and Selkie, and we'll meet you there."

"I'm sorry, Mom."

"Me too, Everly. You have been given the title of a queen, but you are still my daughter. The decisions you make affect everyone around you. It was foolish to meet with Orien alone. After what he did to your father, you should have known better. You put not only your own life at risk but your brother's life as well."

"Mom, please. Darion will understand. I know he will."

"That's not the point. It was reckless, and—" She stopped, and I could hear her exhale a frustrated breath. "We can talk about this later. Just don't call on Orien until we are all there. Is that understood?"

My chest caved at the sternness in her voice. She'd never been so angry at me before. I swallowed hard and said, "Yes."

"Good. I love you," she replied, and hung up.

I dropped my head onto the steering wheel. She was right. I'd been making selfish choices, but it was time to set things right, at least with this one.

⚜

I got to the studio before anyone else. After lighting the candles and cleaning the old blood off the mirror, I retrieved everything I needed for the spell.

Jasper and Anya were the first to arrive, with Freya right behind them.

I waited for everyone before explaining my plan, so I'd only have to do it once.

Freya and my mother were certain that once Orien was trapped in the portal, they could break the magic linked to his ring that protected him from my Empath abilities. I still required his help, so I needed to use magic against him that wouldn't kill him, at least for now.

Anya nodded for me to come close, while my mom, Freya, Calista, and Selkie went over their spell. Once Orien appeared in the tunnel, they would bind him in place, so he would be unable to use his ability to portal jump, and then they would unlink the magic connected to his ring, and he would be mine.

Jasper huddled with Arden and Rhal. I'd hoped Rheya would be here, in case I lost control of my fire magic, but she'd stayed with new guards at the house to look over Malakai, who had regained consciousness.

I clutched my blade tight, eager to get on with my plan. "What is it, Anya?"

She glanced at the others, then whispered, "Your uncle has shown you the truth."

I didn't need to ask Anya how she knew this. Her visions came to her in flashes and glimpses and dreams. On the night

Lucas had died, she had warned me I'd lose someone. Anya had a gift, and her words were not to be ignored.

"He may be telling me the truth about Oria, but it doesn't change what he's guilty of," I reminded her.

"No." She moved nearer, and I breathed in the fading scent of jasmine. Her soft fingers turned my hand over, and she traced the lines on my palm. A violet hue emanated from her aura, and the air grew thick and dewy with her magic. Warm waves of energy pressed against my skin. "You must allow him to show you the moment Orien Ever truly died. Only then will you understand what you need to do." Her wild eyes locked on mine, and I knew she was in the depth of a spiritual connection.

"Ev!"

My body quivered at Jasper's sudden presence. I slipped my hand from Anya's and shook off the shiver that raced up my spine.

Jasper looped his arm around Anya's waist and snugged her to him. He kissed her temple and breathed in the mass of curls bundled atop her head before settling his amber gaze on me. "This plan is dangerous, but if Orien knows anything about the Hunters and how we can save Molly, then I see no other choice."

"I'm glad you agree." I rubbed the goose bumps from my arms.

Jasper nodded behind me.

I turned into a hard mass of muscle.

Arden caught my shoulders as I spun around, and the familiar surge of energy zapped between us, as it always did.

"We'll be right behind you." His grip tightened, and his desire to protect me was hard to miss. Lines creased the edges of Arden's eyes as the green washed away the blue. "Listen." He took a step closer. "About what I said, earlier at dinner—"

"No." I cut him off. "You were right." I thought about how the guards had been attacked tonight, and how we'd almost lost Malakai. If Arden had been there, he might not have been standing in front of me right now. I brushed his fingers with mine, thankful that he was here with me. "You were right about everything." I stepped back, letting his hands drop from my shoulders.

Chalk scraped across the wooden floor. My mom was nearly done drawing the rune she needed for her spell.

"Wait until my signal," I told Arden, and I darted past him, clamping my hand over the goddess pendant at my neck, the weight of it suddenly heavier than before.

Freya eyed me as she stepped into the chalk circle, and I wondered at her expression as she gazed at the pendant she'd given me. She glanced away and began chanting over an enormous, jagged black stone that she had placed directly in the center of the circle.

Her chant grew louder as my mother, Calista, and Selkie joined her. Freya stepped to the outside of the circle and signaled for Anya, who joined the women in their chant.

The air stirred with magic as each woman locked hands with the next. The stone Freya had set inside the circle started to vibrate and bang against the floor. When the final pair of hands were linked, the shining black stone exploded with a bright glow and hovered above the floor.

My mom cast her gaze at me.

I barely noticed the hot sting as I slashed my blade across my palms and smeared my blood over the surface of the mirrored wall. The red eye stared back at me as flames burst from my dripping hands, and I recited the spell I'd used so many times.

My reflection shattered into a million pieces with the glass, and I stepped into the swirl of blackness.

"Orien!"

A crack of light pierced the darkness.

"Back so soon, niece."

"They've taken her! I need answers." I spun to face Orien. "Where would they take her?"

"To his dimension."

"Dimension?" I scowled. "What are you talking about?"

"The Ghost of Time. He comes from——"

Suddenly voices echoed in the dark. They'd begun the spell that would seal the portal and trap Orien inside.

His lips peeled back. "I'm disappointed and impressed at the same time. Unfortunately for you, you'll never find the Hunters now," he whispered as he attempted to use his power to vanish from the portal.

But his spell failed. Magic imprisoned him. He tried again but remained in place. His dark sapphire eyes widened.

"Unfortunately for you"—I used his words against him— "you're trapped here, and your ring can no longer protect you from me."

Heat surged through me. I let loose the rage I'd been holding inside, and a force of energy blasted Orien to his knees.

"Your history lessons are no longer necessary." I circled him. Crackles of electricity rippled down my arms as they had the night I had come face-to-face with Darion at the club after he'd taken our mother captive. I threw my arms out, understanding my magic more now than I had then, and slammed Orien with a blast meant to cripple.

But Orien's back straightened. He pushed against my magic with his own.

A force pressed against me, causing me to stumble backward while Orien got back to his feet.

I thought of Lucas, staring with lifeless eyes, and drew on the hatred I felt for what Orien had done to him and my father. A scream tore from me as my power broke through Orien's and crushed him to the ground.

"Once you're immobilized, my mother will enter your mind and discover all we need to know. Your reign of terror on our family is over."

Orien laughed. "Clever. But you forget who you're dealing with." He crawled into a crouch and lunged for me but slammed into Jasper's shield as Jasper, Arden, and Rhal came into view and circled Orien.

Arden drew his sword and gave Rhal the signal. Rhal trembled, releasing his magic. Wisps of black smoke sifted from the surface of his midnight skin, twisting and turning in a mass as it reshaped itself into multiple shadow forms of Rhal. The forms rippled and crept toward Orien, ready to draw blood at their master's command.

A brief flash of fear shone in the shadowed pits of Orien's eyes before his face twisted with rage.

"We had a deal!" he roared.

"Our deal is done, and so are you." Fire exploded from my palms and walled him in.

"Not before I finish what I started." He shot through the flames, not caring that fire singed his hair and skin.

One of Rhal's shadow forms slammed against Orien, halting him in place.

"You must see what she did to me." Spit sprayed from Orien's mouth as he spoke over the shadow's shoulder.

I gathered energy to me in a massive force and blasted Orien back to his knees.

He yelled and covered his ears, but his resistance was unyielding. The more magic I inflicted upon him, the harder he fought against it, and once again he pushed himself to standing.

Arden arched his sword as Rhal's shadows moved on Orien.

"Wait!" I commanded. Anya's words came back to me as I met my ancient uncle's defiant stare. "Jasper, take down your shield."

He frowned, but the high-voltage energy that surrounded me evaporated.

"Show me." I stepped toward Orien.

The scene rippled like a reflection fading from the surface of the water, and then I stood in another room. A guttural cry came from Orien as he lay across a woman who rested in her final slumber.

I nearly doubled over when his pain hit me. I recognized this agony and knew it well. Orien was being torn apart from the inside.

My hand reached out tentatively to touch his trembling back, but he had no idea I was there as he mourned his beloved. The woman's caramel skin had faded to a pale, sickly color, and sunken eyes and cheeks had replaced what had once been a face of great beauty.

"I'm sorry she did this to you, my love. I promise that I'll make her pay. All of them will pay." His tears flowed onto her cheek as he gently kissed her lips and breathed in her hair.

The doors were flung open behind me, and Orien stiffened. He lifted his head, and when he turned, a coldness crept over his features, and a darkness that hadn't been there before saturated his aura.

"Why, sister? I did everything you asked of me. Zelda was innocent."

Oria flicked her careless gaze at the deceased. "To teach you a lesson, brother. Never forget which one of us is powerful and which one is weak. And never spy on me again." Oria turned from Orien and walked away, offering him no comfort in his grief.

He turned back to Zelda, his fingers threading through long, dark curls that had once been lush with life.

Against my will, my heart ached for the man who would become the murderer of my loved ones.

A chill crept over me.

Dark tendrils snaked through Orien's aura. The sliver of good that Oria hadn't stolen fought against the blackness that consumed him, but the darkness that took root inside him suffocated that part of his being.

Oria had taken her brother's pure-hearted soul and twisted him into a menacing creature.

I wiped the salty tears from my lips and tried to catch my breath. How could Oria have been so cruel to her own brother?

"Now you see, niece." The present Orien appeared before me. "Oria took everything from me and turned me into this monster. She stole what was good in me and left me with her evil. She despised my weakness for love when we were children, so I became the brother she had always desired, and when she least expected it, I struck. I made her pay for what she'd done to my Zelda. I made them all pay for their blind ignorance."

My chest throbbed for all that Orien had suffered. The hate I felt for him distorted into something else ... pity.

"Do not pity me, niece. That was not the point of this lesson. The worst part," Orien continued, "was I still loved my sister even after all she'd done to me, but it wasn't enough to bring me back from the black hole she'd put me in. She had to pay for what she'd done to Zelda, who was a shining light before Oria made her sick. Zelda was my one true love. She was the only person who believed in my goodness. She saw what everyone else was blind to. She never trusted Oria, and Oria knew that and punished her for it."

Orien took a step toward me. "I can't rest until I destroy all Oria cared about."

"But it was so long ago. Can't you let yourself heal and move on?"

"Can't you?" he asked, and a part of me finally understood Orien, and why his need for revenge had consumed him.

Guttural words came from him, and just like that, we were back in the present, and whatever magic Orien used dropped Jasper, Arden, and Rhal all at once. Arden's sword clanged to the ground as he clamped his hands over his ears.

"Stop!" I demanded as blood dripped from their noses. "Just come willingly and help us. Show them the man you were before Oria took everything from you. I know a part of him still exists inside you, or you wouldn't have cared to show me all of this. You wanted someone to see you for who you were, not who you've become, and I think you know why."

Orien's eyes met mine, and for a second, I saw a flash of the eyes from his past, before they had iced over. "I'm sorry. That man doesn't exist anymore." He closed his fists, and screams filled the portal as more blood oozed from the mouths of my friends.

"Tell your mother to end her spell, or this lot dies."

"I'm sorry too." I meant the words as I siphoned the magic Orien used and projected it into him.

Orien had exposed his weakness by showing me his pain. I didn't want to use his heartbreak against him, as Oria had, but it was my only option. I reached into him with my magic and drew forward the pain that he kept buried beneath layers of rage and resentment. He'd had my blood, and I'd discovered that it created a connection between us. Deep down, Orien's heart still ached for the one he'd lost, which meant he was still capable of feeling. I dug deeper with my power, bringing centuries of buried emotions to the surface. Orien's exterior shattered as his agony for the love of his life returned.

He pressed his hands against the sides of his head. "No!

Not this." He dropped to his knees and fell to the floor in a fetal position.

"You've left me no choice." I continued the assault until Arden and the others recovered.

Jasper threw his shield up while Arden bound Orien's arms in bindings that would restrict even Orien's magic.

After centuries, he'd finally been brought down. So why didn't I feel better about capturing the man who had caused my family so much pain and had planned to destroy his entire planet?

As he lay coiled in a ball, I saw a flash of the boy he'd been. That boy had been filled with sorrow and remorse for everything Oria had made him do. Orien had never had a chance at being the man he was meant to be. Oria had made sure of that.

My mother stood with a stony expression, her gaze frozen on Orien as we exited the portal. Her back stiffened when Arden shuffled Orien over to stand before her. She snatched his chin. "Look at me."

The harshness in her words sent a cold tingle down the back of my neck.

Orien's pained stare met hers, but I knew all he saw was the past that haunted his mind. I'd opened a well, and all the emotions he'd buried deep inside it flooded to the surface.

My mom held her hand out to Freya, who produced a silver dagger. "Hold him still."

"Mom! What are you doing?"

Orien offered no resistance as my mom pierced the skin on his forehead with the blade and carved a symbol over his flesh.

"So you never forget what you've done."

Orien's eyes rolled back, and his head fell forward with a moan.

I turned away. I understood how my mother felt. I still

hated Orien for everything he was guilty of, but I also felt something else for him now, something I couldn't deny. He'd been a pawn, as Darion had, only no one had saved Orien before it was too late. I swiped away a tear before anyone saw it and pretended to cough into my arm. I should have been glad we'd finally caught him. This was what I'd been trying so hard to do for so long. I forced away the guilt gnawing at me and wiped the blood from the mirror while Orien was carted to the vehicles to be taken to the cabin.

Anya nodded at me but said nothing as she bent to clean the chalk from the floor, and I wondered what larger scheme her vision belonged to. We would only know as the events unfolded. Premonitions were like a night flower in bloom, giving you just a peek before hiding itself away.

I was the last to leave the studio. Crimson streaked across the sky as I pulled up to the cabin.

My mom waited outside on the porch steps. "You did good, honey." She reached for my hand. A weight had been lifted from her, and her energy vibrated higher than it had in a long time. She'd avenged her love, and with the curse she'd placed on Orien, he would suffer as she had for all his remaining days. There would be no escape from the torturous agony he felt.

"Are you okay?" she asked as I stared up at the changing sky.

"I don't know," I answered truthfully. "A part of me understands him more than I ever expected was possible, and I can't help but feel for him."

My mom put her arm around my shoulders. "You're a royal Empath, honey. You feel others' emotions on a deeper level than most, even other Empaths."

I leaned my head against hers. "It's not just that. He showed me things from his past. Orien was a kind person before Oria ruined him. He loved someone the same way you loved Creagan. The same way I love—" I paused, realizing what I was about to say. "My point is, when Oria took the woman he loved from him, after she'd already taken what made him good when she swapped their auras, it broke him beyond recovery."

Lights flashed through the trees as a car, followed by a motorcycle, twisted around the winding road leading to the cabin.

"There's no excuse for his actions, honey." A hardness returned to her tone. "He has to pay for his crimes."

"I know that, Mom. But you showed Siobhan mercy after everything she'd done to you."

My mom sighed and expelled a breath of fog. "Since this is troubling you so much"—she reached for my hand—"let me see for myself."

Her magic connected to mine as she entered my memories. It was like a tickle in my head as she sifted through the past. Her eyelids moved rapidly, and then she released my arm with a sharp breath.

"How can that be true?" Her dark brows drew down, and she tucked a stray strand of hair behind her ear. "Everything we learned of Oria can't be false." She snugged her arms across her chest, shaking her head.

"I think Oria changed just as Orien had after the aura-transfer spell she performed. You heard what the Hunter told her in Orien's memory. There were permanent alterations."

My mom closed her eyes as a gust of frigid wind surged around us. "This doesn't change anything. Orien is still guilty. He chose to murder innocent people. All Vitarians deserve justice for what Orien did to our families. We have to inform the council of his capture. It's your duty as queen."

I picked at a broken splinter of wood sticking up from the edge of the wooden step. A tightness I didn't quite understand formed in my chest at the thought of serving Orien up to the council. "Orien will be punished, but he has information that can help us. You saw for yourself. Oria conspired with the leader of the Hunters, and just before you started the spell to trap Orien, he was about to tell me something important about him. Right now, Orien is our only hope of finding Molly. We can't inform the council yet. We still need him."

My mom shivered. "It's still so hard to believe. Everything Oria did was treason against her planet and family. The stone she created for the Hunter holds powerful fairy magic, magic that's supposed to be protected. His reason for wanting it can't be good."

I remembered the comment Orien had made after he'd shown me the memory. "Mom, have any other royals in our family had fire magic?"

She turned toward the parking vehicles and waved to Selkie, who was getting out of her catering van. "Yes, there have been others with the gift. Why?"

I exhaled, and my shoulders relaxed. "Never mind. What about Orien? Will you back my decision not to notify the council yet?"

She paused and gripped the edge of the wooden step. "Nothing with our family is ever uncomplicated. You'll need to order the others to remain quiet about Orien's capture. Once the council gets word, they'll want him transported back to Aenoas-Vita for a public punishment."

"Thank you, Mom."

She stood and squeezed my hand, then went to join Selkie, who was lifting Malakai's legs out of the side of her van while Rheya and Dalia supported him between them. Once he was upright, they started my way.

Malakai's bronzed skin tone was still a bit paler than normal, but his energy felt stronger than it had when I'd left my mom's house with Darion.

"You saved me," he said when the trio stopped at the steps. "I'll never forget, Your Majesty." He grimaced as Rheya and Dalia adjusted his weight. "I'm sorry we failed you. I don't know what happened." He stopped to catch his breath. "I was up in the sky." Malakai tilted his head back. "And then I was falling and unable to regain control over the owl I occupied. Its body crashed to the ground, and that's the last thing I remember until I woke up on your mother's couch."

"I'm thankful you're better." I squeezed Malakai's hand and glanced over at Rheya, who wore the largest grin I'd ever seen on her face.

"You finally caught the beast." She beamed. "I'm impressed, Your Majesty," she added with a hint of sarcasm. "Now, can you get the door?" She and Dalia heaved Malakai forward.

I ran up the steps and bumped into Arden just as I opened the cabin's front door. He grabbed my waist as we steadied our balance, then cleared his throat and dashed around me, taking Malakai's weight from Dalia.

A heavy dread settled over me as I watched Arden and Rheya help Malakai inside. Whatever had attacked him was a power unlike anything we'd ever seen.

7

O rien stared past me as if he saw nothing. A week had passed, and he still hadn't muttered a word. He refused to eat and had barely swallowed any of the water or broth we'd forced into his mouth. He was a shadow of the man he had once been. His cheekbones were beginning to protrude, and the skin under his eyes sagged with dark circles. The evil that had once gleamed in his eyes had been replaced with an emptiness so deep and dark that no amount of light could break through.

I'd opened the floodgates of his most painful memories, and my mother had sealed them in place with her curse. Orien would never be free from the torment he felt.

"You're wasting your time." Rheya slammed the tray of food down, causing the broth to lap over the sides of the bowl. "Your mother can't get inside his warped head. He's useless! You should let us transport this monster home, so he can get the punishment he deserves."

Rheya threw up her hands when I answered her with a cold stare. "Fine! But you know I'm right."

When Rheya closed the door behind her, I lifted the bowl

of broth and dipped the spoon into the liquid. Orien pinched his lips tight when I tried to feed him.

I set the bowl back down and slumped in the chair. "Please, Orien. Darion can't find any trace of Molly. Help us before it's too late."

He remained motionless.

"She's carrying twins."

An eyelid flickered, but he still remained silent.

"Huh." I balled my hands into fists. I'd promised my mom I wouldn't ease his suffering, but we were running out of time. Molly didn't know how far along she had been in the vision the babies had sent her, but she knew she'd had a baby bump, and every day that passed was one day closer to the premonition coming true.

I scooted closer and placed my fingers on Orien's temples. His pain gripped me like a nightmare I couldn't wake from. A massive wave of nausea turned my stomach inside out as I siphoned the agony of his memories from him. My body convulsed. I had thought I knew pain, but what Orien felt tore apart my insides.

Fingers tightened around my wrists. "No!" Orien uttered. "Don't take it away. It's what I deserve." His voice was raw and weak.

Orien struggled in his seat to push me away.

I finally released him and bent forward, gagging for breath.

"The Hunter—" Orien coughed.

I pulled myself up. With a shaky hand, I lifted water to Orien's cracked lips. For the first time in a week, he drank without resisting.

"He's from another dimension."

My eyes widened. "What do you mean?"

Orien struggled to hold his head up. His body was weak. "Just as life exists on more than one planet in this universe, so it does in multiple dimensions. Life is infinite, repeating itself over and over."

I knew Orien spoke the truth, but my mind still wanted to resist the idea. "Okay, but how did he get to our dimension, and what does he want?"

Orien squinted and swallowed another sip of water. "How do you think, niece? He used magic to cross over."

"I don't understand. Why would he leave his own dimension and come to ours to kidnap pregnant mothers and murder innocent babies?"

"Why does anyone do what they do? Revenge. Fear. Hate. Love. These are the core motivations that drive us to unspeakable acts, but if you want to know his exact reason, I guess you'll need to find him and ask him yourself."

A crack split open on his lip when he tried to grin, and a glint of the old Orien shone in the devious glare directed at me.

I ignored his taunt. He was trying to anger me, so I'd leave him to his suffering. "If he took Molly to another dimension, how will we find him?"

Orien's head lolled back and then rolled forward. "So persistent. Both you and your mother. Her digging around inside my head, and you with your constant questions. Think back to what I showed you." He paused, looking at me like I should know the answer.

I ran through all the memories Orien had taken me to. "That night in the forest, Oria offered herself to him, but he denied her, and then he spoke of his wife."

Orien nodded. "What else?" he pressed.

I thought back, trying to recall everything I'd heard between Oria and the Hunter that night in the woods, when she'd created the stone of fire for him.

"He's searching for someone! Who?"

"That secret is only his. I never found out," Orien answered.

"Wait!" I leaned over on the edge of my chair. "Oria tasted his blood and told him the one he sought would love another when he found her. Oria must have seen through her gift of premonition. She knows who the Hunter is after. It's time to tell me where her ring is. I need to speak to Oria and find out who the Hunter's looking for. I can't explain it, but I have this feeling the answer can help us."

The look Orien gave me set me back in my chair.

"What is it?" I asked.

"It brings me no pleasure to tell you that the Shimera have Oria's ring."

"What?" I gripped the sides of the chair's seat to keep from lashing out at Orien. "How could you let them have it?"

Orien cringed. "It was part of the deal I made with them. They want to study its magic. They still think magic can fix the genetic disease their kind is cursed with."

It took all my willpower not to throttle Orien. "Can you get it back?"

He shook his head. "They took it back to their planet. It'll take an army to get the ring back from them, and you don't have the time to spare to go to war with the Shimera while the Hunters have your brother's fiancée. She'll be dead by the time you get your precious ring."

The chair crashed backward when I charged to my feet. "Argh!" I shot a murderous glare at Orien and paced to the other side of the room before I did something I'd regret.

Without Oria's ring, there was only one other way to reach the realm where her spirit remained. But that meant finding the Spider Witch first and persuading Darion to go along with my plan.

"I've answered your question," Orien croaked. "Now I need something from you."

My gaze narrowed, and suspicion crawled over me. "If you think you're getting another drop of my blood, you can forget it."

"No." He cast his gaze down. An odd silence settled between us before he lifted his head again. "Take my life. Please."

My breath caught in my throat. That was not the request I'd expected.

"I can't return to Aenoas-Vita," Orien continued when I offered no response. "Not after everything I've done. I'm begging you. It must be you who sends my soul to the pits of darkness for eternity. Set me free from this pitiful existence. It's what you've wanted. It's what I deserve." He looked me straight in the eye, and what I saw surprised me. It wasn't the cruel Orien, who had murdered my father and Lucas and so many others, begging me for mercy. It was the Orien I had seen in his past, the Orien with the tender heart who had loved Zelda more than anything, who was pleading through depths of despair and regret. And then my eye caught something, a shimmer in Orien's aura that hadn't been there before. The last spark that Oria's darkness had suffocated had resurfaced. It was just a sliver, a hint of golden glimmer, so minuscule it was nearly undetectable, but it was there nonetheless, struggling to break through.

I grabbed my stomach and went to stand near the window that looked out over the forest. Raindrops pelted the glass as the wind thrashed, and I thought of Lucas and the bright light that had shone in him before Orien had torn his life force from him. Lucas had been loving and kind. He'd been forgiving. What would he have told me now, when his murderer begged for my mercy? What would my father have done? I had never gotten the chance to know Creagan as my father, because Orien had taken his life before I had found out the truth of my identity. Wild, hot anger seared my insides.

Orien was right. He did deserve death, and I'd wanted to take his life so badly I could taste it, but even now, as he begged me to end him, something within me resisted. I'd suffered his pain. I'd seen his torment. I had to end the cycle of revenge that trapped my family. But if I sent Orien back to Aenoas-Vita, his punishment would be far worse than just death. I pressed my finger to the glass. Waterdrops drew together like magnets at my command. When I pulled my finger away, the ball exploded apart, sending multiple drips raining down.

Orien's head drooped forward once more as I left his plea unanswered and stormed out of the room.

"Did your demon uncle finally give up any information?" Rheya asked. She leaned against the wall in the hall and tapped the hilt of her sword. Her copper braid hung long over one shoulder.

"Yes." I sighed, knowing what Rheya's next words would be.

She pushed off the wall. "Then we can transport him home to face his punishment." She reached for the door, but I slammed my hand over the doorknob.

"Orien remains here under our protection until I decide otherwise."

Emerald fury stared back at me as waves of frustration rolled off Rheya. "I don't understand you. He murdered my king, your father. He tortured and killed your boyfriend. He's taken countless lives over the centuries, and you show him mercy?" She gritted her teeth, then shook her head and stalked away.

I understood Rheya's frustration, but she didn't know the things about Orien that I'd learned. He was broken now. His mind was his own personal torture chamber. I was showing him no mercy by letting him live as he was ... for now.

I sat at Felix's writing desk, using his spelled quill and ink to send Darion a message. Gold letters swept across the thick parchment, and the letter burned to ash as each line was finished, and the letter would appear in Darion's possession.

Now all I had to do was wait for Darion to return. He'd resisted tracking the Spider Witch before. But now we had no choice but to seek her out. Darion had scoured Earth for Molly and had returned to Aenoas-Vita, hoping to find a lead there.

A knock sounded at the door. "Come in."

Dalia cracked the door open and popped her head in. "I brought you some tea and a snack." Her warm smile was like a punch in the gut. Everything about Dalia was absolutely perfect: her kindness, generosity, and she was an amazing cook. If she hadn't continued to bring me meals this week, I wouldn't have made the time to eat.

Arden continued to insist that he and Dalia weren't an item, and he had no plans for them to become so, regardless of my efforts to push him away. But Dalia cared deeply for him, and he respected her. It was obvious when the two were together. Once they left Earth and returned home, I would no longer be an obstacle.

I rubbed at the hot spot burning across my chest. This pain had become a frequent side effect of picturing Arden and Dalia together. But I'd just have to get over it.

I smiled at Dalia as she set the plate of food down on the desk beside me. Despite my resistance, I couldn't help but warm to her, even though she often took advantage of laying claim to Arden when the three of us were in the same room. I couldn't blame her for going after what she wanted when I couldn't. Arden was any woman's vision of a perfect catch. He was devilishly handsome, strong, caring, the commander of the Vitarian guard, and an amazing kisser. Of course Dalia had fallen for him.

I cleared my throat. I really should stop thinking about Arden's kissing skills.

"Thank you, Dalia." I shifted and fanned my face as guilt slithered into the pit of my stomach.

"Has there been any word on your brother's fiancée?"

I placed the quill back into its case and pressed the cork into the bottle of gold ink. "No, but I've sent my brother a message, asking him to return. I may have learned something useful."

"I hope so. It breaks my heart to think of anyone harming an innocent woman with child." Dalia smoothed the front of her silk dress. The fabric matched the larimar stone Dalia wore at her neck and complemented her eyes. "Do you mind?" She indicated the spare wooden chair and sat down when I nodded.

"Thank you." Dalia gently rubbed her abdomen. "I've been suffering bouts of fatigue of late."

The way Dalia's hand lingered on her belly caused knots to twist in my own. I released my mental shield and scanned her aura. The soft pink hue that bloomed around her mirrored the one that had encased Molly. And the hum of her energy … My breath caught, and I struggled to breathe as a lump surged up the back of my throat. It couldn't be. I had to turn away from Dalia before she saw the pain I fought back. She was pregnant with … Arden's baby.

"Are you okay?" She leaned forward, her tone filled with concern.

I pinched my stinging eyes closed. "I ... I have something in my eye is all." I jumped up. "Excuse me, Dalia."

I brushed past her and ran out of the healing room, which doubled as Felix's office and my temporary bedroom.

Rheya scowled at me as I blew past her and rushed out of the cabin.

I bounded into the forest and ran until my lungs felt like they would burst. When I finally stopped, I fell to my knees, and a gut-wrenching cry escaped me. How could he have let that happen? Flames rippled across my skin as fury burned my insides and then turned to something else. I couldn't hold back the well of tears that sprang free. I'd done nothing but continue to push Arden toward Dalia. But now that they had something between them that would bind them together forever, I was filled with so much regret.

I hunched forward and caught the goddess pendant as it dangled from my neck, and I gasped for breath.

A twig snapped behind me, and arms encircled me. I leaned back into Arden's warm embrace, aching with the knowledge that this would be the last time I could allow him to hold me like this. Dalia deserved her chance to be with the father of her child, without another woman standing between them.

"Talk to me, Everly."

I scooted away and swiveled in the layer of dried leaves and nettles and dug my hands into the damp earth. "Have you noticed anything different about Dalia recently?"

A frown darkened Arden's features. "What are you talking about?"

He didn't know. Arden had Empath magic, but it wasn't like mine. He didn't see auras the way I did.

"How long since you two were ... together?"

Confusion rippled across his brow. "It was a month or so before we came here."

"Was Dalia seeing anyone else?"

Worry shone in Arden's eyes as a light of understanding took root. "I—" He glanced in the direction of the cabin. "I don't know. I don't think so. What are you trying to tell me?"

My hands crushed the dried debris, and my fingernails dug into the cool soil beneath. "I think you know."

Arden froze. The blue circle vanished from his irises, and a blaze of green moss stared back at me. "It's not possible. I'm sure I took precautions."

I pushed myself up from the ground. "She's pregnant, Arden. I'm positive. Either someone else is the father, or your *precautions* didn't work, and you're going to be a father. And what do you mean, you're sure? How would you not know one way or the other?"

He jumped up and paced through the leaves toward me. "It's hard to explain. That night is hazy. I have the memory of being with Dalia, but it's more like a dream than reality. I may have had too much to drink." He shook his head. "I'll speak with Dalia. This has to be some kind of mistake." He pulled me to him.

For a moment, I allowed myself to nuzzle my head under his chin and breathe in his scent. His arms tightened around me, and our bodies trembled against each other.

"Mistake or not, if Dalia carries your child, your duty is to her." I inhaled a deep breath of cedar and sandalwood and pushed away from him.

Without looking back or thinking where I was going, I ran until I ended up standing in front of the waterfall that hid a portal between worlds, wishing I could send myself somewhere far away, but that wasn't an option, not when my family needed me.

I sat for hours, lost in misery. A relentless mist dampened my clothes, and my back ached from being hunched over, but I just couldn't bring myself to move. It was dusk before I heard a change in the flow of water, and when I glanced up from the log I rested on, the stream was separating to reveal the large cavern. Energy sparked in the air as swirls of color took shape, and a watery substance stretched tall and wide.

"Sister!" Darion leaped out of the portal and landed next to me with a thump.

I sprang up and flew into his arms.

There was no point in asking if he'd found anything. His expression said it all.

We trekked through the woods in silence. Once inside the cabin, I noticed how thin Darion had gotten over this last week, and he didn't look like he'd slept at all.

Dalia's eyes widened when she saw him, and she filled a bowl with hot broth. I accepted the bowl when Darion refused to even give it a glance.

"Sit down, Darion, and eat this."

Defiance shone in his exhausted eyes. He pushed the bowl away. "Tell me everything."

"Not until you eat something and get some sleep."

Darion's fist pounded down onto the table, and a storm of silver fury glowered at me. "Damn it, Ev. This isn't a game. Molly and my babies are being held captive by murderers, and you want me to eat soup and sleep?"

I took him by the shoulders, and my expression softened. "Yes, I do. And tomorrow, we search for the Spider Witch." I slid the bowl back in front of him.

I hadn't told the others, but Darion understood my unspoken plan. I'd explained everything in the letter. He knew that contacting Oria was our only hope, and without the ring, there was only one other way. I just hoped the Spider Witch would help us. Darion hadn't found a trace of Molly or Ty, and I feared the Hunter had taken them to wherever it was that he came from, somewhere we knew nothing about. But there was one person who knew his secrets and what he was willing to suffer an eternity searching for. I didn't know how, but I planned to find what Cade Wolf wanted and offer him a trade. But in order to do that, Darion and I had to cross into the spirit realm. And the price for that would be our lives. We both needed our strength for what would come.

Darion tore his gaze from me and picked up his spoon. When he finished the broth, Dalia refilled his bowl and brought with it a slice of her freshly baked bread. Darion chewed and eyed Dalia while she mixed him a tonic. Whatever thoughts brewed behind his dark gaze, he kept them to himself, and he mumbled a thanks when Dalia set the herb-scented glass of liquid on the table and went back to storing the leftovers from the meal she'd made in the fridge.

Darion's head drifted forward slightly and then popped back up. He tossed the tonic to the back of his throat and stood, resting his hand on my shoulder. I cupped my hand over his, and we shared a moment of quiet understanding before he left the kitchen. Seconds later, his footsteps plodded up the staircase leading to the second floor. There were still spare bedrooms, since Arden had sent Rhal and most of the guards with my mom to her house. She hadn't wanted to stay under the same roof as Orien, and she'd insisted she would be fine being in her own home. The Hunters had already gotten what they'd come for.

I glanced at Dalia. Steam billowed from the sink while she scrubbed a large metal soup pot.

"Do you need a hand, Dalia?"

She smiled over her shoulder. "All finished up after this one."

Dalia turned back to her task, and I went to stand by the fire in the living room. A silence permeated the cabin. No one but Arden and I occupied the living room. He sat rigid in a stuffed chair. I gathered he'd spoken with Dalia and heard the news from her own lips.

Our eyes locked, and I wrapped myself in a protective shield as I walked past him toward the room I was staying in.

Arden's hand shot out, and his fingertips locked around mine.

"I'm sorry," he whispered. His thumb caressed the top of my hand, causing a flutter to swirl in my belly.

My throat went dry. I reached up and touched the goddess of love and compassion dangling at my neck and thought of the ever stone that was supposed to have taken all these feelings away. I'd left the stone back at my apartment. I had to find out why the spell had stopped working, and how to fix it, and once I did, I would destroy these tormenting emotions for good.

A sharp pain knifed through my chest, and I yanked my hand from Arden's when Dalia's footsteps headed our way. I hurried into my room and closed the door and sank into the twin mattress.

Their voices whispered in the living room. If I listened hard enough, I could probably hear what they were saying, but I didn't want to know. I pressed the sides of the pillow over my ears until their voices faded and I no longer sensed their energies on the other side of the door. Then I made my way to the upstairs bathroom, since the one on the main floor was only a partial and didn't have a tub or shower. I turned on the shower and peeled off my damp clothes, tossing them onto the floor. Hot water pelted my back and soothed my aching muscles. I tilted my head into the stream and massaged shampoo into my scalp.

A cloud of steam had completely filled the bathroom by the time I turned the water off and stepped out onto the padded floor mat. The towel pressed the goddess pendant against my skin as I wrapped my dripping body in the soft fiber.

I sighed and ran my finger along the chain, realizing I

hadn't taken the necklace off since Freya had given it to me, and I had no desire to. I felt a connection to it I couldn't explain, and keeping it around my neck just felt right.

I picked up my bundle of clothes from the floor and tiptoed out of the bathroom. The floorboards squeaked no matter how softly I stepped across the hall and down the steps. The front door to the cabin opened just as I reached the bottom of the staircase.

Arden froze. His eyes roamed over my towel-wrapped body.

Beads of water dripped from the ends of my hair and down my shoulders, and I shivered from the blast of frigid air that followed Arden into the cabin.

The energy that charged between us was like a storm of lightning. Electricity sizzled over my flesh as he trailed his fingers down my bare skin. The bundle of clothes fell from my arms, and my fingers threaded into Arden's hair as he crushed me to him. His mouth landed hard and hungry on mine. My body throbbed with a pulse of desire that was almost painful, and the primal need in our kiss turned deliciously forceful.

A low moan surged up my throat as Arden's hand cupped my breast and skimmed the edge of the towel, untucking it. Wild abandon coursed through me when his fingertips grazed my nipple, and his tongue licked the side of my neck.

A door creaked open upstairs just as my towel slipped loose. I snatched it back in place as footsteps neared the staircase.

It physically ached to separate myself from Arden, but I reached down and grabbed my clothes from the floor and rushed back to my room with a pounding heart.

I threw myself onto the bed and tried to catch my breath. If someone hadn't come out of their room when they had, I wouldn't have been able to stop with Arden. I still didn't want to.

My pulse raced with my heavy breath. I stared at the bedroom door, silently praying the knob would turn and Arden would burst in and continue where we had left off, but he'd leaped up the stairs as soon as I'd bolted, and caught Dalia before she had seen me frantically running off half-naked.

I'd known it was Dalia as soon as she'd stepped into the hall. I'd sensed her essence, as Arden would have with his Empath ability. Dalia definitely had a knack for timing. She'd nearly discovered us that night at the club too.

My arms squeezed around the pillow. I didn't know which frustration was worse, that I couldn't resist Arden or that we'd been interrupted.

The night was restless, and I tossed and turned repeatedly, trying not to think of Arden's hands and mouth on Dalia in the same way they'd been on mine. I knew being angry with Dalia was unfair, but nonetheless, the urge to strangle her for being intimate with Arden and getting herself pregnant was all I could think about, even though Arden had played as much a role as she had.

A tightness ached at the back of my throat, and I forced my thoughts in a different direction.

Orien's memory took shape in my mind.

Oria standing in front of the fire, chanting her spell, while the fairy she'd sacrificed burned, and its life force had been absorbed into the stone she'd collected from the center of the pyre. A light similar to fire had glowed within the stone as she'd carried it to Cade. And the magic inside it had beck-oned to me, somehow connecting to my fire magic. It'd been a strange sensation: a force outside my control, bending the will of my magic. A terrifying pain had consumed me. I still didn't understand how I'd felt it when I'd only been a ghost of another's memory. But the most burning question was why had the stone had any power over me at all?

Cade had called it a "stone of fire." What did that mean, and what did he want with it? It'd been important enough for him to seek Oria's help. And then he'd refused her advances, even when I'd sensed his attraction to her. Oria had discovered something personal about Cade when she'd tasted his blood. It had been enough to make her give up her seduction attempt. And one thing I'd learned about Oria was she wasn't easily deterred from her desires, a trait I was learning ran in our family, so whatever glimpse she'd had of Cade's future must have been significant.

Darion left the cabin early to track the Spider Witch, while I drove home to collect fresh clothes before updating our mom on the plan.

I sat on the edge of my mattress and stared numbly at the nightstand that held the ever stone. Making up my mind, I pulled the drawer open.

My pulse raced. The stone wasn't there. I yanked the drawer out and tossed the contents onto my bed. The stone was gone.

Who would have taken it?

Darion!

He'd been angry when I'd gotten home that night, and had been insistent that I restore my emotions. He had been worried about the cost of erasing such a vital piece of myself. It had to have been Darion. Only he would have been so brazen as to come into my apartment and into my bedroom and steal the stone.

Wait! If Darion has had the stone this entire time, then maybe he has something to do with why the magic stopped working.

My nostrils flared. He had no right! But then he'd only done what I would have done had I been in his shoes. He was being a brother, albeit a thorn-in-my-side brother, but he didn't know about Dalia's condition. I had to get the stone back and destroy it once and for all. My hands clenched, and electrical pulses shot across my skin. *I love Arden, damn it, and if I don't find a way to erase these feelings, I'll never be able to let him go.* I just hoped I was right and it was my devious brother who had taken the stone.

A familiar engine revved outside my apartment, and tires skidded to a halt over the gravel, followed by footsteps rushing up my front porch.

"Ev!" Jasper called as he came into my apartment.

I pulled on my black combat boots and laced them up. "I'm back here."

Jasper towered in my doorway, his dark cocoa waves a wild mess from his helmet. Specks of gold glinted in the amber eyes that narrowed their gaze at me.

"Let me guess. Darion called you."

"I'm your Shield, and you planned to go into battle without me?"

I sighed and bounced off the bed. Darion was going to get an earful when he got back.

"Jasper, you should stay with Anya and keep her safe. She needs you more than I do. We still don't even know how the Hunters learned of Molly's pregnancy, or how they knew where to find her. What if they come back for Anya?"

A vein bulged at Jasper's temple, and I knew there'd be no dissuading him from his decision.

"Anya will have protection, but I'm not letting you go anywhere without me. You've pushed me away enough these last several weeks. I know you think you're keeping me from living my life, but that's not true."

"Isn't it, though?" I shoved the drawer back into the

nightstand. "I can sense you keeping Anya at arm's length, Jasp. You care deeply for her, but you let your duty to me hold you back from letting yourself truly love her, because you know that when I return to Aenoas-Vita, you'll have to leave Anya behind."

Jasper's shoulders drooped slightly. He knew I was right, but he didn't want to admit that his loyalty to me was costing him his own happiness.

"You're my best friend." I squeezed his arm. "You've always looked out for me. Let me return the favor. I want you to stay here on Earth with Anya. Continue teaching music. It's what you love. I won't let you give up your life for me."

Jasper set his helmet on my mattress and gripped my shoulders. "It's not duty or any oath that keeps me by your side. It's love, and I love you even more for wanting me to be happy, but you're my best friend too, and I want those same things for you, and no matter how hard you try to keep me from your side, I will always protect you, and there's nothing you can do about it, so stop trying."

I fell against his hard chest and locked my arms around him. Jasper always made me feel safe. I'd missed spending time with him, and pushing him away hadn't made him change his mind about leaving Earth behind for me. I slipped my arms beneath his leather jacket and buried my face against the soft cotton fabric of his shirt. For a moment, I allowed myself to imagine that maybe everything would turn out okay. We'd get Molly and Ty back. The babies would be safe. Jasper would be happy with Anya. My mom and Sam would go on their planned trip to Mexico. Arden would return to Aenoas-Vita with Dalia. Everyone I loved would be safe and happy, and I'd be … alone, just as I deserved to be.

Jasper's breath tickled wisps of my hair. "Your mom is waiting. She was packing up her car when I pulled in."

I nodded and hesitated before unlocking my arms from around Jasper's back.

He stared down at me, and a smile lit up his face.

"What?" I grinned at the smug glint in his eye.

His thick eyebrow arched, and his lips parted as his smile grew wider. "It's just nice to know I'm still appreciated."

I laughed and shoved him. "Put the ego away, tough guy."

Jasper glanced at my bed and picked up Oria's sword ... my sword. Light danced across the silver blade, and it whispered in a low pitch as he extracted it from its sheath.

"A blade forged for a queen." His expression turned serious as he slammed the blade back into the scabbard and lifted the strap over my head and settled it across my shoulder. "Ready?" He grabbed his helmet and slung my bag over his shoulder and extended his hand toward me.

I laced my fingers through his and followed him out to his bike.

Jasper tossed my bag into the back of my mom's 4Runner.

Luna shot up from the back seat and popped her head out of the open passenger window.

I walked over and scratched her jaw and planted a kiss on the soft fur between her eyes. She lifted her snout high and licked my cheek. I laughed and wiped the dog slobber off with the back of my hand.

The back screen door squeaked open, and my mom, Calista, and Selkie came outside.

"We'll meet you at the cabin," I told them, and I climbed onto the back of Jasper's bike, wrapping my arms around his leather jacket.

"Hold on tight." The bike roared to life, and he hit the gas, spinning the back tire through the gravel.

I'd missed this. I snuggled up to his back, and the bike lurched forward. Brisk air rippled across my skin as Jasper flew down our country road and turned onto the highway, increasing our speed.

There was nothing quite like the exhilaration of traveling at max speed on a motorcycle, and Jasper took full advantage of being in charge. His hand twisted the throttle, and the front of the bike popped off the ground as it lifted onto the back tire. My arms squeezed tighter around his waist, which was tensing with laughter. The front tire hit the tarmac, and our speed slowed as Jasper whipped us off the highway and onto the road that led to Felix's cabin.

I glimpsed Luna's head poking out of the back passenger seat window of my mom's 4Runner, which followed behind us. Calista sat in the front passenger seat, and Selkie was in the back with Luna.

My two surrogate aunts had refused to stay behind, and so all the members that made up my family prepared for a battle with the unknown.

❧

D alia stayed welded to Arden's side and welcomed everyone in as though she were the lady of the house.

My cheeks burned hot when her hand lingered on Arden's arm.

Calista pursed her lips, and I could tell she fought the urge to react. But Selkie looped her arm through Calista's, and I shook my head at their questioning stare.

Calista widened her eyes at me, then slipped her arm from Selkie's.

Oh … no. My head filled with a silent groan when Calista winked at me and sauntered over to Dalia.

"Dalia, dear, why don't I give you a hand?" Calista shimmied between Dalia and Arden in the kitchen. She took the jar that Dalia had asked Arden to open. "Sometimes it just takes a woman's touch." She bumped Arden over farther with her hip.

"Oh," Dalia muttered. "Thank you."

Arden smiled to himself and took the hint.

Selkie pretended to trip as Arden passed us, and knocked me straight into his arms.

"Oh, honey. I'm sorry. I'm getting clumsy in my old age."

Ha! Old age? Right! Selkie was practically immortal, and she was never clumsy. I knew what these two hens were up to, and I loved them for it, but their meddling wouldn't work. There were too many complications between Arden and me now. At least, that was what I had to tell myself to keep up this charade of pushing him away.

A flush crept to the surface of my skin when Arden's arms locked around me, steadying my balance, and a flash of the night before filled my vision. He glanced down at me, and by the look he wore, I could tell he was thinking about it too.

"Ahem." Dalia cleared her throat, and Arden loosened his grip and released me.

My hand slid down his arm and brushed his fingers, sending a jolt of electricity rippling through me at our touch. Goose bumps rose on the back of my neck and down my arms. I caught Selkie and Calista both grinning to themselves.

Dalia coughed louder this time, and Arden and I quickly separated.

I shot Calista and Selkie each a disapproving glare, which they just returned with unapologetic smiles.

"Where's Mom?" I glanced around the cabin.

Selkie twisted her strawberry hair behind her head and secured it in place with a clip. "She took Luna for a walk to the portal to check for your brother."

"Are you expecting someone else?" Dalia asked from the kitchen window.

"No. Why?"

Dalia leaned closer to the glass. "A white Jeep just pulled up, and two women and a royal Shield are getting out."

Freya.

I hurried to the porch.

Jasper was already at the Jeep, berating the Shield he'd assigned to Anya for letting them leave their house without notifying him.

"I'm sorry, sir. They threatened to make my tongue limp." The young man glanced nervously at Freya, who watched him with amusement.

"Leave the poor boy alone," Freya told Jasper. "He had no choice but to do as I said."

Jasper wrapped Anya in his arms, and the two shared a brief kiss.

"Freya, why have you come?" I didn't need to remind her of the current dangers we faced. She had personal experience with the Hunters.

Freya's dark eyes settled on me, and a shadow of fear clung to her. The hem of her dress fluttered at her feet as she walked toward me and took my hands. She smelled strongly of neroli and ever resin smoke. The strong woody scent filled my lungs as I waited for her to answer.

"Anya had a vision," she explained in a somber tone. Deep lines appeared at the corners of her eyes as her eyebrows wrinkled together. "The Spider Witch alone will not be able to bring you both back from the realm of death. We've come to offer assistance."

When Freya said "both," I knew she meant both Darion and me, because if one went to the spirit realm, we both suffered the same fate. I trusted Anya's visions. She'd warned me before and hadn't been wrong. I also knew what Freya risked by bringing herself and her daughter to my aid.

I squeezed my hands over hers. "Thank you, Freya. I

appreciate everything you've done for us. We'll protect Anya."

Freya inclined her head. "Anya is no longer a child. I must respect her choices, but I'm not ready to let my cub wander the jungle alone."

A smile touched my lips. "Anya is lucky to have you for a mother."

The puckered grooves across Freya's brow relaxed as she returned my smile. Her attention wandered over my head as Dalia's energy appeared behind.

"If anyone is hungry," Dalia said with a warm smile, "we have plenty of food inside. I've just made a fresh batch of soup and sandwiches, if you'd like to join us for lunch."

"Heck, yeah," Jasper called from behind, and he tugged Anya toward the cabin, but she told him to go on ahead.

Freya went inside with Jasper, while Anya stayed behind with me.

Anya had that look that told me she had something to tell me in private. Once everyone was safely out of earshot, I asked her.

"What is it, Anya?"

The way her topaz eyes roamed around the cabin and the surrounding woods as if she was expecting something terrifying to lurch out at any moment sent prickles across my skin.

"A wolf stalks you." She tore her gaze from the forest. "I've seen it in my dreams. It hunts you with unsated hunger."

Chills crept over me as I remembered the words Freya had once told me.

Anya studied my reaction. "This is not the first time the wolf has appeared."

My head turned back and forth. "The first time your mother read my cards, she mentioned a wolf, but I never knew what it meant."

"Tell me exactly what she said." Anya twisted a gemmed ring on her finger.

I brought up my mental shield to keep myself from absorbing Anya's growing apprehension. "She said, 'Let the wolf guide you past your fear and into the unknown. Your path into the darkness of the soul will be your family's salvation.'"

Anya gathered the sides of her long, flowing skirt and bunched the fabric in tight fists.

"I thought maybe the reading had something to do with Orien—you know how the spirits like to communicate in riddles. Do you think there's a connection between your mom's card reading and your vision?"

Agitation vibrated within Anya's energy field as she continued to survey the forest. A flurry of chirps came from a nearby oak tree. Several birds sprang from the branches, causing a shower of crisp leaves to swirl toward the ground.

"I can't be sure yet." Anya answered my question as she watched the flock of birds fly away. "But the wolf I saw in my dream desires you. It hungers for your blood." A tremble shook her.

"What do you think it means?" I rubbed my arms, glancing nervously at the woods.

"I'm sorry, Everly." Anya folded her arms across her chest. "The wolf is most likely a representation of something else, but I don't know what. I can't control the visions, but there are herbs I can use to help bring them on."

The sweet, floral scent of Anya's jasmine perfume swirled in the air with a gust of wind.

I touched Anya's arm. "It's okay. I'll worry about this wolf after we get Molly and Ty back. Let's go have some lunch."

Anya didn't budge as her attention fell to the trail that led into the trees. "It's closer to getting what it wants." Her words were ghostlike as she turned toward me.

"Come on." I urged her forward, and we went inside the cabin.

Dalia was once again glued to Arden's side while everyone either sat at the dining table or leaned against the kitchen counters, eating the sandwiches and soup Dalia had prepared.

I took a seat next to Freya at the table and crunched down on a sprout and cucumber sandwich.

Dalia and Arden sat at the other end of the table. When she laid her hand on his, he glanced over at me and extracted his hand from under Dalia's, then left his seat.

Freya watched Dalia with a keen eye when she leaned toward me and whispered, "She's a woman of many secrets."

Dalia abruptly pushed back her chair and took her plate and bowl to the kitchen. She was clearly upset that Arden had just gotten up and left without a word to her.

I watched her rinse her dishes and couldn't help but wonder what other secrets she had besides her pregnancy. My shield dropped as I touched the outer edges of her aura with my magic.

Dalia's shoulders stiffened, and glass shattered in the sink. She turned in my direction just as a blast of cold air blew through the cabin when the front door burst open.

A crackle hissed from the fire blazing in the living room's fireplace.

My mom and Darion rushed inside with Luna on their heels. "I found the Spider Witch," Darion said with a sense of urgency. "But we must go now before she disappears again."

Dalia was unusually quiet while she fixed Luna a bowl of food suitable for a dog. She offered to keep an eye on her as our party quickly assembled.

I rubbed Luna's side and scratched her belly. "Keep a lookout, girl."

Luna whined when I stood to go.

"Thank you, Dalia."

Dalia nodded. Her demeanor had shifted toward me, and I was sure she'd sensed me using my magic on her, but I didn't have time to worry about Dalia's feelings right now.

Everyone was ready and waiting to head to the portal when I exited the cabin.

We followed the trail through the darkening forest. When I heard the rush of the waterfall, I knew we were getting close.

"Are you sure the portal is ready to transport us to the correct location?" Freya asked with an uneasy tone.

"It's ready," Darion confirmed with confidence. As a Tracker, he also wielded the ability to weave portals. Since the night Orien had escaped us in the tunnel by means of portal magic, Darion had been working on strengthening his own ability.

"Let's go, sister." He latched onto my hand, and I reached for our mom's with my free hand. My eyes landed on Arden for a moment before the three of us splashed across the creek and stepped into the cavern and through the otherworldly substance that expanded in front of us.

❧ 8 ❧

My boots sank into grainy sand as we waited for each of our party to come through the portal. Water splashed in the distance, and a warm, salty breeze that smelled of burnt sugar swirled around us.

Night loomed overhead wherever we had landed. Constellations twinkled everywhere the eye could see. They felt so close that it seemed I could almost reach out and touch them. Giant palm trees swayed in the breeze, with long, thick leaves casting shadows over us.

"It can't be," Freya gasped as she spun about, grasping her stomach.

"What is it?" Anya snagged Freya's hand.

Freya stared out over the ocean and then at the jungle behind us, where only a few lights flickered through the dense foliage.

"We've come back to where you were born." Her words were laced with both fear and pain. A cry escaped her. "This was the last place I saw your father before he was taken from me, on this very beach."

I glanced questioningly at Darion.

"I'm sorry, Freya," he said. "I had no idea. This is where I tracked the witch to."

Freya shook her head and sat down in the sand. She tucked the folds of her long dress between her legs and dug her hands into the sand, filling them, and then letting the sand sift through her fingers. "I have not seen this place since my daughter was born and we fled." Haunting memories shadowed Freya as she brushed the sand from her palms and stood.

My mom went to Freya's side. "Freya, I'm sorry. If you want to go back, we understand."

Jasper wrapped Anya in his arms while she bit her knuckle.

"No," Freya answered my mother. "We cannot leave. It will take all of us to bring Everly and Darion back from the spirit realm. I'll be okay." She drew in a deep breath.

Freya reached out a hand and brushed her fingertip over Anya's arm. "I'm sorry, Anya, dear. Seeing this place so unexpectedly was just—" Freya stared up at the sky. "Are you okay being here?" she asked her daughter.

Anya gripped Freya's hand and nodded.

My mom glanced anxiously at both Darion and me. Muddy blue-gray tendrils crept from the surface of her aura. She knew the risk we faced if the Spider Witch agreed to help us, but she also knew we had no other choice; we had to reach the spirit realm and communicate with Oria. She was the only person we knew of who had knowledge of the Hunter's secret, a secret that could very well be the leverage we needed to get Molly back.

Movement came from the trees. Jasper's shield exploded in a burst of energy around us, as did the shield of the other royal Shield Jasper had assigned to Anya. Electrical currents rippled within the surface of the shields, which I could see and sense with my Empath magic.

Arden, Rheya, and Malakai drew their swords and took the front line, while Rhal's shadow forms stalked toward the tree line.

"Show yourself," Arden commanded.

A goat burst from the trees, kicking up sand as it darted back and forth in a frenzy.

Freya laughed. "Don't worry. It is only a farm animal roaming about." She clicked her tongue and held her fingers out. The goat calmed and cautiously stepped toward Freya, nudging her fingers with its nose, then allowing her to pet its fur.

"He likes you," said a deep voice with a rich accent that sounded like a mix of French and Jamaican.

A lanky man of dark mahogany skin stepped out of the woods. He surveyed our group with expectant eyes, then lifted his straw hat and nodded. I got the distinct impression he'd been waiting for our arrival.

"Who are you?" Darion charged forward.

The man's eyes drifted to Freya as though he recognized her. Then he lifted his hand and motioned for us to follow him.

"It's okay," Freya said. "I know this man. He's a farmer. My husband did business with him when he was still alive."

Darion looked to me. I scanned the man's energy and nodded. There was nothing hostile in his vibrations.

"She's expecting you." The man looked pointedly at me before he turned and headed back into the trees with his goat chasing after him.

Darion and I took the lead, flanked by Arden and Jasper. The others trailed behind us as we weaved around and behind single-family huts and farm shelters. Warm drops of water dripped from the leaves above, landing on my hair, skin, and clothes. The air had that moist feeling it got just after rain.

The man slowed his pace when we came to an isolated hut

with no neighbors. Light flickered inside the cabin, and smoke drifted from a chimney. Under the glow of torchlight, I could see that the man was dressed in cutoff pants and a dark tank top, and he was barefoot.

"Only you." He nodded to me.

Arden tensed at my side, and Darion stepped forward. "I go in with my sister."

The front door of the hut cracked open, spilling a soft orange glow onto the porch. The man tilted his head as though he was listening to someone. "You two." He nodded toward the front porch.

My mom latched onto my hand.

"It's okay, Mom. We need her help." I patted her hand before letting it go. Calista and Selkie huddled around my mom as they watched Darion and me walk toward the door.

The door creaked as it swung closed behind us. A fire crackled in a fireplace, adding heat to an already sweltering space. I wiped a trickle of sweat from my brow as I gazed about the room. All types of bones hung from a wall. Most looked to be animal, but some were definitely human. The hair on my arms prickled as I tore my gaze from a jaw attached to razor-sharp teeth and glanced at a set of shelves lined with jars filled with creepy-crawly creatures that wiggled and climbed atop each other.

The furnishings were sparse. The only luxurious item was a plush circular rug that decorated the center of the room, directly in front of the fireplace. Neither Darion nor I missed the line of chalk at the edges of the rug. The wicker chair that stood next to a large window squeaked as it spun. Its occupant sat watching us with curiosity and slight apprehension in her narrowed gaze.

Faint wrinkles lined her light mahogany skin. Though I sensed she'd had an unnaturally long life, her skin remained lustrous. Bright silver that practically shimmered streaked her long, slender braids. She held a staff in one hand, and I recognized the stone that decorated its top. Her energy was not fully human, nor fully Vitarian. She was of mixed race, as was Anya. It all made sense now. That was how the Spider Witch had been powerful enough to channel through Calista that night and latch onto my energy. She had Vitarian magic.

"You sense my Vitarian blood?" she asked me. "And now you know why keeping my identity and location secret is of the utmost importance. I know what hunts you, but your brother is a persistent Tracker, and I fear he will give me no peace if I do not help you. Why do the royal twins of the Ever bloodline stalk me? Have I not already given you guidance?"

"We need your help, witch," Darion blurted tactlessly.

The Spider Witch clicked her tongue and stamped the end of her staff against the wooden planks that made up the cabin's floor. Her eyes hardened. Disdain replaced curiosity.

"I apologize for my brother." I held out a hand, giving Darion a warning glare to back off. "We sought you out because Hunters have taken someone we care about, and we need your help."

She lifted a brow, and her face contorted. "Hunters have nearly wiped out my kind, forcing those who remain into constant hiding. I cannot help you find them." She nodded toward the door.

"Please." I stepped toward her. "I need to cross into the spirit realm and contact my ancestor Oria. She has information that may help us. All I need is for you to guide my spirit in and out. You'll have nothing to do with the Hunters."

"Oh, is that all?" She tapped her staff on the wooden floor, more gently this time. "Traveling to the spirit realm takes a great deal of energy. Do you understand the cost of crossing over?"

I took Darion's hand. "We understand."

The witch studied us. "The curse that binds your life forces will make my task more challenging and my price higher."

Darion seethed. My arm burned with the heat of his emotions streaming into me from our clasped hands. I squeezed his hand tighter, digging my nails into his skin.

"You dare demand payment from your queen?"

I sighed and wished just once Darion could control his ego.

The Spider Witch's mouth twitched. "I am only part Vitarian. I acknowledge your royal blood, but I fall under the rule of no one."

"Of course." I jerked Darion's arm. "We will pay whatever you require."

"Name your price, witch," Darion said through gritted teeth.

The Spider Witch considered Darion for a moment. "You may call me Tilly, and I'll require a vial of blood from each of you."

Darion hissed.

Tilly's thick, sooty lashes drew down as she regarded his response. "You may leave if you don't like my price, but then we all know what's at stake."

I pushed in front of Darion. "We agree to your terms, Tilly."

"That's good, because without your blood, I can't perform the spell. Now"—she lifted herself from the wicker chair—"we'll require the assistance of those with you. Invite in only those who are necessary. The energy in the circle must be focused." Tilly stood facing the door. She exuded a confidence that made her appear much taller than her tiny stature.

Rheya remained outside with Rhal and Malakai to keep watch. Neither Jasper nor Arden would agree to stay outside, so they came into the hut along with my mom, Calista, Selkie, Freya, and Anya.

"It's you!" Freya eyed Tilly with awe. "You saved me and delivered my daughter into this world. I never got the chance to thank you."

Tilly inclined her head, her silver-streaked braids falling forward. "You suffered a great loss. That you and your child survived was all the thanks I required." She cupped Freya's cheeks and then Anya's. "You are stunning, dear."

Anya smiled at Tilly. "Thank you."

Darion and I filled two vials with our blood while Tilly gathered what she needed.

She explained that we would lie in the center of the rug, while she and the others maintained a connected circle around our bodies.

Darion motioned for me to follow him out to the porch before we began the spell. "I took this from your room." He extracted the ever stone from his pocket and whispered over it.

I recognized the words of the cloaking spell that lifted from the stone, and I immediately felt a rush of energy reach out to me. The goddess pendant at my neck vibrated against my skin. I clutched it as suspicion crept into the back of my mind.

"What did you do?" I asked, trying to piece together why the stone and pendant were reacting to one another.

"I couldn't let you destroy a vital piece of yourself," Darion said unapologetically. "The emotions you put inside the stone are tethered to the pendant Freya gave you. As long as you wear it, you're still connected to everything you released into here." He held the stone out to me.

A tight knot formed in my chest as my hand tightened over the ever stone, and I held the pendant with my other hand. It made sense now why I felt so connected to the pendant, and why the releasing spell had suddenly stopped working. It'd been the necklace all along.

I shook my head. "I have to hand it to you and Freya. You both cleverly undermined me. So, why did you cloak the stone?"

"So I could safely keep it with me without you sensing it, and I'm not sorry. And if you're going to be angry, just be upset with me and not Freya. We both knew what losing your emotions would do to you, and you'd have done the same if it'd been me. Admit it." Darion towered over me, challenging me to deny that he was right.

I growled and stepped off the porch onto the large green palm leaves covering the ground outside the hut.

Darion followed me. "Your emotions are a piece of who you are, even painful ones. Without them, you're a fractured part of yourself."

I scanned the jungle surrounding the hut and glimpsed Rheya's shadow moving farther into the darkness.

"Why tell me now?"

Darion placed his hands on my shoulders. "Because I don't want there to be lies between us."

He didn't need to finish the rest of his thought. I felt everything he felt, and part of him worried that we wouldn't make it back from the spirit realm.

I looked up from the stone and pulled my brother into a hug. "Thank you, Darion. I don't know what I'd do without you."

Darion laughed. "Just remember you said that the next time you're pissed at me."

I sniffled into his chest.

Darion's hands cupped my head. "Hey, what are these tears for?"

My breath hitched. "I love you for caring so much. But

Arden and I can't be together, and it's not just about Lucas anymore."

I wiped my eyes and nose on Darion's shirt.

"Jeez, thanks." He pinched the fabric away from his body where I'd left a big wet spot, and he grinned at me. "Tell big bro what's going on."

I laughed through a sob at Darion's reminder that he'd deemed himself eldest twin, and I gazed up at the constellations twinkling in the sky. For a moment, I just enjoyed the tropical breeze on my skin. Then I glanced around and made sure no one was near enough to hear, and whispered, "Dalia's pregnant."

Darion tensed. His face flushed crimson, and his hands balled into fists. "I'll—"

"No, brother. You'll do nothing." I touched Darion's shoulder. "I pushed Arden away. I told him I didn't love him and forced him into the arms of another woman. I only have myself to blame for the outcome."

Darion's features softened. "I'm sorry, Ev. I know how much you love him." He cupped his hands over mine. "But please don't make any hasty decisions. Keep these safe until the spring equinox." He shook our cupped hands and nodded at the necklace tucked under my shirt. "There are irreparable consequences if the stone is not destroyed properly."

I nodded and dropped the ever stone into my pants pocket. "Let's do what we came here to do."

We went back inside. Tilly had everyone seated in a circle and signaled for us to join her in the center.

"Lie on your backs and join hands. It's hard enough bringing one person back from the spirit realm, but two will be an added challenge. I need you to stay connected at all times."

"Wait!" My mom broke from the circle and clung to me

and Darion. "Come back to me. Both of you!" She let us go, then said to Tilly, "Keep my babies safe."

Tilly nodded and waited for everyone to resume their place.

I tilted my head to the side and gave Jasper a reassuring smile, although it didn't seem to comfort him. He had that protective look, like he was ready to blast Tilly back with his shield. Arden's expression wasn't any more relaxed. He watched me like he was thinking of hauling me out of here. I turned away from my two protectors, who would sacrifice their own lives for mine, and focused only on what needed to be done.

I clasped Darion's hand and looked sideways at him. "I won't fail you. We will find them and bring Molly and the babies home safely."

Darion tried to smile, but it turned into more of a twitch of his lip, so he squeezed my hand back instead.

Tilly settled an ever stone atop our hands. She started whispering words in a language that I didn't recognize as Vitarian. It was something else, maybe Latin. Threads of magic twined around the stone, binding it firmly to our inter-locked hands. My legs fidgeted, and I lifted my head.

"To keep your spirits bound while we transition," she explained when I stared at the thin blue sparks intertwining tighter and tighter.

Tilly retrieved three vials of blood from the basket next to her. I assumed two were filled with my and Darion's blood, but I didn't know whose blood filled the additional vial. Since learning about my true heritage, I'd become accustomed to the use of blood in spells. Felix had explained that magic flowed strongly in our Vitarian blood and aided in the strength of our spells.

"What's the third vial?" Darion asked Tilly, as if reading my mind.

"My blood must bind to yours to connect our spirits in the beyond." She emptied the vial of her own blood into the pot, and most of the blood from each of the two that came from Darion and me. She stirred the contents, then ladled the liquid into multiple cups to be passed around the circle, until everyone held a cup. A heavy smoke that I recognized as ever resin permeated the air, and my head spun as my lungs filled with the cloying smoke. My body went numb and tingly all over.

"I've never been a fan of ever resin," Darion murmured. His arm tensed next to mine.

Tilly's chest rumbled with laughter. "Vitarians have harvested the magic of the ever tree since the beginning of time. This particular bark"—Tilly waved the smoking bark chip over us—"is from an ancient tree. The older the tree, the more potent the magic."

My heart thumped against my chest as my senses went haywire. Everything was heightened like it had been the last time I'd breathed the ever resin. Only this time, it was much worse and more intense. A thundering roar echoed deep in my ears as an ocean wave crashed onto the beach. Leaves outside crunched and crinkled under the scurrying feet of tropical creatures in the jungle. A snake hissed as it slithered after its dinner.

My head thrashed back and forth, and nausea bubbled in my belly.

"Just relax and take deep breaths." Darion pumped my hand with his. Through the curse that linked us, he could feel everything I felt, even more so with our hands joined.

I sucked in a long breath and latched onto an emotional thread that came from someone nearby. I recognized the tempo of the vibration and who it belonged to. My chest constricted with the unending longing that seeped into my core, and the chasmic heartache attached to it crushed me like a tidal wave. I gasped for breath and broke the connection to Arden. It wasn't like him to leave his emotions unguarded. The ever resin must be having an uncontrollable effect on all of us. My entire body throbbed from the ache of Arden's emotions and the raw desire and love he felt for me. Now I knew what being near me did to him, and yet he stayed by my side. My free hand clamped over the goddess pendant that kept me connected to every feeling I'd ever had for Arden. I had to fix it. *Even if Arden chooses Dalia. I never want to lose my love for him.* A weight lifted from my heart, and I had a sudden urge to turn and reach for Arden.

"It's time," Tilly said, bringing my attention back to the spell.

She popped the corks from the vials of blood and drank my and Darion's blood, then signaled for the others to drink from their cups.

"With your blood in my system," Tilly explained, "a connection will link us, and that will allow me to guide you into the spirit realm and back out again. The others will also be threaded to this connection through the mixture they've consumed. I will draw on their energy to maintain my connection to you both, but you should know, it will not be easy to leave the spirit realm." Her eyes narrowed into slits. "Some will try to tempt you into staying too long; others may be more forceful and try to trap you. And don't let an unknown spirit touch you. You may unintentionally bring something back not meant to return to this world. You must stay focused and follow my command. Do you both understand?"

Darion and I nodded.

Fear seeped into my thoughts as I remembered the story Freya had told us after Molly's seizure, about the darkness she'd mistakenly brought back to the living realm when she'd still practiced magic using the ever stones.

I inhaled a deep breath to calm my nerves and coughed as I choked on the thick smoke permeating the room. My lungs ached with the smoke, causing my throat to burn. Water dripped from the corners of my eyes.

"You okay?" Darion asked, turning his head sideways to look at me.

I nodded, still coughing up the smoke. "Yeah," I croaked. "I just breathed too deeply."

"Okay, then." Tilly reached back into the basket at her side.

I shuddered when she unscrewed a jar with a venomous-looking spider and dipped her hand inside.

"Since your lives are bound, only one requires the bite." Tilly hovered over us and dangled the enormous spider toward Darion.

"It'll be me," I said before Tilly dropped the spider onto Darion's chest. We were in this mess because of me. Orien never would have gotten his hands on Oria's ring if it hadn't been for my mistakes, and no way was I letting Darion take this bite.

"Ev." Darion's fingers squeezed mine. "Let me—"

"No!" I stopped him. "It has to be me."

I held my breath when Tilly extended the spider toward me. I tried not to look at its thick, furry legs or shining black fangs. It was all I could do not to flinch or twist to fling it off me.

"You must stay still. It will sting just slightly, but once its venom enters your bloodstream, you won't feel a thing. The antidote is here." She held up a syringe of clear liquid that had the consistency of saliva.

I lay frozen while Tilly set the spider on my neck. My skin tickled where its legs crawled. A bead of sweat dripped down my temple, and I nearly bolted up as the spider crawled toward the back of my hair. I squeezed my eyes shut and pinched my lips tight and remained still. Sharp, needlelike pricks punctured the side of my neck, causing my arms to flinch, and then fire spread through me.

Tilly swirled in a haze above me as she lifted the spider and placed it back inside the jar. Her chant echoed in my ears and then drifted away. Everything drifted away as my eyelids drooped like heavy sandbags, and my body floated weightlessly. Or was it just my essence leaving my body?

Bright light whirled around me. Was I dying? I should have been afraid, but I wasn't. A calm spread through me. It was tingly and warm and freeing. An essence of energy brushed my skin, and a rush of euphoria made me lightheaded. I had an overwhelming urge to follow the ball of energy that beckoned me deeper and deeper toward a shadowy mist.

"Stay with me." I heard Tilly's voice in my head. "Stay connected to your body."

The essence that tempted me to follow it vanished, and suddenly my body began to take form before my eyes. My arms floated out in front of me, filled with a warm glow that traveled up and down the surface of my skin. "Where are we?"

"We're crossing over, but you must not lose yourself to the light, or I may not be able to bring you back."

I thought hard about where my body was and remembered that it lay unconscious on Tilly's floor. I focused on how my skin felt, and imagined air pumping into my lungs, just like I had the time Darion had taken me into Molly's dream. A jolt shot through me when someone ... Darion ... squeezed my hand. I glanced down and around me, and then his glow appeared next to me in the mist as the curse that linked our life forces remained strong.

"Continue forward," Tilly instructed once Darion's body

had taken shape next to mine. "Call to the one you wish to speak with, and don't let anything separate you."

"Oria of the Ever bloodline." My voice echoed, repeating itself over and over until a bright golden light appeared ahead. I squinted. The light was blinding. It sped toward us so fast. My breath hitched as I waited to be swallowed by the light.

Darion gripped my hand. We both froze, unsure what to do, while the light catapulted toward us.

"Come on!" Darion yanked me sideways, and we ran.

"Everly …" Oria's voice came from everywhere.

We stopped, and the shimmering gold light expanded as though it were about to swarm us. But then it twisted in a gush of wind that rocked me and Darion backward. It twirled into the shape of a body. Swirls of color burst from its heart center, reminding me of the auras that were harnessed inside Oria's ring.

The being of light pulsed with an enormous amount of energy as shining raven hair grew down its back. Then features formed on the face. I recognized her piercing sapphire eyes, which blinked back at me. The light that shone through them made it painful to maintain eye contact. The auras clung to her, trailing her movements as she stretched her arms and fingers as though she had not seen them in a very long time.

"There's no need for bodily forms in this place, but your minds are still of the living realm, and this is what you're used to." She gazed down at herself, then back up at us. "It's been some time since I inhabited my Vitarian body." She was exactly as I'd seen her in Orien's memory, only slightly aged, and with an otherworldly glow.

"Why have you come here? It is not your time, neither of you." She glanced back and forth between Darion and me. Her gaze paused on Darion. A deep sadness flashed in her eyes and then vanished. "You remind me so much of him." A sorrowful smile touched her lips, and I knew she was thinking of her own twin brother, who she'd betrayed. But we didn't have time to waste, so I got straight to the point.

"Orien gave your ring to the Shimera as payment for helping him escape your punishment and hiding him away all these years. But I had to speak with you, so we found a witch to help us."

Oria sucked air between her teeth, and a frown formed on her beautiful face. "My brother still hates me for what I did to him," she admitted. "You must get the ring back from the Shimera. It holds secrets that could end the Vitarian race."

"The ring is not my priority right now, but I promise, I will try to get it back. We're here because Hunters have taken my friends. They took Molly, Darion's fiancée. She's pregnant with Vitarian twins." I paused, forcing myself to make eye contact with Oria, even though the light that shone through her burned my eyes. "Orien showed me everything. I know who you were before you swapped Orien's aura with your own, and what you did to him after. You conspired with Cade to steal Orien's place on the throne." I couldn't hold back the anger that filled my words or the judgment I felt.

Oria flinched at my accusation. She was the strongest Empath in Vitarian history, and without a doubt, she would feel my revulsion toward her actions as deeply as I felt others' emotions.

Tears pooled in her eyes. "Yes. What I did to my brother was unforgivable. I was atrocious before I took what made Orien who he was and turned him into the monster that he is. If I could change it, I would."

"It's too late for that," I said, growing impatient. "I saw you with Cade in the woods when you sacrificed the fairy and brought him the stone of fire. What did you see when you tasted his blood? Who is he searching for, and how can I find Cade?"

Tilly's voice rang urgently in my ears. "You must hurry, child. The barrier between life and death is shrinking."

Oria stared past me as if lost in her own mind.

"Oria! Please! I need you to answer my questions."

"First, I need to know what has happened to Orien. He told you he gave the ring to the Shimera. You've had recent contact with him?"

I could tell she wasn't going to answer my questions until I'd answered hers. "I have him. His magic is bound, and he's been cursed. His mind is now his own torture chamber. He's awaiting punishment and will never hurt anyone else again. And he asked me to take his life."

A bright glow pulsed from Oria as swirls of colorful energy twisted around her.

"What about the Hunter, Oria? How do I find him?"

She waved her hand through the rapid swirl of pastel colors that clung to her. Her head quirked sideways and nodded as if she was silently communicating with the sources of energy that seemed to be an extension of her being. "I hoped this day would never come. Cade's sole purpose is to find someone he lost in his own world, someone he believes will be reborn in ours. And he's not wrong. His love for this individual makes him deadly. He'll never stop until he has her back."

"Who, Oria? How do I find her?"

Oria's form blurred, and she appeared inches from me. The light that poured from her swallowed me whole. "You are the one he searches for, Everly. He wants you. But you cannot give yourself to him. He will consume you and lead you down a dark path. He wants you to become her—the one he lost from his own world."

The swirls of color shifted frantically, brushing my skin with charged energy.

"How do I find him?"

Fresh tears glided down Oria's cheeks. "I curse the day I ever met that man." She curled her slender fingers and balled her hands into fists.

"If we don't find him," Darion urged, "he'll take the lives of my children. Tell my sister what she needs to know."

Oria faded and reappeared. "I have not seen past the moment you truly give yourself to him, but I have seen and felt his hunger for you. If you go to him, he'll make you his."

Fear clawed at my chest, but I pushed it away. Trading my life would save four. There was nothing else to consider.

"I'll do whatever it takes, even if I have to sacrifice myself."

Oria's expression softened, and her light dimmed as she reached her hand up and touched my cheek. "Yes, I know. That is why you're already a far better queen than I ever was. You have until your next sunset."

"What do you mean?"

Tilly's voice warned me once more that the doorway was closing and time was running out.

"I'm sorry, Everly. Orien wasn't the only one I betrayed. The price for Cade's help was high. He required two things. The first was a stone made of fire and forged with the magic of a fairy, as you saw, and the second was a premonition. You will not need to find him. He is coming for you. He'll bring the young man and woman, and you'll trade yourself for their release. He knows this."

The beat of my heart raced in my ears. "You told him of me before I was born?"

Leaden blue swelled in Oria's aura. "I was different when Cade came to me. I cared for no one but myself. I am deeply sorry, but yes, I gave Cade the answer he needed. He's been biding his time until the day you willingly trade yourself to him."

This was unbelievable. Cade was even crazier than I'd thought he was. "If Cade thinks I'm some reincarnated love of his life, why has he waited this long for me, and why is he murdering Vitarian babies who are part human?"

Oria shrugged. "I only know what I saw."

"Fine. Where, then? Where does he come for me? How does he find me?"

"The trade will take place in a wooded area. There was a cabin. But I presume the location does not matter. He'll find you wherever you are. His spies are everywhere. I gave him the year, and he'll see the premonition through to its end. I am sorry. If there were anything I could do to change your fate, I would do it. I had hoped to alter the course of events by demanding your return to Aenoas-Vita, but you refused to go. I knew he would find you on Earth after your twenty-first year of life, and I thought ... Well, it doesn't matter now. My plan failed. My premonitions have never been wrong. Somehow Cade knew that about me, which was why he came to me. That, and he needed me to make him the stone of fire, so it would be bound to my bloodline." Oria paused as if considering. "There is one thing I can give you before you go, but first, I need something from you."

"What?" Irritation infused my words. I wanted to demand her reason for not warning me sooner, but what was the point now? And her premonitions had never been wrong. So what good would her warning have done?

"Orien."

I blinked, biting back my frustration, and waited for her to elaborate.

"It's time my brother and I were reunited. I will guide his spirit here in this realm, where he belongs, and where he will see his sweet Zelda once again. I owe him peace for everything I've done to him, and the ancestors have agreed to accept him." Oria paused and tilted her head. "Your connection to your witch is fading. We must hurry. Will you do this for me? Will you free my brother from the anguished life I sentenced him to? He does not deserve the punishment he will receive if given over to the council. I am to blame for everything he's done these past centuries."

The part of me that had dreamed of vengeance screamed no, that Orien deserved everything he would get when he was returned to Aenoas-Vita, but my heart knew I'd already decided Orien's fate. "Yes. I'll take Orien's life myself."

Oria closed her eyes and smiled when I agreed to free Orien from the plague she had placed on him.

"One last thing." Oria snagged my free hand. "The stone is both your doom and your salvation. Master the magic in the stone, and the power will be yours." She faded without further explanation, and a new light appeared.

"Wait!" But she was already gone. *Spirits and their cryptic messages!*

Darion sighed and shook his head as if he was thinking the same thing as me.

A bright blue light, the color of a serene sky, caught my eye as it pulsed toward me. There was something familiar and comforting about the color and the warmth of the energy it vibrated with. My knees wobbled as the new form took shape. I'd never thought I'd see him again.

"Lucas …" His name caressed my lips.

His brilliant light embraced me when I flew into his arms, yanking Darion with me.

A hoarse sob exploded from my chest.

"Shh … It's okay."

My head shook back and forth. "It's not. What happened to you was all my fault." A hard lump formed in my throat, and it ached to swallow.

"No, it wasn't. You tried to save me, but it was my time to move on. Now, I need you to do something very important for me." Lucas tilted my chin so that I looked up at him. "I can't move on until you promise." He cupped my face. Beautiful cobalt eyes stared down at me, filled with all the love they'd always held.

How could he still look at me like that after I'd cost him his life? He smiled, and a warmness touched me, like the feeling of sunshine on my skin after a long and cold winter. A fist gripped my heart, and the ache was nearly unbearable. I'd never thought I'd see that magnificent smile again.

"I'll do anything you ask." I drank him in, never wanting to forget this moment or his smile.

"Good." Lucas pressed a soft kiss to my lips.

"I need you to forgive yourself. It's time to say goodbye and let me go. Heal your heart and let yourself love again. You deserve love, Everly."

I shook my head. "I can't."

Lucas breathed patiently, a quality I'd always loved about him.

His smile grew wider, and he kissed my forehead. His fingers brushed my heart. Then he took my free hand and placed it over his own heart. "I release you from your promise. That's not what I want for you, my sweet Ev. Never ... The only promise I ask of you is that you'll find happiness. Promise me, before it's too late."

A flurry of panicked voices filled my mind.

"Your time is running out. You must leave this place. Now!" Tilly's voice filled my head.

My torso jolted, and an invisible force sucked my body backward. I reached for Lucas, clinging to him with my free hand for as long as I could.

Darion's fingertips gripped the hand he held as we were being pulled apart by unseen forces.

"Promise me, Ev. Please! Set us both free." Lucas's voice faded with his light.

My fingers slipped to the edge of his. "I promise, Lucas. I did love you."

"I know," he whispered, and then he was gone from me.

Gasping for air, I sprang up and rubbed my burning chest. Tears dripped from my cheeks, and I realized I was crying. Had I really just seen and spoken to Lucas?

I held my wet cheek where it still tingled from his touch. The heaviness that had clung to my heart had been lifted. Lucas had freed me. Even in death, his kindness and compassion astonished me.

A commotion beside me snapped me back to the present. I spun around. *Darion!*

Darion still lay unconscious. I remembered something tugging us apart just before Lucas vanished.

Oh God! Had I stayed in the spirit realm too long? *No. If Darion were dead, I wouldn't be awake.*

I scrambled to Darion's side. His energy was weak, but he was still breathing, and the curse that bound our life forces still hummed between us.

Darion stirred, and my mom heaved a sigh. "Oh, thank the stars."

"Ev, what happened?" Darion's words were groggy, and his movements sluggish as he pushed himself to sitting. "I was trying to hold onto you, but something latched onto me and tried yanking me away toward the edges of the mist."

My mom pulled Darion into her chest. Then she reached for me and clutched us to her. "I'm so thankful you're both okay. If anything happened to either of you, I—" She squeezed us tighter and kissed our heads.

Jasper paced around the three of us. "We nearly lost our connection to you. It took everything we had to pull you back." He reached out a hand and yanked me to standing when my mom finally released us.

The floor rattled when Tilly thumped her cane against the boards. "It was a wandering spirit. One of the restless ones that stalk the veil between life and death, refusing to move on. They're mischievous and get a thrill out of leading other spirits astray from moving beyond the mist to the intended destination. I warned you. You were lucky to make it out. You stayed too long." She gave me a reproachful glare. "I'm very tired now and need my rest." She glanced at the front door.

"I'm sorry, Tilly. It was just … there was someone I wasn't expecting to see." I peered sideways at Arden, whose vibrations were like a live wire, exposed and shooting sparks. He watched me with a strained expression before striding to the door and leaving the hut. He had a habit of getting upset with me when I put my life at risk, which was why I'd wait for the effects of the ever resin to wear off before I told him what I planned to do next.

I guessed everyone was still feeling the side effects of the ever resin, because the emotions in the room were abnormally heightened and all over the place.

I threw my arms around Jasper's neck. "I saw Lucas." A strange sound croaked out of me. I wasn't sure if I was laughing or crying—maybe a combination of both.

Jasper rubbed my back and just quietly held me for a minute while I gathered myself.

I'd been such a fool. Lucas wanted me to be happy, but I didn't know how that could be possible. Arden was having a child with another woman, and I was about to turn my life over to a ruthless child hunter who thought I was some reborn version of his past love.

"What did you find out?" my mom asked, glancing at Darion and then me.

I peeled myself away from Jasper. "Um …" I couldn't bring

myself to answer her question and tell her that she was about
to lose one of her children—again.

Darion put his hand on my shoulder and glanced down.
His guilt was palpable. He didn't like the sacrifice required of
me any more than I did, but we both knew there was no
alternative. Oria had foreseen my fate.

"Well?" my mom said, her brows pinched and her shoulders tense.

Neither Darion nor I wanted to tell her I was the price to
save Molly and Ty. The Hunter wanted me. Taking Molly had
probably been a part of his scheme to get to me all along, but
how had he known about her pregnancy, and why had they
taken Ty too? Or was he just a bonus captive who had
happened to be in the wrong place at the wrong time?

The fire hissed from the water Tilly doused the flames
with. She gathered the ingredients she'd used for her spell and
began putting things away.

"I'll tell you everything when we get back to Felix's." I
sensed Tilly's eagerness for us to leave her to rest. I turned to
thank her, but she'd already vanished, and I heard a door near
the back of the room click shut.

"I guess we're letting ourselves out." Darion made a face
and shrugged.

"I'm glad to see you haven't lost your sense of humor.
Let's go."

Arden stormed out of the cabin when I told everyone
what I'd learned from Oria.

I took a step toward the door, but I halted when Dalia
darted out after him. My chest tightened with the knowledge
that it would be she who would comfort Arden when it
should be me.

"Mom?" I knelt on the floor and held her while she sobbed into her hands.

"Why must I always lose one of my children?" Her back trembled.

Darion paced. "There has to be another way."

"If there was, Oria would have told us. She saw these events before I was born. It's the only way to get Molly and Ty back safely."

Calista and Selkie sat on either side of my mom on Felix's sofa and comforted her.

"When I get to the afterlife"—Calista swept her long chestnut curls over one side of her head—"I'm going to kick Oria's queenly ass."

Selkie shredded a tissue clutched in her hand. "Why is this Cade Wolf obsessed with finding you?" She picked up the shreds when she realized what she was doing. "I don't understand."

Calista reached across my mom's lap and took Selkie's hand. The three women who had raised me held onto each other.

"I won't allow it," my mom announced, stamping her foot on the floor.

"Neither will we," Calista agreed, punching the sofa's armrest.

Selkie nodded. "No, we won't let you do this. It's too dangerous. We have no idea what he plans to do to you."

I sighed. I wasn't asking their permission, and they knew that, but if it made them feel better to pretend they had a say in the matter, then so be it. I'd explain my point for the umpteenth time.

The words froze on the tip of my tongue when an unusual chill crept over me, and the energy in the room took a dramatic shift.

My attention drifted toward Anya. She stood by the fire,

her body tense and her expression far away. A haunting note filled her words. "The wolf seeks his lost mate. He has bided his time with revenge against those he blames, but only she can fill his unrelenting hunger."

Freya halted Jasper when Anya's head jerked back, and her entire body quivered.

Her head snapped back up, and her eyes glazed over with a milk-white substance. "He will make her his, and when he does, there will be no escape." Anya collapsed, and Jasper scooped her up in his arms.

Anya had explained to me once that sometimes her connection with the spirits took a toll on her, depending on how deep her connection to them was, but she'd be fine after a few minutes.

"No!" My mom grasped for me. "I won't let him have you."

I clung to her as my heart sank to the floor. What would happen to me once Cade got his hands on me?

The front door blew open, and Dalia whisked up the stairs to the second floor, swiping at her cheeks. She was upset, and no one followed her. I wondered what had happened between her and Arden.

Rheya pushed herself up from the floor. She'd been unusually quiet until now. "I'd better go check on Dalia." She settled her green gaze on me and nodded toward the front door.

"I need some air." I hugged my mom, Calista, and Selkie. "I'll be okay. He obviously loved the woman he lost if he was willing to wait centuries for someone he thought could take her place. I don't think he plans to hurt me," I said to comfort them as much as myself.

I locked eyes with Darion as I stood, and saw the fear I kept hidden from everyone reflected in his gaze.

A numbness settled in my bones as I left the cabin. Once

the door was closed behind me, I leaned on it for support. The cool night breeze touched my skin and was a welcome contrast to the heat and distraught emotions consuming the space inside. I stared into the dark forest in a daze while my legs carried me down the front porch steps. I didn't need to use my power to track Arden's energy. I knew where he'd gone.

The glow of the moon lit my way. I walked with my hands lifted out, letting my fingers graze waxy leaves I passed.

Would this be my last night of freedom before the wolf finally captured his prey?

I closed my eyes and latched onto the thread of energy that belonged to the one I desired most in this world. Would I ever see him again after tomorrow's sunset?

Branches shifted apart as my senses guided my body. When I opened my eyes, I found Arden under a beam of moonlight, leaning against the ancient oak that was *our* tree.

His gaze burned my flesh with its intensity, just like it had that night when I'd followed him to this spot, and we'd shared our first kiss.

"Dalia's upset. Is everything okay?" I asked, taking slow steps in his direction.

Arden's brow wrinkled with regret. "I told her I wanted to be alone."

A twig splintered beneath my boot. "And *do* you?"

He pushed away from the tree and stood before me in a flash. "I won't let you do this. I can't let you." His hands cupped my face, and his lips crushed mine.

Knowing that I may never see Arden again after the trade, I abandoned myself to the kiss. It was aggressive and hungry at first, like every frustration we had felt was being expelled by our lips and tongues. Then it slowed and turned deep and passionate and expressed all the tenderness we ached to show one another. When I pulled back, my head spun.

I gazed up at him and affectionately touched his cheek, trailing my fingers over his stubble, and then his lips, which I yearned to spend the rest of my life kissing.

"Trading myself to save my friends and Darion's babies is the only way. Oria foresaw this, and if anything happened to Molly and my brother's twins when I could have saved them, I'd never forgive myself. I'm doing this."

Arden drew me against his chest. "I have a plan."

I leaned back against the tree trunk while Arden explained that he had a guard with the ability to alter people's perception. He would bring this guard here, and when the Hunters arrived with Molly and Ty, the guard would make the Hunters believe they saw me when they looked at him, until the trade was made. Once Molly and Ty were safely returned, the guard would escape with the aid of Arden's soldiers, who would be hiding in the woods, waiting for their signal. And in the meantime, Arden would whisk me off this planet and take me somewhere I'd be safe from Cade's reach.

I had to admit, the plan was a good one. Oria had seen me trade myself, but what if who she'd seen only looked like me but wasn't?

"Maybe this could work," I agreed. "But if I think there's even a chance of anything going wrong, I'm giving myself up."

Arden squeezed me tighter. "We won't let anything go wrong." He released me and wrapped his large hand around mine. My stomach flipped as our fingers intertwined. If this plan worked, there was no way I was giving Arden up without a fight, and we'd deal with Dalia's pregnancy together.

We walked back to the cabin hand in hand and paused at the front door. I stood on my tiptoes and playfully kissed Arden's mouth, tugging at his lip with my teeth. "I'm sorry I pushed you away instead of letting you in after what happened to Lucas. I was wrong, and I know that now. Can you forgive me?"

Arden's fingers slipped inside the belt loops on my jeans, and he yanked my waist against him, causing a frenzy of flutters in my belly. "I'll consider it," he teased as a smile played on his lips.

My cheeks warmed with a flush. "I'm not giving you up again, not if you still want to be with me." The goddess pendant seared my skin as my emotions radiated inside, reminding me of their vulnerability. I had to keep the ever stone safe until I could properly restore my emotions to where they belonged, inside me.

Arden didn't hesitate to show me his answer. His fingers slid past my waist, and he gripped my hips, lifted me up, and pressed his lips to mine.

"We should go inside," I managed to say when his mouth trailed the side of my neck.

"Hmm ... we should," he breathed against my hair.

I laid my hands against his broad chest and wished we were somewhere more appropriate so I could tear his shirt off, but instead, I gave him a small nudge. "We need to tell the others your plan. Tomorrow's sunset will be here before we know it."

Arden sobered at my reminder. His hand slid to mine, but I shook my head.

"Speak to Dalia first. She deserves to know before we make it public."

Arden grinned as a spark of blue flickered beneath the green blaze staring down at me. "You're right. I'll talk to her tonight." He gripped both sides of my waist, sending a burning ache rippling down to my groin. "Then, no more waiting," he growled, his lips claiming mine once more, and I melted against him.

My mom, Calista, and Selkie gained some relief when they

heard Arden's plan. Even Darion agreed it could work. The only person who showed no enthusiasm was Anya. It wasn't just her silence that didn't sit well with me, but her faraway expression. The purples in her aura shifted into muted blues. She set the crystal she held down and frowned. Jasper rubbed her back, and the two talked in hushed voices.

We had until tomorrow's sunset to make preparations for Arden's plan. The one part I rejected was leaving Earth before I saw for myself that both Molly and Ty were safe. I refused to go anywhere until I was absolutely sure we'd succeeded. So we agreed that once I had seen for myself that the trade had gone according to plan, and the Hunters had been captured by Arden's guards, I would escape through a portal that would take us to Aenoas-Vita, deep in the Ever Forest, where the fairies dwelled. Arden explained that the fairies were bound to the Ever bloodline and would hide me with their magic.

❦

I tossed on the sofa, waiting for Rheya, Darion, and Arden to fall asleep. We'd given up our rooms so the others could sleep comfortably. Once I was sure they were fully out, I crept off the sofa and up to the second floor to Orien's room. The guard on duty gave me a questioning look when I approached, but stepped aside without a word.

Orien's head slowly lifted when I sat in the chair facing him. His features were even gaunter than the last time I had come to see him. "Did my sister tell you what the Ghost of Time seeks?"

"She did. But that's not why I'm here."

"You've come to send me to my final punishment?"

No fear or resistance came from his words. Orien was ready to accept his fate.

I inched forward and did something I had never thought I would. I took Orien's bound hands in mine. "No, Uncle. I've come to release you from the prison Oria caged you in so long ago. She waits for you to join her on the other side, with the ancestors. As does Zelda."

"Why?" Orien whispered. "After everything I've done." His eyelids drooped with exhaustion, and the soft skin under his eyes sagged.

I thought of Lucas in the afterlife and the final promise I'd made him. "Revenge has consumed our family for too long. It's time to forgive. Are you ready?"

Orien stared at me in disbelief. His sapphire eyes were an ocean of sadness and regret. All the greed and rage that had once consumed him had gone and been replaced by the grief that trapped his mind.

"I know I can never give you back what I took from you, Everly. But I am deeply sorry for what I've done. I took so much from so many, and yet you're willing to do this for me. You bring honor back to our family. You are the true queen our people deserve."

"Humph," I uttered. I'd refused the idea of being queen for so long, but now a part of me hoped I'd get the chance to prove Orien right.

Orien quirked his head as he studied my reaction. "It's you. He wants you, doesn't he? And you're going to trade yourself for the return of your friends." He shook his head. "Forged in fire and bound with fairy essence. I can't believe I didn't see it before. That's why he refused my sister that night when she offered herself to him, something no one had ever had the willpower to do. He couldn't risk altering fate, had she conceived his child by chance and changed the bloodline."

My shoulders tensed. "What do you mean?"

Orien shifted with effort. He hadn't eaten much, and his

limbs looked frail. "He's gathering what he needs to bring her back, the one he lost. You cannot turn yourself over to him."

I scooted forward. "You can't bring someone back from the dead."

"Not normally. Believe me, I scoured every part of the universe, trying to find a way to bring back my Zelda. But there is one spell I did find. It's old and dangerous and only works to return an Ever to their true reincarnation. That's why he's scoured the worlds. He's been searching for her double, for you. He plans to make you her host by drawing her spirit from the afterlife and sealing it inside you. You will become her if he succeeds, and your own consciousness will be put into a permanent sleep."

My mouth went dry, and my vision blurred out for a moment. I slouched back in my chair. This was too much and couldn't be possible.

"I'm sorry my sister made you a chess piece in her game of power."

The window frames rattled. The storm that had been brewing all day had finally let loose. A burst of light flashed outside the window near our chairs as a crackle of lightning tore through the clouds. I sank into my seat as my brain tried to make sense of this new information. If what Orien said was true, I couldn't tell my mom or Arden. They'd force me to run, and I wasn't going anywhere until I knew Molly and Ty were both safe. No one could know about this.

"No more talk of Hunters and ghosts returning from the dead. I'll deal with whatever comes at me."

Orien leaned back and laughed, but then his laugh turned into a cough. "Oh, niece. I will miss your tenacity. I have to admit, I enjoyed our game of cat and mouse these last few months. I underestimated you from the very beginning, and I think if anyone stands a chance against Cade Wolf, it's you. Just remember that the stone of fire in his possession is bound to the Ever bloodline through both the fairy essence within and my sister's blood, which she used to bind the spell to the stone. Cade has had many years to bend the magic to his will, but you are an Ever. Master the stone, and you master the power."

"Oria said something similar to me in the spirit realm."

Orien glanced out of the window. "My beloved sister and I have had agreeable moments." He turned back to face me. "Well—"

I leaned forward and gripped Orien's arms and latched onto his life force.

He sucked in a sharp breath, and our matching sapphire eyes locked together.

"It's time." I released my magic.

He nodded, and lightning bolts shot across my skin. A spasm trembled through my entire body as I siphoned both his power and his essence into me. It took all my strength to hold onto Orien. Centuries of magic were harbored inside him. My head shot back as his power shuddered through me, becoming one with my own, as Siobhan's had when I'd depleted her of her powers as punishment for her crimes against my mother. A final burst exploded into my chest, and I was slammed against the back of my chair. My head fell forward at the same time as Orien's.

Orien's chest deflated with a final breath. No energy came from him. His body was now an empty husk, slumped and bound to a chair. He was finally free from his cage, while mine awaited me.

I took a moment to catch my breath, then slipped a blade from the strap at my waist and cut the bindings from Orien's hands and ankles, tilting his chair down to the floor so that I could lay him flat on his back. My hand brushed over his eyelids, closing them for the last time. He was a member of the royal family. His life had been taken from him long before his physical death, and I would make sure his body was returned to his home and given the proper burial rights of a Vitarian. I retrieved a clean sheet from a drawer and covered Orien before exiting the room.

"I knew I'd find you here." Rheya was waiting in the hall when I exited Orien's room. "I don't understand your choice to forgive, but I respect it. What will you have me do with his body?"

My hand rested on the doorknob behind my back. I breathed a sigh. "You're a good and loyal friend, Rheya."

She quirked a brow. "Are we friends now, Your Majesty?" Her tone was light, but I sensed something bothered her.

"What is it, Rheya?" I asked when she grew pensive.

She glanced sideways as we made our way back downstairs. "Something's troubling the commander, and for once I don't think it's you causing his issue." She paused at the bottom of the stairs, giving me a look that implied I should tell her everything I know.

Arden normally shared most things with Rheya, and I was sure, when he was ready, he'd tell her the news of Dalia's pregnancy. "It's not my place to divulge Arden's private matters. You are his trusted confidant. He'll tell you when he's ready."

She nodded. "Yes. But for the first time since we've known each other, I've got the feeling he's afraid to talk to me about this. And Dalia won't speak of it either." She sighed. "I'll wait for the commander to come to me on his own."

With that, we headed our separate ways.

Unable to sleep, I spent the remainder of the night writing letters to my loved ones. Before speaking with Orien, I'd had hope of Arden's plan succeeding, but if Cade had been plotting for centuries to use me to bring back his dead wife, I suspected he wouldn't give up so easily. I might escape tomorrow, but what about the next day and the day after that? I had to leave my family behind no matter tomorrow's outcome, or they'd always be in constant danger of Cade using them against me.

By the time I sealed the last envelope, the sun was beginning to fracture the sky. I tied the letters together and tucked them under my pillow. A heavy weight dragged my eyelids low until I felt the sensation of falling into a restless sleep.

A low growl came from the woods as I ran. Fire burned my lungs. My limbs throbbed. My foot tripped over a branch, and I flew through the air. My knees skidded across the forest floor, and when my body came to a stop, the wolf that chased me blocked my path. Its hungry green eyes glinted in the night, and its lips tore back to reveal long, sharp fangs. The wolf lunged for my throat.

My arms thrashed out in front of me.

"Everly!" Rheya whispered. She slapped my cheek, and my eyes snapped open.

"The wolf!" I felt my throat, searching for the gashes from the fangs that had torn through my flesh.

"You were dreaming. You're safe."

For now, I thought, wiping the sweat from my brow as I sat upright.

A crackle of wood hissed from the fire as Rheya tossed in another log. The wood was consumed in a blaze of flames, and a fresh wave of heat filled the room.

I slid the letters from underneath my pillow. "After I leave, will you give these to my mom? Except for this one." I held the bundle in one hand and a single letter in the other and glanced across the room at Arden's sleeping form on the floor to make sure I hadn't woken him.

Rheya eyed the bundle of letters and then the one with Arden's name scrawled across the envelope. She nodded and took them. "You don't think the commander's plan will work, do you?"

A sad smile crested my lips. "It's a good plan. And it may work for a short time, but Oria foresaw my capture, and have her premonitions ever been known to be wrong?"

Rheya's face fell. She latched onto my arm. "Premonitions are a curse." She grimaced. "I refuse to let you accept surrender. You are queen. And the commander will keep you safe."

My expression relaxed, and I smiled at Rheya's unwavering determination. She was a complicated woman whose exterior was practically impenetrable, but once that surface cracked, and she let you in, a fearsome and loyal heart greeted you.

"I'll admit, Rheya, when you first walked out of the woods that day during my training with Arden, I was intimidated by you. And not just because you're the epitome of a fierce warrior and absolutely gorgeous."

Rheya wrinkled her nose at my compliment, and I clasped my hand over hers.

"But I knew by the way you and Arden interacted that you had an unbreakable bond that could never be matched. You are a woman like no other, and I'm honored to have earned your friendship."

A scowl deepened across Rheya's brow as she fought the more tender emotions she tried not to let others see. I grabbed her and pulled her into a hug. She resisted at first but then relaxed against me. Someday, I hoped to be able to find out what caused her to protect herself so tightly, and help her heal the wounds she kept buried so deep that even she couldn't touch them.

I changed and packed a small backpack with necessities. After pulling my hair up, I twisted my ponytail into a braid and secured the end. There was nothing I could do to minimize the sparkling glow that had spread all throughout my skin since I'd siphoned Orien's life force and all his magic with it. This hadn't happened when I'd taken Siobhan's powers from her, but I'd only taken her magic and not her life. And Orien was an Ever; Siobhan's power had been nothing compared to his. I smoothed the skin under my eyes that, despite the lack of sleep I'd had over the last several days, shone bright with the energy that hummed within me. When I'd sent Orien to the spirit realm, I hadn't considered what effect his magic would have on me. He'd been powerful, but I knew very little about his magic, except that he could dream walk, as Darion could, and I'd seen him manifest a travel portal at will, something that I had not been able to do. I'd managed the Sight portal that Freya had taught me, but only Darion had been able to conjure a travel portal. A spark of fear shot through me as I felt Orien's magic course through my veins, and I wondered what surprises lay ahead.

"What have I gotten myself into?" I glanced at the spot where Orien's body had been only hours ago, and rubbed the skin on my arms, but the sparkle refused to fade.

My finger trailed the runes etched into the sword that now belonged to me. I lifted it from the futon mattress and clicked open the secret chamber built into its hilt. *What secrets did you keep hidden inside here, Oria?* I pressed the chamber closed and arched the blade high, slashing it through the air.

I spun, landing in front of the mirror hanging on the wall. Stepping closer to my reflection, I traced the line of my cheekbones and the edge of my lips with my finger.

He plans to bring her back and make you her host. I shivered at the memory of Orien's words. Could that really be Cade's plan, to use my body to bring back someone he loved from the dead? I'd fight to my death before I let him enslave me to a perpetual sleep.

Even though I'd never seen Cade's face in any of the memories Orien had shown me, I couldn't stop wondering why he'd felt so familiar. Did it have something to do with what Orien had told me, that I was the reincarnation of the woman Cade had lost from his own world? *That's crazy!*

The door rattled with a knock. I slammed my sword back into its scabbard and slung the strap over my shoulder.

"Come in."

My mom's eyes widened when she saw my skin. "It's gotten brighter." She ran her hands over my arms with a scrunched brow. "I've sent the letter to Felix, like you asked, explaining about Orien. He'll take care of everything."

I nodded.

"He's finally out of our lives."

"Do you think Creagan would understand why I did it?" I asked.

My mom's cheeks lifted with her smile. Her fingertips brushed my stray hairs behind my ear, tickling my skin. "You made a choice as a leader. Your father would respect that, as do I."

"Knock-knock."

Calista towered over Selkie's petite frame in the doorway. She'd tied her wild chestnut curls up in a floppy bun, which made her appear even taller than she already was. Selkie's hazel eyes smiled at me as the two came into the room and huddled around me with my mom, sandwiching me between them and nearly suffocating me with their hugs.

"I love you, honey," said my mom. "Infinity times infinity infinities forever."

"So do we," Calista and Selkie said in unison.

"I hate this. We should be going with you."

"We talked about this, Mom. Even if everything goes as planned, and we get Molly and Ty back safely, none of you are safe while Cade is after me. Until we're sure we've taken him and all of his Hunters down, I can't risk him coming for one of you again to get to me. Can I count on you three to do as I ask?"

Our heads bumped against each other with their nods.

"Has Bree gotten here yet?" I asked.

"Arden sent Rheya for her," Calista answered. "They should be here soon."

"That's good." *At least Bree will be of some use to me.*

"Now, are you going to tell us what's going on with Arden and Dalia?" Calista asked. Her patience had been stretched near to breaking. And she and Selkie had been scowling at Arden since they'd arrived.

I drew away from them and took a seat on the futon. "Okay, but you have to promise it doesn't leave this room until Dalia's told everyone herself."

"Oh, boy," Selkie said, sharing an "oh no" look with Calista and my mom.

I took a breath and blurted, "Dalia's pregnant."

The air stirred with their gasps.

My mom sat next to me and took my hands in hers. "Oh, sweetie. I'm so sorry."

"Arden was *with* Dalia?" Calista's face contorted.

"Are they still together?" Selkie asked, mussing her strawberry hair—something she often did when she got upset.

I glanced up at Calista. "Yes, they spent one night together. He told me himself."

"And no, they're not still together. It happened just the once," I answered Selkie.

I fiddled with the strap of the blade crossed over my chest. "We were waiting to say anything until Arden spoke with Dalia, but I made a mistake pushing Arden away, and I've told him so. I won't give him up without a fight."

My mom patted my hand. "I'm glad you're working things out with him, honey."

"Yes," Calista added, pumping a fisted hand. "But that doesn't change what the scoundrel did. I'll crush his—"

"No! There won't be any crushing of any part of him. Arden didn't do anything wrong. I told him I didn't love him and that he should find someone else. I can't be angry that he found comfort with Dalia. They were together only the one time. He doesn't love her. He loves me, and I love him." Saying the words out loud released a tension I hadn't even known existed. My heart felt lighter even in the current circumstances.

Selkie's brow furrowed. "But how will it work when Arden and Dalia return to Aenoas-Vita, and she's carrying his child, and you're here?"

My stomach curdled. I hadn't actually thought that far into my future with Arden yet, since we didn't know how this day would end or whether I'd be a prisoner of Cade's or free to be with Arden. I lifted my feet up onto the edge of the futon and tucked my knees under my chin. "I just need to get through today first. We'll worry about the specifics of our relationship when this is all over."

"Right, of course. I'm sorry, honey." Selkie rested her head against mine.

Footsteps creaked outside the room, followed by a loud knock on the door. "Barbie's waiting downstairs," Rheya called from the other side of the door. Then she turned and left, not waiting for a reply or an invitation inside.

I glanced toward the window. A splash of pale orange cut through the sky as the bright yellow sun faded. Fear knotted my insides. I'd never dreaded a sunset before this moment. Before I had a chance to stand, arms wrapped around me from all directions.

"Let us know as soon as you're safe." My mom's tears dripped onto my collarbone as she pulled away.

After receiving another bear hug from each of them, the four of us went downstairs.

"It's about time." Bree flipped her hair over her shoulder. "What's this all about? You sent your guard dog after me"— she sneered at Rheya—"and she wouldn't even tell me why she was manhandling me into your car."

"Ev!" Darion called from the front door, his face a canvas of worry.

I turned back to Bree. "I need you to mask my essence. There's no time for explanations. Just follow me."

Bree tapped her four-inch heel with an air of annoyance until Rheya shoved her forward. "Move it, Barbie. Do as your queen says, or—" Rheya rested her hand on the handle of her battle-ax, which was a permanent fixture on her waist.

"Okay, jeez. No need to get all testy, guard dog."

Rheya's nostrils flared, but she just nodded for Bree to move forward.

"I love you guys." I hugged my mom, Calista, and Selkie once more.

"We love you, honey. We'll be with Freya and Anya, securing the boundary around the cabin. Once we get Molly and Ty, don't hesitate. Run for the portal and don't look back."

"I will."

When I stepped onto the front porch, I stopped short. A petite young woman with raven hair that flowed in waves past her shoulders stood next to my brother. She turned and examined me with her piercing sapphire eyes. She was my carbon copy, but I knew it was just an illusion of perception. The energy shifted around her, and suddenly a tall man with dark hair and brown eyes stood before me. Black trousers and a dark gray pullover long-sleeved shirt replaced the black skinny jeans and gray cotton T-shirt my look-alike wore.

"Astonishing," I said, looking him up and down. "Thank

you." I inclined my head. "Has the risk been explained to you?"

He dipped into a bow, then stood. "Yes, Your Majesty. It's my honor to be of service to my queen."

I tried to offer him a smile but couldn't. I hated that another life was being put in danger for my safety.

"I'm in your debt," I said as Darion urged me forward and rushed me to the edge of the forest, where the force field protecting the cabin ended. I glanced past his shoulder and fumed when I saw Dalia throwing her arms around Arden's neck. *What the hell? Arden said he was going to talk to her. Why is she still touching him like he belongs to her?*

Darion followed my gaze and sneered at the two, then shifted his attention back to me. The gray storm of worry brewing in his eyes made the knots in my stomach throb up to my chest.

"There are no words, sister. You have the heart of a true warrior. If this plan fails, I will find you. I'll never give up, so don't you give up, and don't let him win." Darion pulled me against him. "I don't deserve you."

"Darion," I coughed. "You're squeezing the air from me."

His arms loosened, and I inhaled a deep breath.

"You're my family, Darion, and so are Molly and Ty. I'll always do whatever is necessary to keep those I love safe."

Arden and Jasper came up behind Darion. Their tension could have frozen a lava pit.

"How does he even know to find you here?" Jasper asked, glancing into the forest. "Something doesn't feel right. Anya has a bad feeling."

The trees rustled behind me in the wind. I shivered even though I wasn't cold.

"Has she had a vision?" I asked.

Jasper shifted his gaze from the forest and gave me his full attention. "Just a feeling that we're missing something important. First he knows where to find Molly, and now here. He couldn't have known about Felix's cabin without someone telling him."

I glanced up at Arden, whose jaw clenched. He'd expressed the same concern Jasper had when he'd told me of his plan, and he had already assigned Rheya the task of weeding out our spy if we had one. Outside of Rheya, Rhal, and Malakai, and the rest of our core group, no one else knew about Arden's plan to use the guard with the mind-warping ability to impersonate me. Bree had only just arrived and didn't know what was going on, so if it had been one of Arden's guards who had informed Cade of our location, they didn't know the details of our plan.

"I agree, Jasp. But we already know that Cade is coming regardless, so all we can do is hope our plan works."

"Am I missing something? Argh!" Bree fought to lift her heeled boot from the hole her stiletto had pierced into the ground.

Rheya shook her head as she scowled at Bree's boots. "She asks too many questions, and she wears ridiculous shoes."

Jasper laughed, earning both him and Rheya an eye roll from Bree as she finally yanked her foot free.

"Whatever! Some of us just have better taste than others. Now, is someone going to answer me? You dragged me up here to the middle of nowhere in this bug-infested forest"—Bree shooed away a flying beetle—"to hide your essence from what?"

"Like I said." Rheya shoved Bree forward with her shoulder. "Too many questions! Can we put a binding spell on her tongue so she can't talk?"

Bree twisted around like she was about to pounce on Rheya.

"Sir!" One of Arden's guards ran up.

Arden nodded. "Let's go. Now!"

Darion yanked me into a hug.

"Don't worry, brother. I won't leave until you have Molly."

Rheya and Arden clasped arms. "You can count on me, Commander. Rhal and Malakai will lift the ward, allowing the Hunters to enter at the designated perimeter. Once the trade is made, Cacsha and the others will seal the border of the forest. Our guards will kill any Hunters they track down."

Jasper snagged my hand, and we ran through the woods with Bree and Arden behind us. Branches scraped my skin and snagged my clothes as we pushed through the dense brush until we came to the spot we'd scouted earlier. The bushes were thick enough to hide all of us but close enough to allow us to sneak glimpses of the cabin without being seen.

"What's happen—"

"Shh!" I motioned for Bree to keep her head down and clamped my hand over her mouth. Rheya was right. Bree talked way too much.

Thunder roared in my ears as my heart raced. I sensed Darion's agitation as though it were my own through the curse that linked us. He stood frozen, watching the forest for movement.

Four men emerged from the trees with two bound and thrashing captives. My entire body went rigid. Neither of the two captives was Molly. The Hunters shoved Ty and Kamara ahead of them. How had they gotten Kamara, and where the hell was Molly?

I thought back to what Oria had said about her premonition. She'd said I'd traded myself for the young woman and young man. She'd never said Molly specifically. I'd just assumed that was what she'd meant. But if they had Ty, then they had to have Molly too, but why hadn't they brought her?

Rage radiated through Darion, causing me to snap a thick branch in half.

Crap!

I chewed my lip and dug my hands into the grass to keep from responding to Darion's emotions.

Darion slid the sword free from the scabbard strapped to his back. He was about to do something reckless. I started to stand, but Jasper and Arden pressed a hand to each of my shoulders, holding me in place.

"Where's Molly?" Darion roared.

The brawny Hunter who'd shoved Ty and Kamara eyed Darion and grinned. "We come for your queen," his gravelly voice bellowed. "We offer these two."

Please, Darion, I prayed silently. I was just as upset as he was that Molly wasn't with them, but we still needed to save Ty and Kamara.

My impersonator stepped off the porch as if sensing my silent plea. His magic sifted into the air like a thick cloud of dewy mist as he made everyone believe they were looking at me. "If you want me," he said with a soft, feminine voice that matched mine, "set those two free, and I'll go with you willingly."

I scanned the four Hunters. They were all large men, but none of them was Cade. There had been something in Cade's stance and the build of his shoulders, and the energy he projected, that had felt familiar to me in Orien's memories. I knew I would have recognized him if he had been among the four that stood before Darion. He wasn't here. I was sure of it. Something didn't ... I reached out and felt for energy signatures.

"There are more of them in the woods," I whispered to Jasper and Arden. "They're surrounding us."

Arden nodded, tightening his grip on me. "So are my guards. This is what we prepared for."

My look-alike approached the Hunters. "Let them go."

The brawny man smirked and, without hesitation, whipped his sword through the air and slashed the guard's throat. His spell vanished with his life, and his lanky body slumped to the ground as his hands grasped his neck.

Jasper flinched next to me, and Bree screamed, drawing the attention of the Hunters in our direction.

A raw ache rippled through me as I stared at the blood pooling on the ground next to the dead guard. He'd lost his life, and for what? All so I could try to flee the hand fate had dealt me. I had to put an end to this before anyone else got hurt.

Darion made a dash for Ty and Kamara. He was able to drag Ty away but stopped in his tracks when he tried to grab Kamara. One of the men snatched Kamara and pressed a dagger against her neck.

The gag tied around her mouth muffled her cries.

"Our leader is no fool. Show yourself, Queen, or your brother's unborn filth will pay the price, as will this sweet, juicy thing." He laughed as Kamara's cry fell silent and blood dripped from her neck where the edge of the dagger sliced into her skin.

Heat seared my veins. I pulsed a projection of energy against Arden and Jasper, knocking them back so I could stand.

As if sensing my intention, Arden reached for my wrist, holding me down with an iron grip. "They could kill you."

"They won't. Their leader needs me alive. Just trust me," I told him when he was about to argue.

He pulled me against him and kissed me. "The plan hasn't changed. You'll go with them, but Jasper and I will follow behind. They won't get out of these woods alive with you."

"They still have Molly," I hissed. "I have to leave with them." I yanked my hand free. "Do not attack." I jumped up from behind the bushes before he could waste more time arguing with me.

The trees thrashed as my anger coursed through me.

Flames burst from my palms as I marched toward the Hunters, keeping Kamara locked in my sight. As much as I wanted to burn these animals to ash, I couldn't do anything to put Molly at risk. We didn't know where they were holding her.

I passed Darion, urging him to remain where he was. Ty stared at me wide-eyed and in shock from the ground. His eyes were plastered to the fire stretching from my hands. He scooted backward and away from me, mumbling something, but the cloth tied around his mouth made his words incoherent.

"I'm sorry you got dragged into this," I told him, and I shifted my attention back to the Hunters. "Let her go," I demanded.

Dirt streaked Kamara's tear-stained face. She was barefoot, and her dress was torn.

"I can see the rage in your eyes, Queen. But don't forget, we still hold the most important prize, and if anything happens to me, well ... I'm sure you can put the pieces together. Her life depends on what you choose to do."

I met his hard stare, and he bared his teeth as his lips peeled back with a victorious smile.

Darion stood in my peripheral vision, his body rigid as stone as he struggled to hold himself in place.

"If anything happens to Molly," Darion said through gritted teeth, "I'll kill every single one of you."

The dagger jostled against Kamara's throat as the vulgar beast holding her laughed at Darion's threat. "Good luck finding us."

Darion's energy buzzed like a transformer about to explode. Sparks zapped the air around him.

The Hunter's black eyes gleamed like two glassy marbles. He followed my gaze to his exposed shoulder with the clawed paw tattoo and sneered. His bicep bulged against his dark skin as his arm squeezed Kamara tighter, causing a whimper to escape her.

"I'll go with you." I fought back the rage that seized my muscles, and the flames flickering from my palms retreated.

"Hold out your arms," he ordered. "And don't try anything."

He nodded to the man on his left, who broke their line and approached me, carrying two thick cuff-like bracelets. This one was less bold, and his blue eyes shifted nervously as he held up the marbled stone cuffs.

"Let her go first."

The Hunter holding Kamara loosened his arm and lowered the dagger from her throat.

"Go to Darion, Kamara."

She scrambled away from the Hunter, crashing into Darion's arms as the cuffs snapped over my wrists, hindering my magic.

"Why is your leader not among you?" I eyed each of them. None had the physique of the man who had met with Oria. But their swords had the same wolf head carved into the hilts, and they wore the same maroon cape Cade had.

The bulky one, who seemed to be the leader of the pack, spoke. "He'll be pleased you're so eager to see him." He motioned with his fingers for me to come forward.

Now that my powers were restricted, the Hunter who had cuffed me grew bolder. He lifted my sword strap from my body, tugged my backpack off my back, and slipped the black onyx ring from my finger. Thankfully, he didn't notice the goddess necklace hanging beneath my shirt when he twisted my arms behind me and bound them together, then nudged me forward.

"I'll get her back, brother, no matter what I have to do. Just keep everyone else safe." I thought of Orien's warning. Cade wanted to use my body as a vessel to bring back his wife. If that was what it took to save Molly and the babies, then I'd let him.

Darion seethed. Without the use of my magic, I couldn't see or feel his energy field, but every muscle in his body tensed, and a storm of fury raged in his icy stare. My heart pumped with the curse that linked us, and my pulse sped as Darion's hand tightened around the handle of his sword, and his knuckles bulged.

I shook my head at him and gave Kamara a pleading look. She yanked on Darion, trying to pull him toward the cabin. His eyes flashed down at her and back at me.

"Think about Molly." My ears pounded with the rush of my blood as the Hunters all reached for their weapons and faced Darion.

I heaved a sigh when his hand relaxed, and he stepped back with Kamara tucked under his arm.

"I'll find you both. I promise." His narrowed gaze fell on the Hunter giving the orders.

The burly beast grunted and shoved me ahead of him. "Let's go."

Darkness spread through the forest as night crept into the sky, and the trees closed in around us. My foot tripped over a rock on the bumpy trail, and I flew chest-first onto the ground. Hands that were hard as stone yanked me to my knees, and I glimpsed glowing gold eyes stalking us from the shadows.

"Get up," the Hunter barked, missing the sound of the low growl that came from the unseen animal.

I fought the urge to slam my head back into his nose as he dug his nails into my shoulder.

"No!" I yelled at the cougar that I knew was being controlled by Malakai.

The Hunter, assuming I was yelling at him, ripped me to my feet.

"You're lucky our lord wants you unharmed, or I'd—"

But he didn't get the chance to finish. The cougar leaped from the bush and clamped its jaw over the Hunter's neck, tearing out his throat. Blood sprayed down on me as the body crashed to the ground next to my feet.

A guttural scream came from ahead.

Damn it! It was too late to stop Arden's orders.

Another mountain lion burst through the trees, tearing flesh and bone from the shoulder of the Hunter in front of me. Rhal's dark shadow forms twisted between tree trunks and branches, raking unseen claws across the backs of my remaining captors until they were all dead.

Shrieks and the coppery scent of blood pervaded the forest as Arden's guards attacked the hidden Hunters.

Jasper sprang toward me, his shield expanding.

In an instant, he cut the rope binding my arms and cracked the bracelets from my wrists, tossing them into the trees. He grabbed my backpack and sword from the ground, where the Hunter had dropped them after being mauled by the cougar. "Come on." He snagged my hand and dragged me behind him.

The wind soared, responding to my will, halting Jasper's progress.

"What are you doing?" Jasper turned back to me.

My braid whipped across my face. I pulled it back. "I need to go with them. They still have Molly."

Jasper shook his head. "It's too late for that. They're all dead."

Arden burst from the forest onto the trail and pulled me to him. "We're leaving. Now!"

"No!" I yanked myself free. "I promised Darion I'd get Molly back, and now you've killed them all. I told you not to attack." The wind roared with my fury. "How am I supposed to find Cade now?"

Arden scowled down at me. "We'll figure that out later. I'm getting you to Aenoas-Vita so the fairies can hide you."

I refused to budge.

"Damn it, Everly. Just come with me. I swear we will find Molly, but we need a new plan." He latched onto my hand.

"Fine!" I let him pull me along. Arguing was pointless, since they'd already killed Cade's men.

Arden kicked aside a corpse that lay across the trail. His shoulders tensed, and he drew his sword when twigs crunched underfoot and shadows moved from the trees. His arm relaxed when Rheya appeared, dragging a Hunter who was still alive.

"I caught this one trying to escape. I think I'll have a little fun with him before I send him to his maker." She grinned, wiping her brow.

Blood smeared the Hunter's face. His nose was smashed and definitely broken. The same clawed wolf-paw tattoo the others had marked his right shoulder.

"Keep this one alive, and take him to my brother to be questioned. They still have Molly, and we need to find out what he knows."

Rheya nodded with a hint of disappointment as she stroked her bloodstained ax.

"We need to go," Arden said. "My guards are waiting on the other side of the portal to accompany us. Are you good?" he asked Rheya.

Rheya's green eyes glowed from within. Electric pulses of adrenaline radiated in her energy field. Her lips pulled wide when she glanced down at her captive. "All good, Commander." She pumped her fist against her heart. Arden, Jasper, and I did the same before leaving Rheya on the trail.

We tore through the trees, and I had nearly collapsed by the time the waterfall came into view.

"What are you doing here?" Arden asked Dalia, who waited at the cave entrance.

She recoiled at his grimace, and I couldn't help but feel bad for her.

"I—" She paused and then started again. "I wanted to make sure the portal was ready for you, and I'm ... I'm coming with you. I want to go home." She lifted her chin, daring anyone to deny her this.

Arden cursed under his breath.

Movement came from somewhere nearby. Arden grabbed Dalia by the arm. "Go!" He ordered me ahead of him.

Jasper threaded his fingers through mine, and we leaped through the portal together.

The weightless sensation lurched through me as it did every time I entered a portal, and I fought back the wave of nausea.

When we tumbled out of the other end, Jasper still gripped my hand tight. Dalia and Arden came out right behind us.

Jasper's shield exploded around us. It took me a second to orient myself and understand why he'd gone on guard. Hooded figures surrounded us, and blood dripped from their swords.

Slain soldiers belonging to the royal guard lay across the ground, all dead.

Arden hissed and pressed Dalia behind him as he closed ranks with me.

"How did they know?" I whispered.

The deathly stare that hardened Arden's face sent a shiver through me. He drew his sword. "You won't have her," he growled at the Hunters, who watched us wordlessly.

One stepped forward.

Every muscle in my body tensed as the hood of his cloak drifted back, revealing his face. "I will."

My breath caught. It was him. Cade Wolf. I recognized his voice from Orien's memory, and the way he stood, emanating power and confidence. Glowing emerald eyes scorched my skin, raking over me with their unsated hunger.

My eyes fell on the wolf head carved into the hilt of his sword as he stepped closer, and Anya's words rang in my ears: *He will make her his, and when he does, there will be no escape.*

I stumbled back a step, fear clawing its way through me. "How is this possible?"

"Is he a shifter?" Jasper asked, just as stunned as I was.

Arden's expression went from shock to rage in an instant. "Don't take another step."

Cade stopped, his gaze never leaving me. Something about the way he looked at me froze me in place. A slight grin creased the corner of his mouth. He knew what effect he was having on me.

My eyes trailed the scar on his left cheek, drifting down to the familiar lips that parted just slightly as he whispered, "Mila."

Arden stepped in front of me. The two men studied each other. So similar, yet so different. They drew their swords in the same moment, one with his left hand, and the other with his right.

Cade's Hunters began to tighten their circle.

The ground rumbled beneath us as I sent out my silent command. Tree roots snaked through the forest floor and wrapped around the Hunters' ankles, keeping them from coming any closer.

Jasper's shield stretched as I took a step away from him and spread my fingers wide. Heat singed my skin as the flames I released were forced to recoil.

"I'm sorry, my love, but I'm afraid I can't allow you to do that." Cade twisted a ring on his finger. Its fiery stone flashed, and an ache spread through me as an invisible force repressed my fire magic.

I narrowed my gaze on the stone welded to the ring. It had to be a chunk of the same stone Oria had forged for him that night I'd seen them together in this very forest. Cade had called it the stone of fire, and it had power over me.

"I'm not your love," I spat. "I'm not Mila."

Cade was undeterred by my words. "You will be."

My thoughts raced as his men cut at the roots binding them in place. I glanced around the familiar forest from Orien's memory.

Orien!

I had his magic inside me. Orien could summon a portal at will, which meant I now had that capability, but how? My mind fumbled through flashes of spells I'd seen in my mom's grimoire, but none were of summoning portals. And then I remembered the spell Orien had chanted when he'd escaped me in the tunnel that night after he'd taken Lucas's life.

Cade watched me with curiosity, and a smile played across his mouth as I repeated Orien's words, and magic sizzled in the air.

"You always loved playing hard to get, my darling. But you'll submit in the end."

I ignored the strange sensation Cade's words caused in me as I focused on the spell.

"If you let my friends leave unharmed, I'll go with you."

Cade eyed Arden and Jasper. When his gaze fell on Dalia, I swore I noticed a glint of approval, but then his expression darkened as he nodded.

The last words of Orien's spell left my lips as a charge of air swirled beside me.

Jasper kept Cade and his men pressed back with his shield as the portal took shape near us.

"Go!" I yelled to them.

Dalia yanked Arden's arm, but he shrugged her off and pressed her into the portal alone. He and Jasper shared a look before Jasper turned, shoving me toward Arden, who tossed me over his shoulder and held onto me with an unbreakable grip.

My legs and arms flailed. "Let me down! Now!"

"No!"

"Please! Arden! If anything happens to Molly, I'll never forgive you."

Arden launched off the ground. "I'll have to take that risk." And then we were diving into the portal.

I lifted my head as we entered the watery substance and met Cade's hard stare. The fiery stone on his finger reflected in his furious gaze, but his mouth lifted in a malicious grin as Jasper followed us into the portal, and we tumbled through space.

✾ 9 ✾

I had no idea where we would end up, but when I lifted my head from the sand and glanced at the sparkling blue ocean, and breathed in the scent of burnt sugar, I had a feeling I knew where we were.

Sand sifted from my hair and stuck to my skin as I sat up and spotted Jasper shaking sand from his clothes and rinsing his arms in the ocean water. His bronzed skin sparkled under the streaks of early-morning sunlight.

"Not bad for your first portal," he mused. "It takes most Portal Weavers years to master creating a travel portal on the fly like that."

I jumped to my feet and shoved him in the chest. "Why did you do that? That was my chance to go with him and find Molly." I stormed around him and marched toward the water. I snagged the band loose from my hair and undid my braid, threading my fingers through my tangled hair.

Jasper rushed in front of me. "I'm sorry, Ev, but I'm your Shield. It's my duty to protect you, even from yourself if I have to."

"ARGH!" I screamed and stomped away from him. "I'm

going to strangle Arden when I get my hands on him. Where are they?" I shielded my eyes from the glare of the sun and peered at the stretch of beach.

Jasper pointed. "They're way over there. Dalia's tearing Arden a new one for tossing her through the portal by herself."

The glare reflecting off the water made my eyes sting.

I spotted Arden and Dalia a way down the beach. Dalia flung her arms in the air and twisted her feet in the sand, storming away from Arden in our direction. They definitely seemed to be in the middle of a heated discussion. I quickly averted my attention and dipped my hands in the water, pretending to scrub sand away as their voices came into earshot.

Jasper shook his head, then tore off his shoes, pants, and shirt and dove in a perfect arch, splashing into the water. His head popped up, and he smiled from ear to ear. "Come on, Ev. You brought us to this gorgeous island. We might as well enjoy it while we can."

I took another glance sideways. Strangling Arden would have to wait. When I saw the look on Dalia's face as she neared us, I shook off my jacket, leaving my tank top on, then peeled off my boots, socks, and pants and ran into the water. It was even warmer than I'd expected. I jumped up and dove in headfirst. The water felt like a liquid blanket as I swam toward Jasper.

When I came up, Jasper circled me in the water, like a shark stalking its prey.

"Are you ready to launch?" Jasper asked, wiggling his eyebrows.

"Jasp, I'm not in the mood, and I'm pissed at you."

"Oh, come on, Ev. Did you really expect me to let you just give yourself to the wolves? I love Molly as much as you do, but we'll find her another way." He dove beneath the water, then came back up directly in front of me. "You always loved this game. Besides, it's either stay in here awhile and have a bit of fun or join those two."

I peeked over toward the beach. Arden had almost caught up to Dalia. His expression was complete misery as he reached for her arm. I tore my gaze away and swallowed the lump forming in my throat, thinking about Dalia's pregnancy. She'd be a constant presence in our lives as the mother of Arden's child.

"Okay." I held onto Jasper's shoulders and propped my foot in his hands. "But this doesn't mean you're forgiven."

"On three," he instructed.

At the count of three, he propelled me up, high over his head. I dove deep, blowing bubbles out of my nose and opening my eyes. The salt stung at first, but then I got used to it as I swam low, running my fingers along the pointed edges of conch shells poking out of the sand, before arching up and swimming back to the surface.

"Your turn." I locked my hands together for Jasper's foot.

We laughed and did this several more times before finally swimming to shore.

Dalia and Arden were sitting in silence on the sand when Jasper and I finally came out of the water. Arden's gaze lingered on me, traveling the length of my body while I reached for my clothes, causing my traitorous pulse to race.

My body didn't seem to care one bit that I was mad at him for ignoring my orders.

Dalia shot up out of the sand and stormed off toward the forest of palm trees behind us. But this time Arden paid her no attention. I hadn't pegged Dalia as a tantrum thrower, but I supposed the pregnancy hormones were having an effect.

"We need to talk about Cade. He's not a shifter. Did you know?" Arden asked me.

I shook my head and spread my jacket out so I could sit

next to him without getting a fresh layer of sand stuck all over me.

"I never saw his face in Orien's memory, but I'd sensed something familiar about him, and now I guess we know why. Maybe this other dimension he comes from is a replica of ours, and that's why he thinks I'm a reincarnation of his dead wife."

"What?"

Crap! I hadn't planned on telling Arden what I'd learned from Orien the night prior, but I had no choice now, not after seeing what Cade looked like.

Arden listened while I explained what Orien had suspected Cade was up to by making the stone of fire and binding it with fairy essence and Oria's blood. His jaw clenched, and a vein bulged at his temple, the same as Cade's had when he'd watched Arden take me through the portal.

I shivered at the likeness between the two men.

"He won't give up. I felt his desire and ... love for you. It was the same as my own." Worry lines appeared around Arden's eyes, and his brow furrowed. "He'll tear apart the universe to get to you." Arden stretched his long arms out and lifted me onto his lap. "I won't let him have you." He cupped my cheeks and gently kissed my lips, making me forget I was angry with him.

I rested my head on his chest. Sweat dripped down my arms and between my breasts from the scorching heat. "Maybe the Spider Witch knows something more about him. I must have opened a portal back to this place for a reason."

"Maybe," Arden agreed, tightening his hold on me.

I was about to ask him if he'd told Dalia about us when a piercing shriek came from the tropical forest behind us.

"Dalia!" I jumped off Arden's lap, my heart racing. Dalia wasn't my favorite person, but I didn't want anything to happen to Arden's child.

He leaped to his feet, kicking up waves of sand as he rushed toward the dense line of palm trees.

Jasper and I followed Dalia's shrieks as we pushed through the bushes and shrubs growing between the palms and dodged cactuses with sharp needles.

We found Dalia pressing herself flat against a palm trunk while Arden shooed away the wild boar that snorted in protest.

The boar bolted in the opposite direction when Arden withdrew his sword, and Dalia threw herself into his arms, clinging to him.

I groaned as she buried her face in his chest and he consoled her. "I was so scared," she said, and rubbed her stomach.

My irritation turned to a deep ache.

Jasper widened his eyes. "You just scared away our breakfast."

I snorted and covered my mouth. Jasper had a one-track mind when it came to his appetite. "I'm sure we'll find something to eat, Jasp. Maybe Tilly can offer you a roasted spider."

Jasper stuck out his tongue. "That's one snack I think I'll pass on, unless, of course, there isn't anything else to eat. Then bring on the creepy-crawlies." He crawled his fingers up my shoulder, neck, and ear.

I laughed, slapping his hand away. "Come on." I looped my arm through his. "Let's go find Tilly's."

Arden led the way, following in the same direction we'd gone when we'd come here the other night.

In the light of day, we could see how luscious and alive the forest was with brilliant green hues. Palm and banana trees grew in abundance. Gorgeous flowers bloomed everywhere in an array of vibrant colors. Coconuts, mangoes, and papayas filled the tropical trees above us. The island was a paradise.

The hum and whistle of many birds serenaded us as we

meandered on the path we'd found.

Jasper moaned when a decadent breeze swirled and caressed our skin. He'd left his shirt off, and sweat trickled down his muscled back. "This place is like a sauna during the day."

"Yeah," I agreed, swiping streams of sweat from my forehead and the sides of my face.

When we finally reached the familiar hut, the door opened, and the man who had guided us here the first time stepped onto the porch. He wore the same straw hat as before, with a tank top, cutoff shorts, and sandals. In the light of day, his dark skin was wrinkled with age.

"Hello." He greeted us with a warmth that matched his relaxed vibrations. "Tilly has gone," he informed us. "But she has left you use of her home in her absence. She says to make yourselves comfortable and to stay as long as you need."

My shoulders drooped forward. I'd hoped Tilly could help us.

"I hope Tilly left her fridge stocked," Jasper said, darting inside.

Dalia and Arden followed him in, but I lagged behind, unable to shake my disappointment. Cade would never stop searching for me, and the longer I stayed with my friends, the more danger I brought to them. And he still had Molly. I had to find a way to get to her without anyone else getting hurt.

The gentleman came down the porch steps and held out a folded piece of paper. "For you."

"What—"

He pressed his finger to his lips. "Ms. Tilly instructed for your eyes alone."

I nodded. "Thank you."

"There is plenty of food and water, and I left some bottles of my own rum. It's exceptionally aged. We grow our own sugarcane here on the island." Pride shone in his eyes at his declaration, and then they dimmed with sadness. "Mr. Silus built a distillery near the field, where we do our fermenting and bottling for our neighboring islands. He sure is missed. How is the lovely Freya?"

I smiled. "She's well, and so is their daughter, Anya."

"Glad to hear it. Well, if you need anything, I'm not far." He pointed through the trees. "Second hut on the left. When you've spotted Marge, you've found me. She's the largest goat on the island." Deep lines formed under his eyes with his bright smile.

"I'm Everly. Thank you again for your help."

The rough surface of his hands cupped mine as he pressed the paper into my palm. "Harold." He turned and left in the direction he'd pointed to. A giant iguana darted onto the trail, following behind him like a house pet. Its large stomach nearly brushed the ground as it ran with its short legs and a long, leathery tail swaying behind it.

I sat on the top porch step and unfolded the note.

There is no escape from the wolf that hunts you.

Tension knotted my stomach and seized my back as I continued to read.

Not until he believes he's succeeded. Give him what he wants. Master the power of the stone and set yourself free. Your path into the darkness of the soul will be your family's salvation.

I crinkled the note in my hand as my throat went dry. The last line of Tilly's note had the same words Freya had said to me the night she'd performed my first reading. The spirits had tried to warn me even then. Cade had always been a threat. I just hadn't known it. He would never stop. I had seen it in his eyes as he'd watched me escape through the portal. He'd waited centuries to get her back, his Mila, and he'd go after everyone I loved until she was returned to him.

I put the crumpled note in my pocket with a heavy heart, then stood to join the others inside.

⚜

A rden got the woodstove fired up, while Jasper helped Dalia prepare a stew. The sound of chopping coupled with the sizzle of wood lulled me into a thoughtful trance. I opened the windows to let out the heat from the fire, but it was useless, since the island was still boiling from the heat of the sun.

At least the generator worked, and there was ice in the freezer. I filled a cup with some of the cubes and went to sit on the porch.

Cade had known I'd have fire magic. He'd asked Oria to forge the stone even before she'd given him his premonition of my future. How had he known so much about me before I'd even existed?

I'd been so lost in thought that I hadn't heard Arden come out to the porch. The wooden steps creaked as he stretched his long legs on either side of mine and sat behind me, taking an ice cube from my cup. The cold sensation felt amazing when he slid the dripping cube down one of my arms and then the other, then trailed the melting cube up my neck. He scooped my hair to the side and cooled the back of my neck with the ice. Drops of water trickled down my chest underneath my shirt, sliding between my breasts. Arden's fingers kneaded my shoulders, and I relaxed against him. He leaned down and licked the melted ice from the side of my neck. My skin burned, but not from the heat of the sun. I arched back, and Arden's mouth found mine.

"Chow time," Jasper announced, popping his head out of

the front door.

I was so stunned by the interruption that my body jolted, and my head bumped into Arden's jaw.

"Sorry," I said as I got up.

He laughed. "It's okay. Are you hungry?"

I shrugged. "Not really, but I guess we should eat."

Jasper and Dalia carried bowls filled to their rims over to a rickety wooden table that barely fit the four of us.

My knees bumped up against Arden's on one side and Jasper's on the other while we ate. The goat meat tasted a bit gamy, but the stew was delicious.

My cheeks were flaming. Each time I glanced at Arden, his eyes were on me, and all I could think about was the feeling of leaning against him while he ran the ice down my skin.

Dalia's gaze darted from me to Arden. The room was beginning to feel as though it were shrinking with each passing second.

Jasper finally broke the tension. "Who knew of your plan?" he asked. "To portal Everly back to Aenoas-Vita."

Arden crushed his bread in his palm. "Besides those at this table, only those I trust with my own life. It would seem the traitor is closer to us than we thought." He dropped his annihilated bread onto a plate without having taken a bite. "When I find out who they are, they're going to suffer a long, agonizing death."

Dalia coughed up her drink of water. "Wrong pipe," she wheezed, and covered her mouth.

"So, I guess I'll address the elephant in the room." Jasper took a sip of his rum, and his eyes closed as he swallowed. Then he continued. "Is Cade a relative of yours?"

Arden's chair scraped back against the wooden floor. "I've never seen him before today."

"Okay, well ... either he's using magic to look like a

rougher, war-weathered version of you, or he's your—"

"It wasn't magic, and he isn't a shifter." Arden's voice was low. "I don't know who he is, or how it's possible that he's ... me."

Jasper drained his bowl of stew broth as though we were discussing the weather and not the fact that Cade and Arden could be twins.

Dalia brought over the tray of custard she and Jasper had made using the goat's milk. She seemed to share the same enthusiasm for food as Jasper, who didn't waste any time digging in.

"Let's say," he said in between bites, "that you two have more in common than it looks. What would be your next move?"

Arden glanced at Dalia, then settled his gaze on me. Not a speck of blue had remained in his eyes all day. He pressed his hands flat on the table, his tendons straining against his skin as his eyes glowed green. "I'd do whatever it took to find her, and I'd annihilate anyone who stood in my way."

I swallowed hard, and Dalia pushed her custard away and stood abruptly. Her pale skin flushed all the way from her cheeks to her chest as she gathered the empty bowls and carried them to the kitchen sink.

Jasper made an "awkward" face, and the two of us got up and gave Arden and Dalia a moment alone, while we looked around the rest of Tilly's hut.

We found a bedroom with a single cot, and another small room that was used as a study. Ancient books lined a shelf on one wall, and another shelf was stocked with all sorts of bones and spiders kept in jars, which gave me the jitters.

"Look what I found." Jasper held up a bottle of gold ink with a dripping quill. He grabbed a few pieces of the parchment stacked under the quill and ink.

"Let me see those."

I scrawled out a quick message to my mom, letting her know what had happened. Then Jasper sent Anya a message, so she'd know he was safe.

Minutes later, a sheet appeared out of thin air, and I recognized my mom's handwriting.

"Ty and Kamara are okay. Besides being shoved around a bit, they weren't harmed." Relief flooded through me. When I'd seen Kamara's torn dress, I'd worried the worst had happened. I kept reading. Hot anger coiled in my belly. "Bree was the one who lured Molly outside the night she was taken. Ty says she showed up out of the blue at his place. They ate pizza and played video games. And that's the last thing he remembers before my mom did a spell lifting the block Bree created. Bree apparently typed the messages on Ty's phone and used her magic to persuade him to go to my house and meet Molly." The coiled anger churned to boiling as I kept reading. "She also lured Kamara into a trap outside Neil's club."

"Where is she now?" Jasper asked.

I scanned the rest of the letter. "Sounds like she disappeared during the chaos, and Darion's gone after her." My hand balled into a fist. "When I get my hands on her, I'm going to make her wish I'd burned her to ashes."

"But what about the blood oath?" Jasper asked.

The note burned away as I finished reading it. "She didn't break her oath to me directly by giving Molly up. That little snake is going to pay. But I don't know how she knew about Molly's pregnancy or the Hunters. We never talked about either in front of her."

"I'm sure your brother will get it out of her. I almost pity her."

I smirked. Jasper was right. Bree was going to wish she were trapped back in her studio with me when Darion found her. She didn't stand a chance escaping him.

We left the study and updated Arden on our findings. I was telling him that Darion was tracking Bree when glass shattered, and Dalia scrambled to pick up the broken pieces of the plate she'd dropped.

Arden sent his own message to Rheya. The two agreed we would stay where we were for the time being and that our location should remain a secret while Rheya worked to find out who our traitor was. She would report back to Arden when she learned something.

I found some extra pillows and blankets, which we laid out on the floor. We insisted that Dalia take the room with the cot, and after some protest, she agreed and excused herself. I couldn't help but notice the strange nervous energy that overcame her, but I supposed her life had been turned upside down overnight.

Jasper slept deeply beside me, his breathing a series of long, steady breaths. I kept my eyes closed and listened to Arden's restless steps as he paced. When the front door creaked open, I got up, and followed him outside.

He didn't need to turn around to know it was me. His Empath abilities would sense me.

When I took a seat next to him, he reached for my hand. "Did you feel it too?" he asked.

"Yes."

"Who is he?"

"I don't know." I squeezed his hand and rested my head on his shoulder.

Arden stood, drawing me up with him. "Walk to the beach with me." His fingers laced through mine.

The tropical forest was a symphony of nightlife as we followed the path to the beach. Birds sang a haunting lullaby, while frogs croaked and crickets chirped as though they collaborated in a harmony.

When we broke through the tall palm trees onto the sand

and open beach, the sky twinkled overhead with brilliant constellations, like I'd never seen. Sweet, salty air swirled around us as the wind stirred its own midnight melody.

Arden wrapped his arm tight around me, and we walked in peaceful silence with the ocean gently lapping the beach and caressing our bare feet. Even late at night, the temperature felt like warm bathwater on my skin.

We stopped and gazed at the full moon. Its luminous glow reflected across the ocean's surface. Arden shifted and slid his hand over the side of my face.

"How is it possible that he can love you as fiercely as I do? He'll rip apart the galaxy to find you, the same as I would. How are we the same?"

I reached up and caressed his stubbled cheek. The same cheek where a scar hardened Cade's appearance. "You're not him, and he's not you."

Arden's forehead touched mine. "I won't lose you to him." His lips brushed against mine. "I will find a way to beat him."

My lips parted as Arden's tongue found mine, and I surrendered to his kiss.

"I love you," he whispered.

I stood on my tiptoes and skimmed my fingertips up the back of his neck. The goddess pendant burned hot against my skin as my emotions responded to Arden. "I love you too."

His hands ran down my waist, and he gripped my sides, lifting me so that my legs wrapped around him.

My fingers combed through his hair as our kiss deepened.

Arden held onto me and walked us up toward the trees.

"Where are we going?" I breathed.

He pulled his head back and nodded. "I spotted a hammock up there earlier."

I slid off him when we got to the hammock and trailed my fingers under the hem of his shirt, lifting it over his head. I traced the definition of his muscled torso and kissed his chest, grazing his hard nipples with my teeth. Goose bumps flushed across his skin as my lips trailed down his abdomen.

His hands went into my hair, and he guided me back up until his mouth was on mine. Gliding his hands beneath my shirt, he managed to unclasp my bra and remove my top all at once. He lowered his head, trailing his tongue down my neck and chest until he captured my nipple in his mouth, sucking and nibbling on it. Violent waves of pleasure rippled through me. He continued moving his mouth lower and lower, until my entire body trembled. Gripping my hips, Arden lifted me so I straddled him once more.

"Is this okay?" he whispered.

I answered him with my kiss, wrapping my tongue around his and squeezing my legs tighter around his waist.

Arden moaned and dug his fingers into my thighs as he lowered us onto the hammock.

My head shot back, and a soft scream parted my lips.

Our bodies quivered together over and over until it was almost too much to endure, and we cried out at the same moment. I collapsed forward onto his muscled chest. Strong arms wrapped around my back, and we shifted our bodies.

We lay sideways, breathing heavily and completely entwined in each other's body, dripping with delicious, sweet sweat. I kissed his chest and nuzzled my head under his chin. My eyes drifted closed as a succulent breeze blew over us and the hammock gently swayed above the sand. For the first night in months, I fell into a dreamless and peaceful slumber.

The breeze tickled my ear, and I twisted my body, snuggling my face against Arden's chest and breathing in the scent of him.

"Hmm." He stirred and ran his hand down my leg.

A warm ray of sun heated my skin and felt scrumptious.

Our bodies swayed weightlessly in the hammock as I shifted slightly.

Soft lips caressed my forehead, nose, and then my lips.

"This is how I want to wake up every morning." Arden smiled, the blue shining brightly in his eyes once again. His fingers kneaded the aches in my back, shoulder, and then my neck.

"Me too," I said, wishing there were no more obstacles in our way, and I pressed a kiss to his lips. "But right now, I have to go to the bathroom." I sprang up, almost flipping the hammock over.

Arden laughed and scooped me up into his arm, pulling me back into him. "Not yet."

His honeyed hair lifted in the breeze, and he reached out, lacing his fingers through mine, sending a flurry of butterflies scattering in my belly.

"I want you to know that I told Dalia about us. She knows I love you." He kissed my nose. "I told her I'll be there for our child, but that's as far as our relationship will go."

I rolled on top of him. The look he gave me made my spine tingle. His hands roamed every part of me, fondling and teasing until I couldn't take it any longer. He laughed, pleased with himself, and gently lifted my hips. His moan sent wild pleasure pulsing through me. I arched back as he massaged my breasts, and my body rocked against his until it shook with complete ecstasy, and I fell forward, utterly depleted. I didn't think I'd have the energy to move for days, but nature was calling.

"I'll be right back." I kissed him.

He propped his hands behind his head and smiled at me.

"What?" I scrambled into my clothes.

"I just like watching you squirm around with nothing on."

I shoved his leg, sending the hammock swinging away. "Ha ha!" I took off toward Tilly's, barely escaping Arden's attempt to recapture me.

"Hey! Where'd you disappear to last night?" Jasper piled a mountain of fluffy egg onto his fork. "I noticed a certain someone else missing too." He winked, balancing the enormous amount of food on his fork all the way into his mouth.

I couldn't stop the smile that stretched across my face. "We went for a walk and slept on a hammock."

Jasper's brows shot up, and a grin tugged the corners of his mouth. "I hope that means you're finally going to let yourself be happy for once."

I glanced around the room. "Where's Dalia?"

Jasper shrugged. "She got up, cooked breakfast, and then said she was going for a walk."

I spotted my backpack next to the pillow I'd been lying on before following Arden outside last night. The zipper was partially open. *Hmm …* I remembered zipping it all the way closed when I'd opened it last night to get my toothbrush.

"Did you get in my bag for anything?" I asked Jasper.

He scraped the remaining food onto his fork. "Nope."

"Huh."

"Is anything missing?" he asked, getting up and rinsing his plate off.

I dropped to my knees and rummaged through my bag. Everything appeared to be there. *Wait.* I checked the inside zipper pocket, where I'd stashed the ever stone from the releasing ceremony. My heart skipped a beat. *Where is it?*

"Are you sure you didn't get in my bag?"

A worry line furrowed Jasper's brow. "I'd tell you if I did. What's missing?"

Jasper didn't know about the releasing ceremony or about the stone. I was going to tell him. I just hadn't gotten around to it yet.

"I had an ever stone in my bag. It was zipped up, and there's no way it could have fallen out. And the Hunter never opened my bag."

"Why would you have an ever stone? You know how dangerous they can be."

"Yeah." I dropped my head into my hands, feeling dizzy. *How could I be so careless?*

"Jasper. I have to find this stone. It's very important. I did something that can't be undone if the stone isn't destroyed properly."

Oh my God! My hand latched onto the goddess pendant. I still felt connected to my emotions, so the stone hadn't been damaged.

Jasper's eyes narrowed. He knelt and tucked a strand of my hair that had fallen across my cheek behind my ear.

"What did you do, Ev?"

My body trembled as I blurted it all out. "This necklace is keeping me attached to my emotions, Jasp, but if something happens to the stone before the spring equinox, every feeling I've ever had for Arden will be gone … forever."

He fell silent. "Okay. Let's think. Do you think Dalia would have taken it? She was the only one besides me who could have been alone with your bag."

I shook my head. "I don't know. I mean, she has no idea about the spell or the stone, so even if she went through my bag, why would she have taken it? Maybe it did fall out somewhere when we first got here."

"Are you sure you packed it?"

"Yes!"

Jasper stood up and looked around the hut. "Okay. Let's retrace our steps from the beginning." He held out a hand and pulled me to my feet.

I stood on my tiptoes and threw my arms around his neck. "I love you, Jasp."

"I know." He kissed my cheek. "I'll head back to where we popped out of the portal."

He left, and I ran to the bathroom and did a quick search while I was in there. No ever stone.

I dashed back outside, nearly stumbling down the steps in my haste.

My heart thundered in my chest as I ran toward the beach. I had to tell Arden. Before anything happened to the stone, I had to tell him again how much I loved him and always would until my last breath. Dalia's voice stopped me in my tracks.

Blood rushed to my ears. I panted, trying to catch my breath, and tucked myself behind the trunk of a palm tree.

Arden stood facing Dalia. Her hands cupped his cheeks.

"You made love to me, Arden, and we created a child together." She dropped her hands from his face and gripped his wrists, bringing his hands to her belly. "A part of you grows inside me, and *we* need you."

Arden's hands remained on Dalia's belly. His expression was strained as he stared at his hands on her abdomen.

A pain like a knife wound ripped down my chest. Dalia was right, but I needed him too, and I wouldn't lose him to her.

Arden stepped away from Dalia just as a warm breath touched my cheek, and a twig snapped behind me.

I froze, sensing his energy.

"He'll never be yours again," Cade whispered in my ear. "He might not love her now, but as they raise their child together, a bond like no other will grow between them, and where does that leave you?"

Hot fear crawled over me. Not fear of Cade but fear of the truth he spoke.

"You belong with me." He touched my arm, and a memory flooded my mind.

It was *me*, but it couldn't have been. I was laughing and taunting Cade, letting him chase me around an enormous chamber until I threw myself into his embrace and we tumbled together, entangled as one.

When Cade took his hand from me, shock reverberated through every bone in my body. *How ...? What was that?*

I glanced back at Arden and Dalia. She was crying now, and he was comforting her. She was the mother of his unborn child. Her needs would always come before my own.

My eyes stung, but I wouldn't let Cade see my weakness.

"You're wrong," I growled. "Arden loves me, and I love him. We can get through this."

Cade slipped his arm around my waist and squeezed the breath out of me, but I refused to let him know he was hurting me.

"Maybe you could." His lips brushed my ear as he breathed in my hair. "But what about Molly and her unborn babies? Are you willing to risk their lives for your happiness?"

I spun to slap him, but he caught my hand and twisted my wrist. I grimaced, and he loosened his grip, his eyes softening.

"I didn't mean to hurt you. It's just ... I've waited so long." His eyes roamed over my face and drifted to my lips.

Tilly's letter flashed in my mind. If I wanted to save my family and free Molly, I had to let Arden go, give myself to Cade ... at least until I could find a way to master the magic of the stone of fire.

He smiled when my arm relaxed, and released it.

The bracelets I allowed him to clasp over my wrists glowed with fire, and I knew they'd been forged from the very stone Oria had created for him. The magic seeped into me like venom.

"Ev!" Jasper yelled as he barreled toward me.

Cade's Hunters blocked his path, surrounding us in a shield of armed soldiers.

Jasper blasted them with his invisible energy shield. He tore his sword loose and threw it to Arden, who burst through the trees with Dalia at his heels.

Arden caught the handle with a growl and slashed through the line of Hunters who kept him from reaching me.

Energy charged the air beside Cade as a portal took form.

Cade's soldiers continued flooding in from everywhere. Jasper and Arden were vastly outnumbered, but I knew they'd both give their lives trying to save me.

"Call off your men."

"You'll come willingly?"

I held up my wrists. A shimmer of orange and red flickered across the surface of the bracelets. Cade would know if I lied. He had some kind of connection to the magic wielded in the stone of fire, the same magic infused into these prison cuffs I now wore. I sensed it as the magic invaded my body. It was like a whisper in my head, warning me. Was it the fairy magic Oria had put into the stone that was bound to the Ever bloodline? Did it recognize me? A new hope filled me. If the magic was trying to warn me, then I could learn how to control it and beat Cade at his own game.

But as long as my heart truly belonged to Arden, I could never fool Cade. Not if he had some empathic connection to the magic that was spreading through every cell in my body. I clasped the Quan Yin pendant hanging at my neck and sucked in a sharp breath. My hands trembled violently as I watched Arden fighting with every ounce of strength he had to get to me. He slashed through guard after guard, but when one fell, another appeared.

"Don't do it, Ev." Jasper met my eyes and stared at my hand, shaking his head. "Don't!"

A heart-wrenching cry escaped me as I yanked the chain from my neck and let the goddess slip from my grasp into the sand. In a flash, all the emotions that bound me to Arden

were gone, just as they had been that night after the ceremony. I rubbed my chest, feeling the empty ache, but nothing
else for the man who called out my name as he cut down
body after body.

"I'll leave with you willingly."

The Hunters pressed back toward us as one, and I realized they were responding to a silent command given by
Cade. He communicated with them telepathically.

"Ev! Please! Don't leave with him," Jasper pleaded.

"I'm sorry, Jasp. It's the only way." I tore my attention
from Jasper and finally looked at Arden as Cade backed us
toward the portal.

Rage and confusion contorted his face, and his eyes
glowed green with fury when he glared at Cade. "If you hurt
her in any way, I'll tear you to pieces."

Cade's chest rumbled against my back. "I couldn't have
said it better myself."

"I'll find you!" Arden fell to his knees in the bloodied
sand.

Dalia dropped beside him and wrapped her arms around
his chest. An odd expression glinted in her gaze as she turned
toward me, and then a grin crested at the corners of her
mouth. He was all hers now.

My eyes fell on the ever stone clutched in her hand. She
had taken it, but what did it matter now?

"Don't come after me," I told them. "Just ... let me go."
The words seared the tip of my tongue like acid, and an ache
settled deep within me. What I was doing felt completely
wrong, but fate had given me no choice, and Molly's life
depended on me.

Cade lifted me into his arms.

"No! Ev!" Jasper thrashed against his barricade as Cade
turned and carried me through the portal.

THANK YOU

Thank you for reading Stone of Fire! If you loved this book, please take the time to write a review. I'd love to know what you think, and so will other readers. I value your time and opinion. Just a line or two is all it takes. Thank you for being a part of the Vitarian adventure. Your support helps keep the story alive.

Stone of Fire (Vitarian Chronicles Volume 3)

Don't forget to grab your free short story prequel to the Vitarian Chronicles if you want to read more over at my website :)

Fate of Fury: Vitarian Chronicles Volume 0.5 (Free Short Story Prequel at my website)

Join my newsletter to be notified of upcoming releases.
www.slwatsonauthor.com

ALSO BY S. L. WATSON

Fate of Blood (Vitarian Chronicles Volume 1)

Last Descendants (Vitarian Chronicles Volume 2)

Stone of Fire (Vitarian Chronicles Volume 3)

Visit at www.slwatsonauthor.com for upcoming releases and
newsletter giveaways.

ABOUT THE AUTHOR

S. L. Watson is an author of young adult fantasy. Stone of Fire is her third novel in the Vitarian Chronicles series.

S. L. grew up in Oregon, where she currently resides with her husband, daughter, boisterous German Shepherd, and two feisty cats. As a lover of all genres, it's not unusual to find stacks of her current reads scattered throughout her home (Sorry friends and family for the constant clutter, but I love my books!). If she's not deep in developing plot twists, lost in the story realm, or wandering nature trails with her daughter, she's lifting heavy barbells, practicing muscle-ups, or glued to a UFC match with her husband.

S. L. believes reading keeps the imagination alive and that shared stories bring communities together. She would love to hear from you! Please connect with her as she regularly gives out sneak peeks, prizes, and other freebies to her friends and newsletter subscribers. Don't miss the next giveaway.

CONNECT WITH S. L. WATSON

Visit my website for exclusive updates and newsletter goodies:
www.slwatsonauthor.com

Come hang out with me on:
Facebook: https://www.facebook.com/slwatsonauthor
Instagram: https://www.instagram.com/slwatsonauthor/
Join Fans of S.L. Watson's Vitarian Chronicles for more fun games and prizes: https://www.facebook.com/groups/1040089066815333

ACKNOWLEDGMENTS

A special thanks goes out to everyone who worked directly with me and behind the scenes to make this book the best version of Stone of Fire. This has been a work of passion, blood, sweat, tears, and countless sleep deprived mornings. And I wouldn't trade a second of it! Getting up at 4:00 AM has become a daily ritual, and I love the peaceful quiet of these early creative mornings, and the pot of coffee helps :) My German Shepherd, Chloe, loves her early morning romps in the yard too!

A huge thanks to Leonora Bulbeck, whose top notch editing and precise eye saved my sentences from my obsessive incorrect use of commas and grammatical errors. Thank you for the meticulous detail you put into polishing Stone of Fire.

Another huge thanks to Fiona McLaren, whose honest and detailed edits helped pushed my writing to a new level. Thank you, Fiona, for keeping me aware of passive vs active voice, setting details, cliche phrases, tedious dialogue bubbles, and for being honest when you didn't agree with a story detail.

An enormous thanks to Rena Violet. Thank you, Rena, for taking the details I gave you and bringing my imagination to life on the cover. You have an amazing talent!

And to my incredible husband, Adam. There aren't enough thank you's in the world to express my gratitude. Thank you for taking the time to read this book and sharing your thoughts. Thank you for all of the input and advice you offered every step of the way. Your support kept me going. Thank you to my precious daughter, Rowan, whose creativity, imagination, and kind heart inspires me every second of my day. I'm so grateful for you both. I love you, infinity times infinity infinities forever!

Printed in Great Britain
by Amazon